Cole had taught himself to sleep lightly.

He snapped to awareness when he heard a car door close with deliberate softness. Lying rigid, he listened. The digital clock Erin had put at the bedside said 2:33. Anyone coming or going in the middle of the night wouldn't want to disturb the neighbors. Especially if that person was stealing a vehicle.

When the engine started, he knew it was Erin's Jeep. He jumped out of bed, reaching the front window just before the dome light went out. In that instant, he saw her. While he watched, Erin reversed, then drove down the driveway. Brake lights flickered before she turned onto the street.

He didn't welcome the uneasiness he felt as he stared out at the yard and street dimly lit by streetlights, the closest half a block away. Where was she going? Wouldn't she have woken him if she had some kind of emergency?

His mouth tightened. Why would she? What was he but her charity project, after all?

She might have just been restless. He was projecting to think that whatever ghost haunted her and shadowed her eyes had sent her out into the night.

And, damn it, Cole didn't want to feel any responsibility for another human being. Even so, he knew with icy certainty that he wouldn't sleep again until she came home.

Dear Reader,

I've been interested for a long time in the experiences of the many men released from prison after very long terms because DNA evidence not available when they were convicted now proves their innocence. How Rip Van Winkle is that? What would it be like to rejoin the world after such a long absence?

Imagine going to bed one night and waking up years in the future, as he did in Washington Irving's story. People you loved would have moved on without you or died; your children would be grown. What work history you have is outdated. Is there a place for you at all?

At least Rip had the advantage that day-to-day life hadn't changed much. Now transfer that experience to the modern world. Something as simple as standing on a sidewalk with traffic rushing by can be terrifying when you've been shut away for so long. You've forgotten how to make conversation (especially with the opposite sex). And then there's technology, which changes with breathtaking speed. You're bewildered by smartphones, touch screens, car dashboards that look like they belong in the cockpit of a Boeing jet. And, oh, yeah, you don't have a driver's license, or a bank account, or acceptable credit history. Now take a deep breath, and best of luck out there.

Falling in love? That's a whole other complication (and I so love to complicate the lives of my heroes and heroines).

So, here's my Rip Van Winkle story.

Janice

USA TODAY Bestselling Author

JANICE KAY JOHNSON

The Hero's Redemption

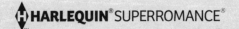

Recycling programs
for this product may
not exist in your area.

ISBN-13: 978-0-373-64049-2

The Hero's Redemption

Printed in U.S.A.

An author of more than ninety books for children and adults (more than seventy-five for Harlequin), **Janice Kay Johnson** writes about love and family— about the way generations connect and the power our earliest experiences have on us throughout life. A *USA TODAY* bestselling author and an eight-time finalist for a Romance Writers of America RITA® Award, she won a RITA® Award in 2008 for her Harlequin Superromance novel *Snowbound*. A former librarian, Janice raised two daughters in a small town north of Seattle, Washington.

Books by Janice Kay Johnson

HARLEQUIN SUPERROMANCE

Her Amish Protectors
Plain Refuge
A Mother's Claim

Brothers, Strangers

The Baby He Wanted
The Closer He Gets

Because of a Girl
The Baby Agenda
Bone Deep
Finding Her Dad
All That Remains
Making Her Way Home
No Matter What
A Hometown Boy

Anything for Her
Where It May Lead
From This Day On
One Frosty Night
More Than Neighbors
To Love a Cop

Two Daughters

Yesterday's Gone
In Hope's Shadow

The Mysteries of Angel Butte

Bringing Maddie Home
Everywhere She Goes
All a Man Is
Cop by Her Side
This Good Man

Visit the Author Profile page at Harlequin.com for more titles.

PROLOGUE

"No guy is ever going to be interested in me! I *tower* over all of them!" Alyssa Enger wailed from near the back of the extended van.

The other nine girls cried out in denial.

"Why did I have to take after my dad?" Alyssa moaned.

Erin Parrish hid her grin as she changed lanes on I-5 in northern California to pass a slow-moving RV. As head coach of Markham College's women's volleyball team, she also did the driving for away games. Her assistant coach, Charlotte Prentice, was considered too young at twenty-three to be trusted behind the wheel of a vehicle insured by the college.

Alyssa was the team's middle blocker *because* she was six foot one. Erin had met her parents—a mom who, at only five-eight or so, was the shrimp in their family, a dad who had to be six foot six and two younger brothers who'd already shot past Alyssa in height.

"Boys are scared of you because you're so

beautiful," declared Stephanie Bell, a setter. "And there are lots of guys taller than you."

Maybe not "lots," but some.

"Have you met Emmett Stark?" someone asked.

"Eeew!" several girls squealed.

Outright laughing now, Erin glanced at Charlotte, whose face was lit by laughter, too. Emmett Stark, freshman and Markham College's JV basketball center, would surely grow into his body eventually. Right now, he was so skinny he looked ridiculous.

"We should dress you up as an Amazon for Halloween," another girl said. Ella Pierce? "Maybe we could use gold paint, and you could carry a spear."

"Where can we get a spear?" someone else asked eagerly.

"Ohh! I know." Ginny Simacek bounced in delight. "My brother's girlfriend did this volunteer thing in Africa, and she brought one home with her! I bet I can borrow it."

Erin narrowed her eyes at the rearview mirror. Was Ginny wearing her seat belt? *Could* you bounce if you were wearing one? The girls had a way of taking their seat belts off for "just a minute," because they had to grab a bag from under a seat or find a shoe that was kicked off, and then, oops, forgetting to fasten them again.

"Charlotte..." Erin began.

Motion caught from the corner of her eye spiked her adrenaline. She turned her head. All she took in was a swirl of dirt and the monster cab of a semitruck roaring straight at them across the median, rearing bigger and bigger. She wrenched the steering wheel and her foot sought the brake, even though she knew it was too late.

Then crunching metal, stabbing pain, screams. And nothingness.

CHAPTER ONE

JOLTED AWAKE, ERIN lay utterly still, her heart pounding. What— But the shuddering sense of horror answered an unfinished question. Which nightmare had it been? The crash itself? What she'd seen as she was extracted from all that was left of the van? The faces of parents? The empty seats in her classroom?

She stared at the ceiling, unable to make herself move. She could stay in bed all day. Never get up. No one would notice; no one would care. She had no place to be, not anymore.

Voices played in her head, as they so often did.

You're so lucky. Yep, that was her—lucky.

God must have saved you for a reason. Because He'd condemned her to purgatory?

You still have the chance to do something extraordinary.

Make your life count. That one had come with an encouraging squeeze of her hand.

Who'd told her she owed it to the dead to be

happy? She couldn't remember. Probably hadn't been able to look that person in the face.

Nope, of course she wasn't to blame. She was only the driver. The one all those girls had trusted to get them safely where they were going. They'd trusted her in other ways, too. As an assistant professor of history, lecturing from the front of her classroom, she maintained an invisible distance. But with her team, it was different. She knew every girl—her strengths, her vulnerabilities, her fears, her dreams.

There'd be no more dreams. Just her own nightmares.

The ceiling, she slowly realized, needed painting as much as the walls. What had probably once been white had yellowed, like pages in an old book, even showing the brown spots a book dealer would call "foxing."

Eventually she rolled her head enough on the ancient, flat-as-a-pancake feather pillow to see the clock—7:26. She'd slept for maybe three hours.

Erin both craved sleep and dreaded it. The oblivion called to her, but the nightmares always took her back to the worst moments.

The screams, metal and human. She would never forget.

Be happy? Really?

Unfortunately, she *was* alive, which meant she

had to pee. Aching, moving as slowly as an old woman, she pushed herself to a sitting position, swung her feet over the edge of the mattress and looked for her slippers. The wood floors were chilly. Plus, she kept thinking she'd get a splinter. Those floors needed stripping, sanding and refinishing as much as the interior of the house needed painting. The exterior, too—but it would have to be scraped and pressure-washed first.

Sometimes she wondered if Nanna just hadn't seen the deterioration. Maybe her vision had been going. She'd lived here most of her life, and in recent years, she hadn't gone out much. If Erin's dad was still alive, he would have seen to the maintenance, but Erin had been too far away to be aware of how badly Nanna needed someone.

"I'm sorry, Nanna," she whispered.

Thank you, Nanna, for leaving me this house. She had no idea what she would've done if she hadn't had this refuge waiting for her. Familiar, filled with memories and an occasional moment of comfort that felt like the touch of a small, arthritic hand.

Once recovered from her injuries, she'd returned to her classes, sticking it out until February, when she and her department head realized at about the same time that she couldn't stay on at the college. She'd been at Nanna's house now for…almost three weeks? Made meaningless by grief, the days ran together.

In the bedroom again to pull a sweatshirt over her sleep tee, Erin said aloud, "I'll start today, Nanna, even if it's only one project. I promise."

There was no answer, of course, and yet Nanna felt more alive to her than— Nope. Not going there. Couldn't go there, not if she was going to be able to choke down a piece of toast and actually accomplish something like pulling a few weeds.

And she did manage, although she had trouble believing she'd lived for no reason but to save her grandmother's hundred-year-old house from being bulldozed so some new structure could be built in its place.

Over my dead body, she thought, and wished she could laugh.

A MONTH LATER…well, she was taking better care of herself, which was something, and had painted the parlor, the library and the downstairs hall, as well as the small bathroom tucked under the stairs. She'd stripped the fireplace surround, sanded until her hand and arm ached, and finally stained it and applied a Varathane finish. It looked really good, if she did say so herself. Too bad the molding and floors still looked so bad.

But in early April, spring could no longer be denied, and today she was going to assess the tools her grandmother had owned, and what needed to be done to get the yard in shape. Of course, she took her life in her hands every time she went down the rotten porch steps. She didn't think the siding had rotted, except the porch skirt, but couldn't be positive.

Erin was acquiring a library of how-to books, since she had zero construction experience and didn't even know how to replace a washer in a dripping faucet. She'd never refinished a piece of furniture—or floors—and barely knew a dandelion from a peony. She could afford to hire some help, but right now she didn't want workers in and out of the house, blocking the driveway, wondering about the young woman who probably looked like she'd been rescued from a life raft that had drifted in the Pacific Ocean for three months.

To get to the detached garage, she couldn't cut across the yard because it was, well, a thicket. Fortunately, the driveway had been asphalted at some point, although the cracks in it allowed grass and weeds to send down roots. The garage had been updated more recently than the house, probably when an upstairs apartment had been completed. Of course, that was something like forty years ago. There'd been a time when her grandparents had rented out the garage apartment for extra income. Erin remembered from visits when she was a child that a young man not only lived in the apartment but did yard work, too. After Grandpa died, though, Nanna had quit renting it out. Maybe she hadn't liked the idea of a stranger so close. Erin hadn't thought to ask.

She should have visited more often, seen that Nanna needed help. One more reason to feel guilty.

Join the crowd.

Now the apartment was dated, to put it kindly. The refrigerator was harvest gold. There was no dishwasher. The showerhead had corroded, the fiberglass walls of the shower showed small cracks and the toilet and sink were both a sort of orangey-yellow that might also qualify as harvest gold. The apartment was at the absolute bottom of her list of needed updates, however.

Heaving the garage door open, she mentally moved a remote-controlled opener a few notches up on her list.

The workbench probably hadn't been put to use in decades. Unfortunately, the tools she located obviously hadn't, either. Rust was crumbling the teeth of a handsaw. The pliers might work, but the blade of the shovel had long since separated from the handle. The rake lacked some tines, and the clippers... She squeezed with all her might and nothing happened except a shower of rusty dust.

Along with the smaller tools, drawers contained tin cans filled with miscellaneous screws, nuts and nails, a hose nozzle, a couple of mousetraps and some object that looked like a branding iron. Very useful.

The lawn mower... Well, if she could ever scythe the overgrown grass, weeds and blackberries down into something that resembled a lawn, she would need a new mower. This one was destined for the junkyard.

Today, she decided, hardware shopping she would go. Hi-ho, the derry-o...

And if she was lucky, the store would have one of those bulletin boards covered with business cards advertising useful people like electricians, plumbers and handymen.

USUALLY, SOMEONE IN a hardware store would buy a particular tool. Clippers with a longer handle than the ones she had, say. Or replace a shovel.

As he waited for the elderly man leaning on the counter to quit gossiping, Cole Meacham idly watched the woman pushing a cart. She barely hesitated over her choices. Far as he could tell, she bought one of everything. Who didn't have the basics?

Her, evidently. She had to be a new home-owner.

He watched out of curiosity, but she'd caught his eye because she was a woman—and appealing. Long hair somewhere between red and blond, caught up in a messy bundle on the back of her head. She was too thin for his taste—although he wouldn't swear his taste had remained in cold storage and therefore unchanged—but long-legged and still curvy. A baggy denim shirt hid enough of her breasts to leave him wondering—

A brusque voice had his head snapping around. "Done with that application?"

"Yes, sir."

In this small-town hardware store, the manager had been running the cash register while chatting with his customers. A notice in the window had said Help Wanted. When Cole asked about the job, the guy had hardly glanced at him, but handed over an application.

Filling it out had taken Cole a whole lot longer than it should have. His hands had shaken, and sweat beaded his forehead and trickled down his spine. All those little boxes. Some of them he could fill in, some he couldn't. He had no current driver's license. The employment history made him clench his teeth. He either had no recent jobs to list—or he admitted what kind of jobs they'd been. *Where* they'd been.

But inevitably he came to the question he dreaded, the one asking whether he'd been convicted of a felony crime. It never asked if he'd *committed* a crime. He marked "yes," as he had on all the other applications he'd filled out these past days. Lying wasn't an option; employers could, and would, do a criminal background check before offering a job. Cole's father always had.

The manager bent his head to read Cole's application, revealing a small bald spot on the crown. Waiting without much hope, Cole stared at it. Behind him, the wheels of a shopping cart rattled on the uneven floor in the old building.

He saw the exact moment when the man reached that "yes" mark. His eyes narrowed and he looked up. "How long you been out?"

"A week."

Shaking his head, he crumpled the application and tossed it toward what was presumably a trash receptacle behind the counter. "Don't need to know what you did. Can't have an ex-con working here. Now I'll ask you to be on your way."

Cole nodded stoically and turned to find himself face-to-face with the woman he'd been watching. Of course she'd heard. He didn't let himself see her expression or what would be shock and distaste in her eyes. He said a meaningless, "Ma'am," and walked past, taking the most direct route to the front door.

Outside, he turned left and walked twenty feet or so, until he was no longer in sight through the hardware store windows, before he stopped. He flattened his hands on the wood siding and allowed his head to drop forward.

Maybe he'd have to give up on this shit town. West Fork. He'd refused to stay anywhere near the penitentiary on the east side of the mountains. The Greyhound bus had taken him to Seattle. Overwhelmed by the city, he had hitched north, looking for a smaller town he could handle, one that seemed friendly.

He made a guttural sound. *Friendly.* What a joke. He needed to move on, but why would the next town be any different?

"Excuse me."

At the sound of the voice, Cole whirled, his right hand balling into a fist. He *never* allowed himself to be unaware of his surroundings.

It was her. The woman from the hardware store. Green-gold eyes widened and she retreated a step, making him realize his lips had drawn away from his teeth and every cord in his neck probably showed. It took him a couple of deep breaths, but he managed to straighten, and he outwardly relaxed even if his heart still raced.

"Sorry," he mumbled. "You startled me."

"That's all right." She studied him. "I heard. In there."

Cole schooled his face to blankness. He didn't say anything.

"I'm wondering what kind of job you'd consider. And what you know how to do."

He stared at her. What did he know how to do? That was what she'd said.

"Because, well, this wouldn't be long-term, but…it might tide you over for a while, and I really need someone. That is, if you know anything about yard work or basic construction. Like building porch steps or scraping siding." Pink crept into her cheeks, as if his blank expression was getting to her, making her babble. "Not that scraping siding takes any experience or skill, I guess."

"I can build porch steps." His voice came out rusty. Was she offering him a job? "And scrape and paint. And yard work?" He shrugged. "As long as I know what's expected."

"If you're interested, I can pay ten dollars an hour, maybe up it once I have a better sense of what you can do."

"Is this…a business?" he fumbled.

She shook her head. "I inherited an old house

from my grandmother. It's...well, not falling down, but in need of a lot of work. Since it's spring, I thought I'd start with the exterior and yard. It's a mess."

"You have a husband or...?"

"Nobody. And my spirit is willing, but I've never done this kind of work. I need help—someone with muscle and at least some know-how."

"I can provide that." He still sounded like he had a hairball caught in his throat, but she'd taken him by surprise. No, more than that. Was she *nuts*, hiring an ex-con she knew nothing about to work on her house? With apparently no man around to protect her?

His conscience kicked in. "You did hear. I just got out of prison."

Here was where she'd ask what crime he'd committed. But once again, she surprised him. "How long were you in?"

"Ten years."

She blinked. "You said you've only been out a week."

And he felt like a toddler abandoned in the freeway median. Everything whizzing by, with him too terrified to move.

"Yes."

"Do you want the job?"

His throat almost closed. Even a day or two

of work would give him the means to eat for a week. He had nothing to fall back on. Ten years ago, he'd spent every cent he had on his defense.

"Yes." After a moment, he added a belated, "Thank you."

"Well, then, will you help me load this stuff?"

"Yes, ma'am."

"Erin. My name is Erin Parrish."

He nodded.

"And yours?"

"Cole Meacham."

"Cole."

He trailed her to the front of the hardware store, but then his feet stopped moving. "Where are you parked?"

"Out back."

Was there a parking lot behind the building? He hadn't noticed. "Why don't I meet you there?"

"Oh. Sure. See you there," she said, matter-of-fact. She disappeared inside, and he turned to circle the corner.

A job. Maybe only a few days, but real work. Basic work, the kind that hadn't changed in the past ten years. A hot little burn in his chest wasn't pride or even hope, but might be kin to either.

Unless she changed her mind, or had it changed for her by the man in the hardware store, who must've been horrified when the pretty woman customer chased the ex-con outside. Yeah, that was what would happen. His steps slowed. She'd say something like, "I'm sorry, but I just got a call from a guy who decided to take the job, after all." She might offer him a little money, which pride required him to refuse. Shit, why was he going to meet her at all, setting himself up for more disappointment?

But as he started across the parking lot, Cole saw her struggling with the glass door as she tried to back out with her overloaded cart. He broke into a trot, firmly taking the handle and saying, "Hold the door."

She glared inside. "With what I just spent, you'd think that jerk could've offered to help."

"He's afraid of me." *The way you should be.*

She sniffed. "I may have to drive out to the freeway next time and shop at Lowe's."

A smile wanted to break across Cole's face. Erin Parrish might be a little strange, but what the hell?

His stomach growled.

ERIN BACKED HER Jeep Grand Cherokee up to the garage, never so glad she'd bought it last year instead of the Mustang she'd had her eye on. Back then, she'd told herself she wanted a burly vehicle, with a powerful engine. Hauling anything but a new piece of furniture had been the last thing on her mind.

She sneaked a sidelong look at the man beside her. There'd been a time when she thought through every decision before acting. The old Erin Parrish was the antonym of *impulsive*, but that woman no longer existed.

She knew what had triggered this impulse. It wasn't so much that he'd been turned down for a job he obviously needed desperately or even the reason he was rejected that got to her. No, she'd been watching his face, assuming she'd see disappointment, shame, perhaps anger. Instead, she'd seen only resignation. He hadn't expected to be hired. She'd found herself wondering if this man expected anything good from anybody.

And then she'd heard herself say, "Will you ring up my stuff? I'll be right back," and had gone racing after him.

When she approached him on the sidewalk, his head was hanging so low she couldn't see his expression, but his body spoke of despair. She'd been conscious of how powerful that body was, noticed the tattoo peeking out above the collar of his white undershirt. When he whirled, prepared to fight, wariness finally kicked in, but then she saw how gaunt his bony face was, that his shirt was wrinkled, his boots worn. His brown hair was cut brutally short, and his expressionless eyes were an icy blue. She had the kind of thought that would once have appalled her.

He could be a murderer. Maybe he'd kill her.

I should be dead. If he corrected that little mistake, so be it.

Here she was at Nanna's house. *Me and the ex-con.* Nanna had to be shuddering, wherever she was.

She turned off the engine and set the emergency brake. "Home, sweet home." They were the first words out of her mouth—or his—since she'd determined that he had no transportation of his own.

He nodded and got out, going to the rear and waiting until the hatch door rose. When she started muscling the garage door up, he moved fast, taking over before she even heard him coming.

In the garage, he walked a slow circle. "I see why you needed the tools. Although—" he picked up an ax "—some of these can be salvaged with some steel wool and oil."

Me and the ex-con, who is now holding an ax. She cleared her throat. "Really? They're so corroded."

"Just rusty." He set it down. "I'll unload."

Of course she helped. They leaned the old

rake and shovel and whatever else against the wall and used the hooks and nails to hold the new tools. The smaller tools hung above the workbench.

"Okay," she said, "let me show you around."

He followed silently, his expression no more readable. She was slightly unnerved to notice he carried a screwdriver. When they reached the front porch steps, he stabbed the screwdriver into the wood, which made a squishy sound. He removed it, straightened and looked at her. "Your foot'll go right through."

"I have been worrying about that. The back steps aren't so good, either."

He shook his head, poked at the porch apron, then gingerly climbed to the porch itself, where he did some more stabbing.

His verdict? "Whole porch should be rebuilt."

Her shoulders sagged. "Can you do that?"

"Sure."

"Well, then." Gosh, buying lumber might have been a smart thing to do. She'd bought a circular saw with the vague idea that she could use it for small projects. Was that what he'd need?

"Can you drive?" she asked.

Not wasting even one word, he shook his head.

"Then I guess I should go to the lumberyard."

"Did you buy a measuring tape?"

Oops. "I'll…go see if I can find one inside."

"I'll check the workbench. If you can get a pencil and piece of paper…"

Feeling awkward, she went inside, aware that he'd disappeared into the garage. The best she found was an old wooden yardstick. But she stepped out onto the porch to find him crouched, a metal measuring tape already extended across the porch steps. "I can do the writing," she offered.

He reeled off dimensions and what kind of board was needed. Two-by-four. Four-by-four. Two-by-two. Nails. Primer. Brushes. He asked if she'd bought paint for the house yet. No.

"Might be good to decide what colors you want," he suggested. "Then I can paint the porch as I go, while the weather holds."

She could do that.

He said he hadn't seen a ladder. She told him she had a stepladder inside. A faintly condescending expression crept over his impassive face. Three steps wouldn't get him very high on the side of the house, he pointed out. Um, no, they wouldn't.

"Tell you what," he said finally. "If you want to run to the lumberyard, I'll get the clippers and start cutting back the growth that's crowding the house. Can't scrape it if I can't get to it."

"Will you recognize the lilac and…there used to be a big climbing rose to the right of the porch?" she asked, remembering the garden in bloom so many years ago. "Oh, and some rhododendrons."

"I'll recognize them."

They agreed she could pick up paint chips today and think overnight about what colors she wanted for the house. When she left, clutching the piece of paper with the materials list, she told him the front door was unlocked if he needed the bathroom. But she saw his face. He wouldn't be going in.

Now was a fine time to wonder whether she'd crossed the line to crazy.

CHAPTER TWO

COLE SWUNG THE machete in a smooth rhythm, glad Erin had thought to buy one. The sharp blade sliced through blackberry canes, salmonberries, fireweed and other nuisance weeds, baring the foundation and clapboard siding of the old house. He used the ancient clothesline he'd found in the garage to pull salvageable shrubs away from the house.

When he heard the Jeep turn into the driveway, he walked around the corner of the house to meet her.

The first thing he noticed was the aluminum extension ladder tied to the roof. Lumber was piled in the back of the Jeep, extending beyond the bumper. A strip of red cloth dangled from the end of the longest board.

He forgot everything else when Erin got out, carrying a pizza box.

His stomach cramped and saliva filled his mouth. Pride made him want to thank her politely and refuse her offer of lunch, but he was too damn hungry. If he didn't get more to eat, he wouldn't be able to do the work she'd asked of him.

"Let's eat before we unload," she said.

He managed a stiff, "Thank you."

She handed over the pizza. "I have bottled water and some Pepsi in the fridge. Milk, too. What would you like?"

When was the last time anyone had given him a choice? He didn't want milk, he knew that, but only said, "Anything."

She disappeared into the house, returning with two cans of pop and a bottle of water, as well as what looked like a wad of paper towels. When she saw him sitting on the bottom porch step, legs outstretched, she put the drinks down within reach and sat, too.

"We aren't going to end up on our butts in the dirt if we move wrong, are we?"

He felt a tiny spark of amusement, which surprised him. "There's not far to fall."

"Well…that's true." She picked up a slice of pizza and started eating.

She'd bought a half-meat, half-cheese pizza. He sank his teeth into a slice heaped with sausage, pepperoni and mushrooms, almost groaning with pleasure.

"How far did you get with the weeding?" she asked eventually.

"About halfway around." Did she realize it

might take a couple of weeks to do the job she'd talked about, rather than the two or three days he'd originally expected?

"Any surprises?"

"Some siding that'll need to be replaced." He'd used the screwdriver to check for rot as he went.

She scrunched up her nose. "Figures."

Two pieces later, he said, "The gutters are in bad shape."

"I noticed rain was running right over them."

Without a ladder, he hadn't been able to look closely, but they were obviously packed full of leaves, fir needles and debris. They'd also torn away from the eaves in places. She might decide to hire a company that specialized in gutters to replace them instead of keeping him on.

He stopped eating sooner than he would have liked, and began unloading the Jeep. Erin came to help him. The lumber went in the garage. He propped the new ladder against the house, figuring they'd need it today. When she put on gloves and started scraping, he went back to taming the wild growth.

By now, there was some burn in his muscles as he swung the machete. Lifting weights built muscle, but this required a different kind of motion. To block out the discomfort, he turned his thoughts in another direction.

He hadn't let himself speculate about another person in a long time, but as the next couple of hours passed, Cole did a lot of thinking about Erin Parrish. How could he help it?

Despite his wariness, he spent some time savoring the pleasure of watching her. Whenever he passed behind her, his gaze lingered on the long, slim line of her back, the subtle curve of her waist and hips, her ass and astonishing legs. He had a feeling he'd have no trouble picturing her face tonight when he should be trying to sleep. Her eyes were beautiful, the gold bright in sunlight, the green predominant in the dimmer lighting of the garage. The delicacy of her jaw, cheekbones and nose turned him on as much as her body did. He hadn't seen anything this pretty in ten long years.

But mostly he tried to understand what she'd been thinking.

Why would a lone woman hire someone like him, no questions asked? He could be a rapist, a murderer; how would she know? She might have assumed she was safe, midday in a residential neighborhood, but he could have pushed her into the house more quickly than she realized. Or yanked the garage door down while they were piling lumber in there. Done whatever he chose, then walked away.

He wanted to ask why she'd hired him, but he

wanted the job more. Encouraging her to have second thoughts wasn't in his best interests.

Yeah, but this could be a setup. What if she got what labor she could out of him, then refused to pay him? He'd have no recourse. Although, considering what she knew about him, it seemed unlikely she'd take the risk of pissing him off.

A darker scenario occurred to him. He could get some of the hard work done, and then she could cry rape or assault. Whether there was any physical evidence or not, her word would be taken over his.

Hell, he thought. Accepting this job hadn't been smart. But he circled back to hard reality—he was desperate. No one else would hire him. He'd already run out of the limited amount of money he'd been given on leaving the joint. And he was flirting with trouble, anyway, because one of the conditions of parole was having a place to live and a job. His sister had agreed he could say he'd be able to stay with her, but that had never been an option. Her husband wanted nothing to do with her ex-con brother, refused to let Cole near their kids.

He had to contact his parole officer soon and have an acceptable alternative, or he'd find himself back in his cell.

Whatever Erin Parrish was thinking, she was

a hard worker who made good progress scraping the siding while he continued beating back the jungle. When he finished, he returned to find her standing high on the ladder, stretching as far as she could to reach a spot beneath the eaves.

"What should I do with the piles of stuff I cut?" he asked.

Turning too quickly, she lurched. He lunged forward and grabbed the ladder to steady it.

Gripping the ladder herself, she blew out a breath. "Sorry. I didn't hear you coming."

Despite a temperature that was likely in the midsixties, he'd worked up a sweat, and saw that she had, too. Damp strands of hair clung to her cheeks, and she wiped her forehead with her forearm. Flakes of white paint looked like confetti in her hair and on her shoulders.

"I have no idea," she admitted after a minute. "I noticed when I put out my garbage can that a couple of neighbors had big green ones, too. I wonder if they're for yard waste? I'll call the company and find out. Otherwise, I might need to get a Dumpster of some kind. I think it's possible to rent one."

"You might need both. There'll be nails in what I tear off the house. Some of that wood's been treated or painted, too. It can't go in yard waste."

"Oh. Right."

"Why don't you come down? I'll deal with what's up there, above your reach."

She looked mulish. "I'm doing okay."

"I'm taller and I have longer arms." And if she fell and was injured, he'd be up shit creek. How could he ask for his pay while she was being loaded in the ambulance?

"Oh, fine." She climbed down with extra care.

Cole saw that she was trembling, and it couldn't be from cold. Suddenly angry, he said, "You're exhausted."

She glared at him. "I can keep working."

He plucked the scraper out of her hand. "You've done enough for one day."

"It's none of your business if I want—"

Something froze inside him. He set the scraper down on a ladder rung and stepped back. "You're right."

He'd started to walk away when she said, "I'm sorry. I'm being stupid."

Stupid? Cole turned around. He thought it was shame that colored her cheeks.

"I don't have much upper body strength," she admitted. "It's been a while since—" She broke off. "I don't like feeling useless, but you're right. I've reached my limit."

He didn't dare say anything.

Her eyes shied away from his. "I'll go in and

call the garbage company. And look at the paint samples. Um, if you'd like to stay for dinner—"

He shook his head.

"Well, then…"

"I can get a couple more hours in."

She backed away. "Okay. Thank you. Don't take off without knocking. I'll pay you as we go. Cash for now, unless you'd rather have a check—"

"I don't have a bank account yet."

She nodded and disappeared around the corner of the house. A minute later, he heard the front door close.

Cole shifted the ladder and started in where she'd left off.

ERIN DIDN'T SLEEP any better than she had the night before, or any other night in months. This was different only because she had something new to think about.

Some*one*.

Cole Meacham disturbed her.

The irony was, she could hardly bear being around people who wanted any kind of normal interaction with her. Whether it was chatting about nothing or an exchange of deeply personal information, either had her longing for escape. Cole asked for neither. He seemed to have no more interest in chatting than she did. Less. He

answered questions as briefly as possible, and
sometimes she sensed him struggling to pull
a response from somewhere deep inside him,
as if he'd forgotten how to make conversation.

That was fine with her. He was a day laborer,
that was all. She hoped she was helping him
out, as he was helping her. And maybe her self-
consciousness around him, her constant awareness of him, was only because of his history. As
far as she knew, she'd never met anyone who
had served a term in prison, or if she had, they
hadn't looked the part as completely as he did.

The nearly shaved head emphasized the sharp
edges of his cheekbones, the hollows beneath,
the strong line of his jaw. She wondered about
the tattoo reaching toward his collarbone. Today,
he hadn't removed the chambray shirt he wore
loose over a ribbed white undershirt or tank,
she wasn't quite sure which. He'd rolled up the
sleeves, exposing muscular, sinewy forearms
dusted with brown hair but exhibiting no ink.
Was his entire back or chest covered with tattoos? What about his shoulders?

Moaning, Erin flipped over in bed. The knowledge that he had a tattoo increased her visceral
knowledge that he could be dangerous. That, and
his complete lack of expression.

Every so often, she imagined she saw a flicker
of something, but *imagined* was probably the

right word. Did he not feel anything? Or had he just become adept at hiding any hint of emotion or vulnerability?

Even when she'd paid him shortly after five, he had only nodded and stuffed the bills in his jeans pocket without counting them first. He'd thanked her in that gruff, quiet voice, asked what time he should start in the morning and refused her offer of a ride.

Where was he staying? Had he been able to rent a room somewhere, or did he have a friend or family in West Fork? Most places in town were within walking distance. Erin might have asked, except she'd known how unwelcome any personal question would be. And she'd learned to hate intrusive questions herself, so she had to respect his feelings.

Would he show up in the morning? If he didn't... Of course she could find someone else, but Erin knew she'd hate not knowing what had happened to him. Despite her prickling sense that he could be a threat, he had been almost painfully polite all day, even gentlemanly. The way he'd leaped when he thought she might fall from the ladder, and then urged her to stop work when he could tell she was tired, seemed like the behavior of a guy whose protective instincts were alive and well.

Or else he didn't want her to overdo or hurt

herself because he was afraid of losing even this short-term job. She made a face. That was more likely. He was an ex-con.

Only, she knew too well that everyone made mistakes. A life-shattering mistake was never more than a heartbeat away. Sometimes, the mistake was no more than a moment of inattention.

ERIN FINISHED BREAKFAST and a first cup of coffee, disappointed that Cole hadn't knocked to let her know he'd arrived. She was sure she would have heard him if he'd started in without waiting for her. Maybe one day's pay was enough to allow him to drift along.

But she decided to look outside, and when she opened the front door, she saw him leaning against the fender of her Cherokee. He straightened and walked up the driveway as she descended the porch steps.

"I hope you haven't been waiting," she said.

"Not long."

His tongue hadn't loosened overnight.

"You could have started. Or come up to the house for a cup of coffee."

"I didn't want to wake you."

Couldn't he tell how little sleeping she actually did? Or…maybe he had.

"Would you like some coffee?"

"Had a cup on my way here," he said briefly.

"Oh. Okay." She couldn't ask if that was true. "But you're always welcome—"

"I'll get started." Apparently, they were done talking. Except he didn't move, but shifted his weight from foot to foot in what might be a hint of uncertainty. "Thought I might work on the porch today instead of the siding." Pause. "If that's okay with you."

"Yes. Oh! That's probably a good idea. I keep thinking a step will give way."

He nodded.

"Thank you. Do you need help?"

"Not now."

So she retreated to the house for a second cup of coffee that *she* needed, and brooded about the fact that he was wearing the same clothes as yesterday. She recognized the tear on the right knee of his jeans, and a stain on the tail of the chambray shirt. No reason that should worry her; given how dirty the job was, putting on clean clothes every morning didn't make sense. She had on yesterday's ragged jeans herself. Chances were good he'd only have a few changes of clothing. Even if he had plenty of money, running out and buying a new wardrobe probably wasn't a priority.

Besides, she'd embarrass him if she said anything.

Since he obviously didn't need assistance, she

went back to scraping. Sore muscles screamed; if they didn't loosen up, she'd have to find something else to do.

She stuck to it for about an hour before whimpering and letting her arm fall to her side. Coaching volleyball and softball, she'd stayed in condition. The weight she'd lost since the crash, plus six months of idleness, were apparently exacting a cost.

From where she was working, she hadn't been able to see Cole, but the screech of nails and the ripping sound of boards being torn up hadn't stopped. Walking around the house, she stopped at the sight of a bigger-than-expected pile of splintered lumber.

He'd finished with the porch floorboards and now had one knee on a step as he pried up a board on the step above. It didn't come up cleanly. With a sodden sound, one end separated.

Erin winced. She'd been careful to stay close to the edge and cling to the rail as she went up and down the steps, but still...

His head turned and he fastened those icy eyes on her.

She approached. "You've made good progress."

"This part doesn't take long." He kept watching her. "The supports are rotting, too. I'm going to have to rebuild from the ground up."

"I guess that's not a surprise. I think the porch is original to the house."

"The steps aren't as old as the rest of the porch."

"My grandfather kept things up until his health declined. Even then, he made sure the work got done."

"When did he die?"

A little startled that he'd actually asked, she said, "Fifteen years ago? No, more than that. Seventeen or eighteen."

He nodded, then changed the subject. "Did you order a Dumpster?"

"Yes. They'll deliver it either today or tomorrow. I also asked for two yard waste bins."

He had that brief dip of his head down pat. Saved a lot of words.

She gazed upward. "I'll have to buy shingles." She assumed he would rebuild the porch roof.

"And some plywood. Different kind of nails, too."

He agreed he'd make her a new list or accompany her to the lumberyard, although an even blanker than usual face suggested he'd rather not go on an outing. With her? Or at all?

At his request, she ended up pulling nails out of a pile of boards he'd set aside because he thought they were reusable. At lunchtime, Erin shared the remainder of yesterday's pizza with him, although Cole didn't look thrilled about that.

Erin kept trying to think of some way to ask about his accommodations, but failed. He wouldn't welcome nosiness.

"It almost looks like rain," she finally ventured. "Scattered showers" was what her phone had told her.

He squinted up at the gray sky. "Probably not until evening."

"If it's raining tomorrow, I can put you to work inside."

He barely glanced at her. "I'll set up the saw in the garage, cut the lumber for the porch to size. Might even slap some primer on and let it dry."

He had to be staying *somewhere*. He must have at least a few possessions. Or would he? She couldn't believe the correctional institute released inmates who'd completed their sentences or were on parole with nothing but the clothes on their backs and maybe what they'd had in their pockets when they were arrested. Or did they?

By five o'clock, the front porch was gone. The house seemed oddly naked without it, Erin thought, surveying the result of his work. Behind her, the garage door descended with a groan and bump. She'd noticed before that Cole wiped each tool with a rag and returned it to its place when he was done with it.

She knew he was walking toward her only because she looked over her shoulder. She never heard him coming. Somehow, even wearing boots, he avoided crunching on gravel or broken branches the way she did. His walk, controlled, confident and very male, was part of what made him so physically compelling.

"I won't tear out the back steps until I've replaced this," Cole said.

She found herself smiling. "Climbing in and out of the house on a ladder would be fun."

Was that a flicker of humor in his eyes? No, surely not.

She dug his pay out of her pocket and handed it over. Feeling the first drizzle, she said, "Would you like a lift tonight?"

"I'll be fine." He inclined his head and then walked away, turning right at the foot of the drive.

Going where?

COLE HAD DECIDED to take a chance tonight and wrap himself in his blanket beneath a picnic table in the county park. It was on the river about a mile out of town. He'd be less conspicuous hidden in the shadow under the table than he would lying between tables on the concrete pad.

Previous nights, he'd stayed in the woods, out of sight of any patrolling officer. A couple of times, he'd seen headlights swing slowly through the small park during the night. Cops wouldn't want homeless squatters using the facilities here, limited though they were. There was a restroom, unlocked during the day, but locked by the time Cole got here after work. Wouldn't have done him much good, anyway, since it lacked showers. He could clean up a little with river water come morning. Thanks to the pay in his pocket, he'd stopped at a mom-and-pop grocery store this evening and bought a bar of soap and deodorant, as well as food. If he stayed here long, he might think about picking up some charcoal and using the grill in the pavilion. And if he had transportation at some point, there was a state park a few miles upriver, where he could get an actual campsite and have the right to use restrooms that did have hot showers. But until he could afford a motorcycle, or at least a bike, that was out.

Cole pillowed his head on the duffel bag holding his only change of clothes. To combat the claustrophobia he'd felt the minute he squirmed beneath the picnic table, he thought about the day's work and what he hoped to accomplish tomorrow. His effort at distraction didn't entirely work. Built out of really solid, pressure-treated wood, the table was bolted to the concrete. The only way out was to roll under one of the benches. What might have felt cozy to him when he was a kid now felt like a trap. The patter of rain on the pavilion roof persuaded him to stay put, though. Not that he wouldn't be soaked by the time he walked to Erin's in the morning. He debated whether he should wear his other shirt and pair of jeans. Damned if he wanted her feeling sorry for him.

He grunted. Who was he kidding? Why else had she hired him? And, by God, he should be grateful that she *had* let pity overcome her common sense. If she kept him on even a couple of weeks… For about the hundredth time, he calculated how much money he'd make. Eight hundred dollars sounded like a lot right now, but if he couldn't find another job immediately, it wouldn't last long, especially if he added rent to his expenses. He'd looked at the local weekly paper, but the classified section listed only two apartment rentals, both way more than he could afford, even with a full-time job paying minimum wage. Especially if first and last months' rent was required up front. There ought to be rooms available, but if so they were listed somewhere else. He'd have to hunt for bulletin boards that might have ads for rentals. And from what he'd heard, there might be online listings. He mulled over the idea of going to the library tomorrow night, but imagined how people would look at him, wet and dirty. Learning how to navigate the internet would take time and energy. It could wait.

Tonight, though…tonight his stomach was full, and he wasn't being rained on. He could have used another blanket, but the concrete wasn't much harder than his bunk in the pen had been, and he felt safer here in the dark by himself than he had during his ten years in Walla Walla.

And tomorrow, he had a purpose. He liked building. He particularly liked building for her, an uncomfortable realization. Even so, he let himself fantasize a little. Thinking about a woman's softness and sweet smell didn't hurt anything, did it?

CHAPTER THREE

"YOU'RE SOAKED," ERIN said behind him.

In the middle of nailing together some of the lumber he'd salvaged to form crude sawhorses, Cole straightened and slowly turned to face her. The rain was little more than a drizzle now, but droplets shimmered in her hair like scattered pearls. Damp, it looked darker, more red than blond.

"I'll dry," he said with a shrug. Yeah, it had been coming down harder when he started his walk. He hoped the contents of his duffel remained mostly dry where he'd stashed it beneath the undergrowth at the base of a big cedar.

She crossed her arms and scowled. "Where are you staying?"

"What difference does it make?"

"You have to be miserable!"

"Getting wet is nothing."

She huffed and he half expected to see steam coming out of her ears. "It's not nothing! What if you get sick?"

"I won't—"

"Why don't you want me to know where you're staying? Do you think I'll come knocking on your door or something?"

He wished. "No." A brief hesitation later, he surrendered. "I'm camping out. It's spring, not that cold. It'll do until I can afford a place."

Her eyes narrowed. "Do you have a tent? A sleeping bag? A camp stove?"

In another few days, he might be able to out-fit himself.

"I guess the answer is no," she said.

Yes, it was.

They stared at each other, Cole making sure no emotion broke cover.

She turned her back on him, appearing to study the tools hanging on the wall. "There's an apartment upstairs."

"I can't—"

"It's crappy," she went on, as if he hadn't spoken. "But it's dry, and there's electricity, and I think the plumbing works."

"I can't accept—" The words died on his tongue when she swung around to glare at him.

"Do you know how much I *hated* seeing you walk away in the rain?"

Something did crack then, not in the shell he'd perfected but deep inside him. It was a strange, wrenching experience.

Why would she care?

"Here's the deal. Once I finished with the house, I intended to get the apartment remodeled. If you'll eventually do the work, I'll take that in lieu of rent. We both benefit."

He couldn't look away from her. The freckles scattered across her nose and cheeks were pronounced with her color high. He wanted to touch them. He wanted a lot of things he couldn't have.

Would it be painful to look out the window at night and see a light in her bedroom window, her shadow moving behind the curtains? Maybe. But if he had a place here in town, he could walk to the library, or any other place open evenings. Perhaps make some friends.

"I'll take a look," he said abruptly.

"I'll get my keys."

He finished constructing the sawhorses while she was gone, only able to accomplish it because nailing a few two-by-fours together didn't demand much concentration. When Erin returned, he followed her to the outside staircase and up to a small landing, where she fumbled getting a key in the lock and opening the door. Had she noticed this staircase needed replacing, too?

He stepped inside and studied the space. It was furnished, although thrift stores would probably say *no, thanks* to the sofa with sagging cushions and a television that might qualify as an antique. The kitchen at one end was small but complete, including a table with two chairs. She stayed by the door when he stuck his head in the bedroom—double bed, closet, dresser. He went into the tiny bathroom. Water ran when he turned the faucet handles. Ditto in the shower, although the spray was more of a dribble. Would there be any hot water? He could live without, but— Damned if it wasn't warming up.

Cole went out to find her opening and closing the kitchen cupboards.

"I'll grab some cleaning supplies."

"I'll clean," he insisted.

"No. I can't do your work so it's only fair. In fact, there isn't much I *can* do while it's raining. Paint inside, maybe, but I'm still deciding on colors." When he didn't argue, she said quietly, "Let me do this."

Kindness from strangers was easier to accept than from a woman he was getting to know. Even so, after a moment, he nodded and said hoarsely, "Thank you."

She couldn't have any idea that this shabby apartment looked like paradise to him. A space he'd have to himself. Being able to shower without listening to every word spoken around him. Staying constantly aware of who was nearby, maintaining a state of readiness. He could keep a light on all night if he wanted. He wouldn't have to hear snores and grumbles and occasional shouts, remain aware that guards were checking in on him.

If she intended to rent out the apartment in the future, it would need work. The impulse might have been charitable, but he wouldn't have to feel indebted to her. She'd been careful that way, he thought, treating him like a man who deserved his dignity.

She gave him the key, which he tucked carefully in his pocket. How long since he'd had a key that opened any door?

"Will you let me drive you to pick up your stuff tonight?"

Cole's instinct was to refuse help he didn't absolutely need, but she knew his real circumstances now. "I don't have much."

"Why should you have to walk?" she asked simply.

He dipped his head, choking a little on another "Thank you." As he returned to work, Cole realized that this gave him an address that would satisfy his parole officer. If the job was going to last even a few weeks, it would be enough, at least for now. Except that meant the parole officer would be calling Erin, which Cole hated.

Live with it, he told himself, locking down

the angry sense of outrage and humiliation he'd felt from the minute the jury foreman had said, "Guilty as charged."

THE DRIZZLE NEVER did let up. Working in the apartment, Erin heard the on-and-off buzz of the circular saw in the garage below. She started with the kitchen, scrubbing the sink, the stove and the inside of the refrigerator, which—to her astonishment—hummed when she plugged it in. She cleaned the countertops, the interior of the cheap cabinets, the floor. She vacuumed the sofa and wiped cobwebs from corners with a broom. The television didn't come on. She'd have to see that cable service was hooked up for the apartment, anyway. Cole wouldn't be happy to have her buying a new TV, but if she offered a furnished apartment down the line, she'd have to include one, so why not now?

The bedroom didn't take long, except for mopping the vinyl floor. She bundled up the rag rug, curtains and mattress pad and started a load in her washing machine at the house. Exploring Nanna's linen closet, she found a set of worn but soft flannel sheets in the right size. She'd have to buy a bath mat to replace the one she'd thrown away, but had plenty of towels to supply the apartment.

She persuaded a reluctant Cole to accept a

sandwich, pop and potato chips for lunch. When she suggested he come inside to eat, he said, "I'm wet and dirty." Carrying their meal, she trailed him to the garage, where she hopped up on the workbench and he sat on a pile of lumber. Instead of pushing him to talk, she reminisced about her grandparents and long-ago visits. He didn't seem to mind.

By the time he was ready to call it a day, he'd built the framework of her new porch with pressure-treated beams and four-by-fours resting on the original concrete blocks. He agreed she should make another trip to the lumberyard in the morning.

"This costing more than you expected?" he asked, not quite casually. He pulled the seat belt around himself.

Erin started the engine, eager for the heater to kick in. "No, if I'd had to hire a contractor, I'm betting the job would've cost a whole lot more," she said frankly. "In fact, I'm bumping up your pay."

He shook his head. "Not when you're letting me stay here, too."

"That's a separate deal—"

"No." Completely inflexible.

She put the gearshift in Reverse, but kept her foot on the brake. "Has anybody ever told you how stubborn you are?"

"Could be."

"Hmph."

Giving him a suspicious, sidelong look, she could swear she saw the corner of his mouth lift. Even the idea that he'd smiled made her heart feel weightless. Which was dangerous territory. Falling for an ex-con because he had gorgeous blue eyes, sculpted cheekbones and awe-inspiring muscles would be incredibly stupid. Always law-abiding, she'd been the quintessential good girl and was now an educated woman, a college professor.

Had been a college professor. Every time she thought about returning to the classroom, she hit a concrete wall. Couldn't see through it or around it. She'd had no success imagining what she might do instead, either. To keep her heart from racing and panic from prickling her skin, she reminded herself that there was no hurry. She wasn't spending any more money working on the house than she would have paying her former mortgage. She could afford a year off before she had to worry about the future and still have investments, thanks to the inheritance from her parents and Nanna's savings, too. By then... But she hit the same blank wall when she tried to see any future.

"Where to?" she asked abruptly, refusing to turn her head to meet his scrutiny.

"County park on the river." Erin nodded, remembering summer picnics there. Grandpa had taken her fishing, too, an enthusiasm she never came to share. Were his fishing pole, waders and tackle box still in the garage? She hadn't paid attention to anything that wasn't immediately useful.

The drive passed in silence, as so much of her time with Cole did. It was restful, except… she increasingly found herself wondering about him. What had this quiet, hardworking, patient man done that had earned him ten *years* in prison? Her mind balked when she tried to picture him committing any of the obvious crimes.

He had her pull into the day-use area at the park, and he disappeared into the mist clinging to the old-growth trees preserved by the county. He returned with a canvas duffel bag, which he deposited behind the seat. Erin opened her mouth but managed to close it before she said something stupid like, *That's all?*

He hadn't even had a sleeping bag. Horrified, she pictured him lying on the ground. At most he had a blanket of some kind in that bag—but if he did, it meant he didn't own much of anything else.

And wouldn't take anything more from her. She'd have to keep biting her tongue. She'd lose him if she tried to make him an object of charity.

And no, she wouldn't let herself examine what she meant by "lose him."

"Okay if we stop at the grocery store?" she asked when they were close to town.

She felt his swift glance. "Sure."

He followed her inside and picked up a basket, separating from her right away. Erin tried not to mind as she filled a cart with perishables. When she carried her bags out, he was already waiting with two grocery bags of his own. They stowed them together in the back of the Jeep. During the short drive, she struggled for a conversational opener and came up short. The first words she spoke were when she pulled into the driveway.

"It would be nice to park in the garage someday."

"You might want an automatic opener before you try that."

"No kidding. I'd never realized how heavy a garage door could be."

"The rails might be rusted," he said thoughtfully. "I'll take a look."

"You're a handy guy, aren't you?"

He grunted and got out. The only other words he had for her were "Good night."

HE COULDN'T BELIEVE everything she'd done in the apartment. Cole was uneasily aware of how personal it felt, knowing she'd been thinking of him when she cleaned, hung a pair of thick towels in the bathroom and made the bed. Every so often his nose picked up some unidentifiable perfume in the air that had to be hers.

Earlier, he'd hauled the old TV down to the garbage can. She'd said, "I'll replace it," in a tone that told him not to argue. Being able to choose what to watch would be a novelty. Maybe he could pick up a DVD player at a thrift store. Tomorrow night, he might walk to the library. If he couldn't get a card yet, libraries usually had donated books for sale. He'd start checking out garage sales, too. Erin got the local weekly and the *Seattle Times*, both of which she recycled. She wouldn't mind if he took them from the recycling bin. Lying on the lumpy sofa, stockinged feet propped on one of its arms, his head on the other, he thought about going downstairs right now and digging out a few papers, but couldn't work up enough interest to make the effort. After a meal and a hot shower, he felt too good. Too relaxed. Too safe.

This is temporary. He shouldn't have needed the reminder. He'd become accustomed to living one day at a time, not letting himself think even a week ahead. If a man couldn't live without hope, he didn't survive a long prison term in his right mind.

Not that Cole was certain he had.

Happy just to be clean and comfortable, he dozed for half an hour, rousing to decide he might as well go to bed. He'd been looking forward to that ever since he saw it made up with baby-soft flannel sheets, a wool blanket and a beautiful old quilt. More luxury.

He turned off lights as he went, brushed his teeth and stared at himself in the mirror. For a second, he almost didn't recognize the face looking back at him. He still saw a death's head instead of the face he'd once known, but... less so. Despite the rain, he'd acquired the beginnings of a tan since he got on that bus out of Walla Walla. His hair hadn't grown very much—he ran a hand over the stubble—but maybe a little.

It was the eyes, he thought, leaning closer to look. They weren't empty anymore. Someone was at home in there. He wasn't sure he liked it, but he *felt* again, and not only rage and despair. He'd have to watch that, not let his emotions get out of hand.

Finally, he turned out that light, too, and walked across the dark bedroom to the window that looked toward the house. He could tell from the shiny reflection that Erin had washed the inside glass, and the curtains smelled fresh. With one pulled aside, he found that he could indeed see the golden square of an upstairs window that had to be Erin's bedroom.

Cole stood there longer than he should have, both grateful and disappointed not to see even a shadow of movement or the silhouette of the slim, womanly body.

THEY WORKED IN harmony the next morning, Cole appearing relaxed. He didn't go so far as to waste a smile, but once, when she was returning for another load of debris to toss in the Dumpster, he raised his chin up, to guide her gaze to the roof of the house. Bright eyes in a furry face looked back at her. A squirrel. The tail gave an agitated jerk, and the squirrel vanished.

Erin chuckled. "I hope his food stash didn't get thrown out with the porch."

"I'd have seen that." Cole placed another nail and swung the hammer.

Smiling, she went back to her job. With his strength, he would have finished it a lot faster, but she couldn't have done a single, useful part of what he was doing. Transferring the pile of splintered, rotting boards to the Dumpster was at her skill level.

At lunchtime, he refused her offer of a bowl of chili and went up to the apartment. Probably to have something like a bologna sandwich, but she understood his need to be self-sufficient.

It didn't seem worth heating anything just for herself. With little appetite despite her labors, Erin cut a few squares of cheese and ate them with crackers, calling it good. When he came out, she was already at work.

His stony face sent a chill through her.

"I need to buy a phone," he said, "but I'm wondering if I can use yours to make one call."

"Of course you can."

Still with that utter lack of expression, he looked at her. "He'll want to talk to you. I'm... due to check in with my parole officer."

"Oh. I see." Did he expect trouble?

"Do you mind if I give him this address?" he asked stiffly.

"It *is* your address as long as you live in the apartment." She pulled her phone from the kangaroo pocket of her sweatshirt. "Here."

He took the phone but didn't move, only stared at it. Erin had started to turn away to give him privacy, then stopped. How long had iPhones been around? Would he ever have used a smartphone of any kind? If not... God, it probably looked like a slab of polished stone to him.

She turned again, careful not to meet his eyes. "Push this button to wake it up."

Without a word, he continued to follow her

instructions, his jaw clenched so tight muscles quivered. He took a business card from his pocket and tapped out the numbers, then said a gruff, "Thanks."

Guessing how hard it had been to say that much, Erin nodded. She went to get one of the yard waste bins, rolling it up the driveway to the first heap of cuttings. Cole had walked a few feet away and stood with his back to her, talking.

She succeeded so well in ignoring him, she gasped and jumped six inches when he touched her shoulder.

"Mr. Ramirez."

Taking the phone, she willed her heartbeat to slow down. She aimed for a brisk tone. "Mr. Ramirez? This is Erin Parrish."

"Ms. Parrish. I'm Mr. Meacham's parole officer. He tells me you've rented him an apartment."

"That's right. He's also working for me."

"So he says."

"He's currently rebuilding the front porch on an old house I inherited. Unfortunately, my grandmother didn't maintain the house or yard very well, so they both need a lot of work that's beyond my skill level. Cole's doing a great job." Wow, listen to her. Bouncy, upbeat. Would she be more believable if she scaled it back? Still, she had to finish. "We came to an agreement that he'll stay in the apartment above the garage in return for working on that, too, once he has the time and I buy the materials."

"So you're satisfied with his work?"

Hadn't she said so? But skepticism was probably part of his job description. "Yes."

"Were you acquainted with Mr. Meacham before his prison term?"

"No, I overheard him applying for a job in town, and thought he might be willing to take on short-term work for me."

He had more questions. How long did she expect to employ Cole? She guessed at least a month. Yes, he was welcome to stay in the apartment after that, provided he did the work on it. She verified the address. West Fork was not in Whatcom County, where Mr. Meacham was supposed to go. Did she know why that hadn't worked out? No, she had no idea.

Yes, this was her phone. She didn't mind if Ramirez called from time to time. She walked into the garage and scribbled his phone number on a sheet of notepaper, below the list Cole had come up with for her next lumberyard run.

When she pocketed the phone again, she went out to find Cole swinging the hammer with short, violent motions. *Wham. Wham.*

"I'll come up with a rental agreement," she

said to his back. He quit hammering but didn't turn. "That way, you can show it anywhere you need to."

He nodded. *Wham. Wham.*

O-kay.

An hour later, he barely glanced at her when she told him she was heading out. When she returned, she showed him the two different kinds of roofing nails she'd bought because she hadn't been sure which was the right one.

"These," he said, taking the bag.

That was the extent of their conversation for the rest of the afternoon.

Erin knew she shouldn't feel hurt. She understood why he detested needing help and how he must've struggled with himself to accept her offer of the apartment and then have to ask her to vouch for him. Friendship wasn't part of their deal. He hadn't really even been rude, just withdrawn.

But it was as if she'd become invisible. She had felt more alive since she brought Cole home with her, more purposeful, less isolated. Now she had to retreat. She excused herself early and went inside, taking a hot shower that didn't warm her at all, not where it counted.

Rationally, she knew she had friends, if she didn't shut them out. Aunt Susan left an occasional phone message and emailed daily, her worry obvious. Erin's mother had died of breast cancer, her father in an accident, both way too young. Maybe they could have anchored her to the present, if they were still alive. As it was, the people who had died felt more real to her than the ones still living. Especially the girls. It was as if nothing but a semitransparent veil separated them from her. In this mood, she imagined they were waiting for her to step through the veil to their side. They couldn't go on without her.

Erin lay on her bed, curled on her side, gazing at the square of bright light that was her window. She stopped hearing the hammering or the occasional scrape of a handsaw. Napping now would be a mistake; she'd never get to sleep tonight. But that was okay. It had been a couple of weeks since she'd gone for a drive.

Tonight, she thought, and closed her eyes.

COLE HAD TAUGHT himself to sleep lightly, to awaken at the slightest sound that was out of the ordinary.

He snapped to awareness when he heard a car door close with deliberate softness. Lying rigid, he listened. The digital clock Erin had put at the bedside said 2:33. Anyone coming or going in the middle of the night wouldn't want to disturb the neighbors. Especially if that person was stealing a vehicle.

When the engine started, he knew it was Erin's Jeep. Shit. He jumped out of bed, reaching the front window just before the dome light went off. In that fraction of an instant, he saw her. While he watched, she reversed, then drove down the driveway. Brake lights flickered before she turned onto the street.

He didn't welcome the uneasiness he felt as he stared out at the dark yard and dimly lit street. The closest lamp was half a block away. Where was she was going? Wouldn't she have awakened him if she had some kind of emergency?

His mouth tightened. Why would she? What was he but her charity project, after all?

She might have been restless. Or she'd started her period and gone out for supplies. Or a friend had called and needed her. There were plenty of logical explanations. He was projecting if he thought that whatever ghost haunted her and shadowed her eyes had sent her into the night.

And, damn it, Cole didn't want to feel any responsibility for another human being. Any real connection. Even so, he knew with icy certainty that he wouldn't sleep again until she came home.

CHAPTER FOUR

"YARD WASTE BINS are full." Stopping at the foot of what would be the porch steps, Erin peeled off her gloves. "The rest will have to wait until Thursday." Astonished at how much progress Cole had made, she asked, "Did you do this kind of work in prison?"

Kneeling on the porch proper, he'd paused at the sight of her and straightened. For the past hour, the rhythmic sound of his hammer striking nails had begun to remind her of a heart beating.

"No." He watched her warily.

She knew he didn't like her asking questions, but this seemed innocuous enough. "Then... how do you know what to do?"

"My father's a contractor. I worked for him some."

"Oh. That makes sense."

He didn't say a word. An eyebrow might have twitched at what was, admittedly, an inane comment.

"Um, did you have jobs while you were serving time?"

He lowered his head.

She waited.

He rolled his shoulders. "Different ones." Pause. "Machine shop."

"You mean, you can fix mechanical things, too?"

"Probably."

"Have you ever done wiring or plumbing?"

"I could do simple jobs. Replace an electrical outlet or a light fixture. Same for plumbing. If you need the house completely rewired or the plumbing replaced, you'd be better off hiring an expert."

"I don't think I do." She hoped. "But my shower drips and plugs are too loose in some of the outlets. Plus, the light in the pantry doesn't work. I tried different new bulbs."

"I can take a look." He moved as if preparing to stand up.

"Not now. There's no urgency. Just something to get to later."

He studied her, nodded and, after a decent interval, reached for a nail.

Wham. Wham.

She'd been forgotten.

Except Erin knew that wasn't true. She suspected Cole was hyperaware, not only of where she was and what she was doing, but also his surroundings in general. She'd seen his head turn before she heard the sound of an approaching car. An elderly neighbor walked her slow-moving pug several times a day. Cole always turned to look. She wondered if his caution would slowly abate, or whether in ten years it had become part of his makeup. Cops were probably the same—although Cole might not like the comparison.

They didn't exchange another word until their lunch break. After yesterday, she didn't offer him anything, just went inside, aware that he was heading toward the garage. But as she peeled a carrot, she saw him coming down the stairs from the apartment with a can of pop and what looked like a sandwich. So she carried her plate outside, too.

Most of the porch boards were laid. Cole sat at the top of what would be the steps, his lower legs dangling. His sweat-dampened T-shirt clung to a broad back and shoulders. A screwdriver poked out of a pocket of his jeans, drawing her gaze to his muscular butt. Feeling a little shy, she joined him, seeing him glance at her lunch.

"You don't eat much," he said after a minute.

A carrot and a serving of cottage cheese were more than she'd had for a midday meal a month ago. Taking a page from his book, she merely shrugged.

After finishing the cottage cheese, she said, "This porch is going up fast."

"Long way to go." The supports were in place, but he hadn't started on the roof.

It occurred to her that getting heavy sheets of plywood up there wouldn't be easy. Could they do it, just the two of them?

Cole seemed to be assessing the work still to be done when he said, "Heard you leave last night."

She'd hoped to be quiet enough that he'd sleep through her departure, but wasn't surprised that he hadn't. She chose not to answer.

Now he looked directly at her. "Thought someone might be stealing your car."

Of course, that was exactly what would leap to mind, given his background. Had *he* stolen cars? That was a more bearable possibility than some she'd considered, although a ten-year sentence for car theft seemed extreme.

"Or you'd had an emergency," he added.

Astonished, Erin studied him in profile. Had he been worried about her? How unexpected. Unless, she reminded herself, he'd been concerned about his employment and not her personally.

"I just went for a drive." She would have been ticketed if the state patrolman had caught her. She'd managed to turn off the highway and quickly disappear down a driveway leading to a rural property, killing her engine and headlights before the patrol car went by. Stomach clenched, she'd driven home at a sedate pace. Her need to speed, to lure death, warred with the law-abiding good girl still in her. Unwilling to talk about what she barely understood, she scooted back from the edge of the porch, stood and went into the house, where she dropped her half-eaten carrot in the trash.

Her emotional health was nothing to brag about, but she was getting better. Wasn't she?

BEING NOSY HAD gone over about as well as it would have in the pen. Cole couldn't imagine what had gotten into him to ask that kind of question.

He finished his lunch and went back to work, half expecting Erin not to reappear until she came out to pay him. He heard her scraping the siding again, but around the corner where he couldn't see her. It was all he could do not to go and see, to reassure himself that she was working from the ground, not teetering on top of the ladder.

None of my business. Why did he have to keep reminding himself?

Being unsure of the answer made him uncomfortable. Something was eating at the woman, and he didn't like not knowing what. Self-preservation, he told himself. Hiring him had been odd behavior to start with. He'd give a lot to know why she had.

But he made himself keep working, just the way he did when she walked by and he couldn't help noticing the sway of her hips or her breasts beneath a T-shirt that should be baggy but wasn't.

When she paid him at the end of the day without comment, Cole nodded his thanks and stuffed the bills in his pocket, the way he always did. But in his head, he tallied the total, feeling a subtle relaxation that worried him. Yeah, he was making money, but she wouldn't need him for more than a month or six weeks at most, unless the inside of the house was a disaster demanding another few weeks. Once she cut him loose, he'd face the same odds he had while job-hunting.

A recommendation from her might help. The idea of asking for one tasted bitter, but he had a suspicion he wouldn't have to ask. He remembered that she'd offered a rental contract; he wouldn't have thought of needing one, but it would open some doors.

Since it wasn't raining, after dinner he walked the mile to the library, answered the library clerk's questions and got a card that he placed carefully in his wallet. The one awkward moment had been when she asked for his phone number, and he had to say, "I don't have a phone."

After, as he browsed books, she seemed to be watching him. Did she think he was going to steal a book? Maybe he just made her nervous. A few patrons, from a stout older woman to a huddle of teenagers, kept watching him, too.

He gritted his teeth, pretended he didn't notice and checked out several books. On his way out, a bulletin board in the foyer caught his eye. Cole studied the various postings, from scraps of paper to glossy notices about upcoming community events. Nobody seemed to be looking for help, but garage sales were being advertised. There was a bike for sale, too. He would've preferred a motorcycle, but as long as he stayed in West Fork, he could get around pretty well on a bike. He borrowed a pen from the nervous clerk and jotted down that phone number. Maybe it was time he got a phone, too. The ones he'd studied at Safeway didn't cost much, and he couldn't imagine he'd use a lot of minutes. Other than the obligatory calls to his parole officer, who would he want to talk to?

Not his father. Dad had abandoned him, and Dani's claim that Dad had changed his tune didn't ease his resentment.

Dani, sure. Cole could just hang up if his sister's husband or one of the kids answered. She'd want to know he was doing okay. On the other hand, what was the hurry?

Now that it was dark, he was happier walking back to Erin's house than he'd been going. He made people working out in their yards anxious when he went by. Even passing drivers stared. He regretted not growing his hair a little longer before he got out. Would that make a difference? Different clothes might help, too. Cargo pants, like he saw the men here wearing, instead of his tattered jeans? Maybe. Cole made a mental note to find out if there was a thrift store in town. He hated to part with a cent he didn't have to. He looked back now with disgust at the time when he'd spent money as fast as he could earn it.

Erin's Jeep was still parked in front of the garage, and lights were on inside the house. He wondered what she'd do if he rang her doorbell. Would she invite him in?

Good thing he wasn't dumb enough to do anything like that.

Having missed the early news, Cole decided to read rather than turn on the TV. Most of what the other inmates watched had seemed stupid to him, so he'd ignored the TV except when news or sports came on. Baseball was his least favorite sport to watch, though, and the first exhibition football games weren't until late summer.

Clasping his hands behind his head and staring into space, Cole decided that, come fall, he'd go to some of the high school football games wherever he was. He'd loved playing. He'd even been recruited by college scouts. Not by any of the big names—Alabama or USC or the University of Washington—but he could have accepted a scholarship to play for any other state school and gotten an education while he was at it.

Turning them all down—well, that *was* stupid. He'd paid and kept paying for that mistake.

Cole shook off the darker memories. Next time he went to the library, he'd use the computer. Nobody would notice if he struggled to figure out the internet. Patrons were limited to fifteen-minute segments if anyone was waiting, which was fair, since there were only eight computers, and half stayed available so people could use the library catalog. Still, if he could manage a search, even fifteen minutes would be long enough to look up his father's construction company and get an idea of how it was doing, and how his dad was doing, too. Dani hadn't said in her occasional letters or visits. Cole wasn't 100 percent sure why he cared, considering that after his conviction, his father had said he no longer had a son and walked away. Cole wanted to think that all he felt was curiosity, nothing more, but he knew better.

Putting his father out of his mind, he decided he'd figure out how to set up an email address. Cole couldn't help feeling renewed frustration. If he'd been allowed to learn this stuff as an inmate, transitioning to the outside would have been a lot smoother.

Since he had only Dani to exchange emails with, he felt no great urgency. But down the line, who knew?

If he could get to garage sales, he might look for a cheap stereo system, too. Right now, he didn't feel the lack; one of the greatest gifts Erin had given him was this silence, the closest thing to peace he'd had in ten years.

Lying on the lumpy couch, he opened the first of his books, a mystery called *Bitter River*. He felt an odd tingle, as if something inside him had opened along with the book cover. He'd read the first chapter before he identified that feeling. Anticipation.

ERIN DIPPED HER brush into the peach-colored paint she'd selected for some of the trim on the house. It would be accented by a much deeper coordinating color. She smiled, remembering Cole's reaction.

"That's pink." He'd looked stupefied.

Naturally, she'd argued. "It's not. Anyway, it'll be perfect." She thought. Since she'd never owned a house, only a condo, she'd never had one painted, either. But he was currently spray-painting the clapboards a warm, midbrown, and she could already see that the trim colors worked.

He'd finished building the front porch and the smaller back stoop. Yes, getting those heavy pieces of plywood high enough off the ground had been a job and a half. She didn't tell him how much her arms, neck and back had ached the next day. They should've found someone with more muscle to help him, but Erin didn't know anyone in town except for elderly neighbors, and Cole didn't know anybody but her.

Well, they'd managed, and she loved her new front porch. She'd resolved to buy a couple of Adirondack chairs and a porch swing, too. Cole was confident the beam would support one.

At the sound of a soft footstep behind her, Erin realized she hadn't heard the sprayer for several minutes. She finished the swipe of the brush she'd begun, then set it on the paint can and turned to look down from the ladder.

Open amusement and even a glint of white teeth as Cole grinned made her heart seize up. In the ten days he'd worked for her, she had yet to see more than a faint twitch at the corners of his very sexy mouth.

His grin faded at whatever he saw on her face.

No, no.

"What's so funny?" she asked, pretending deep suspicion.

Another curve of his mouth betrayed him. "You look like you have chicken pox."

"I can hardly wait to see myself in the mirror."

He laughed, a low, rusty sound that seemed to startle him as much as it did her.

To keep him from retreating, she said hastily, "You've sprayed yourself, too, you know. Except around your eyes. You have the raccoon thing going."

He shrugged. "It's latex paint. It ought to wash off."

"But not from our clothes." Dismayed, she said, "I should've bought you coveralls." He couldn't possibly have had more than one change in that duffel bag.

Seeming unconcerned, Cole glanced down at himself. "I'll keep these for messy jobs. The jeans have about had it, anyway, and T-shirts are easy to replace. I picked up some more clothes the other day."

She nodded. "What do you think? Is this color not perfect?"

"I don't know. I would have liked a nice cream…" He smiled again at her expression. "Yeah, it looks better than I thought it would. Kind of different, in a gingerbread-house way."

She sniffed. "And I'm the wicked witch."

"Well, you said it, not me."

Erin grabbed her paintbrush and brandished it. "I'll polka-dot *you*."

Another rusty chuckle, and he backed away. "I put a roast in the Crock-Pot." *Now or never.* "Will you have dinner with me?" He'd taken care of his own meals since those first few days.

He went still, in that way he could, his blue eyes unreadable. The moment stretched. Erin suddenly realized that the brush was dripping down her front and she hastily moved it over the can.

Pride had her shrugging and turning back to the window. "Or not."

"No." Cole cleared his throat. "I mean, yeah, that'd be great. I'm…not much of a cook."

Having seen the frozen meals he bought each time they'd gone to the grocery store together, she wasn't surprised.

Without looking at him, she said, "Give me half an hour or so after we knock off for the day. I want to shower and put some biscuits in the oven."

"Thanks." He sounded hoarse.

Erin didn't look back, even though she knew he was walking away. Usually, she couldn't re-sist any chance to watch him when he wouldn't notice. He was just so damn beautiful, whether in motion or at rest.

By the time she tapped the lid back on the can a couple of hours later, she expected to be exhausted. To her astonishment, there was still some spring to her step. Maybe she was regaining her strength.

She'd brought some plastic bags out to the garage, and now used one of them to wrap the brush. This seemed to work, saving her from having to clean it every evening. She'd seen Cole using the hose to do something to the spraying assembly, which they'd rented. She'd learned some creative new profanities from him every time the nozzle plugged up. Thank goodness he growled them almost under his breath, or he might have shocked a few neighbors.

Erin could tell that a young family lived three doors down, judging by the small bike with pink streamers on the handles and the big plastic tricycle often left lying on the lawn. Kids seemed to live in the house on the corner, too. Presumably, there were other neighbors younger than eighty, but she hadn't seen them. She'd bet the folks within a four-block radius could fill a good-sized retirement home, if they were all willing to give up mowing their lawns and walking arthritic pets. Nanna had been happy here partly because she had lifelong friends. Even the neighbors she disliked were part of the landscape of her life. She could tell stories about every one of them. Erin knew all the older folks, but hadn't yet tried to make herself part of the neighborhood.

Yesterday afternoon, she'd heard a mower fire up and looked over to see Mr. Zatloka across the street wrap his knobby hands around the handle of his mower and totter forward. She'd heard him mow before but hadn't seen him. Would he let her do it for him? She knew the answer. A young lady—no, that would offend his masculine pride.

Even as she was hesitating about trying, anyway, Cole trotted across the street, spoke briefly to Mr. Zatloka and took over. In twenty minutes, he mowed the Zatlokas' entire lawn. He dumped the clippings in Erin's yard waste bin—she'd seen Mr. Zatloka put theirs in the garbage can—and wheeled the mower into the garage. He and the elderly man laughed about something, and then Cole returned to work on her house.

His kindness was the reason she'd decided to ask him to dinner again. Maybe she was being foolish, but she wanted to know him better. Be friends. Not anything more.

One dangerous habit was enough.

ERIN HAD LONG since disappeared into the house by the time Cole showered, changed clothes and made his way from the apartment to her front door.

They'd worked longer than they should have. He'd suddenly become aware that the quality of the light had changed and he was having trouble seeing. Now, full night had descended.

Seeing the porch light left on for him stirred uncomfortable feelings. He should've politely thanked her and headed out for fast food and a visit to the library.

Erin had hired him for a dirty job, but it seemed she wanted something else. Cole didn't get it, didn't trust the lures she kept throwing out.

Did she just want him in her bed? If it was completely uncomplicated, there was nothing he'd like better. He wasn't having a dry spell; he'd had a dry decade. But he had trouble believing Erin was a woman who'd have sex with an ex-con only to scratch an itch. However, raising the subject would make her wary of him.

He bounded up the new porch steps, liking their solidity beneath his weight and the non-slip treads they'd applied. They'd keep her from taking a tumble some icy day in winter, when he was long gone.

Uncurling his fingers to ring her doorbell, Cole discovered his palms were sweaty.

Should have said no.

From within, she called, "Door's unlocked."

It was. Once he'd opened it, he hesitated before crossing the threshold. The act felt momentous, even dangerous. He hadn't been inside a house, any house, since the police cuffed him. Wasn't welcome at his father's home—he couldn't think of it as his—or his sister's.

"I'm in the kitchen," Erin added.

He followed the sound of her voice and the fabulous smell of meat cooking, glancing into a living room lit by a single lamp and then a dark dining room. She was right. The place was seriously dated. *Was* the wiring safe?

The kitchen looked 1940s. Truly ancient linoleum, metal-edged counters, not enough cabinets, a small wooden table with two chairs in the middle of the extensive space.

"The stove isn't bad, but the refrigerator—" He stopped himself.

Looking over her shoulder as she pulled a cookie sheet covered with golden-brown biscuits from the oven, Erin wrinkled her nose. "Is an antique. I know. I've been here something like two months, and I've had to defrost the freezer twice. And chip out ice creeping down into the refrigerator compartment."

"Why haven't you replaced it?"

She straightened. "I don't know. It works." Her shoulders sagged. "It seems wrong just to throw it away."

He already knew her sentimental side, but discovered it went deeper than he'd realized. "It makes you think of your grandmother."

"I guess so." She sighed and turned her back to him as she used a spatula to deftly lift the biscuits off the cookie sheet and into a basket.

He watched her, staggered by how beautiful she was. Usually, he tried not to notice, but now her cheeks were pink from the oven heat; she was clean and her red-gold hair was shiny, bundled at the back of her head with some stretchy thing holding it in place. Above the collar of her T-shirt, her neck showed, long, slender, pale. Were those faint freckles on her nape?

Cole caught himself taking a step to close the distance between them. No.

He rolled his shoulders and backed up. "Anything I can do?"

"Um…" She looked vaguely around. "Get yourself something to drink. I'll take milk, if you don't mind pouring."

His stomach growled, although if he'd had a choice… His hunger for the meal wasn't the first he would have satisfied. In fact, he managed to keep his back mostly turned to her as he poured milk for them both and set the glasses on the table, then took a seat so she wouldn't see that he was aroused.

It was the setting, he tried to convince himself. Sexy woman in snug jeans cooking for *him*. Didn't explain why he'd been so damn tempted earlier to lift her off the ladder, strip her and lay her down on the grass.

Brambles, he reminded himself. He'd have hurt her delicate, translucent skin.

Crap. He cast a single, desperate glance toward the hall and escape.

CHAPTER FIVE

ALREADY SEATED AT the small table, Cole realized that standing up and walking out wasn't an option.

A huge, crockery bowl held the pot roast with potatoes, carrots and other vegetables. Now, Erin set butter and the basket of fresh-baked biscuits on the table, sighed and sank down in her chair. "This does smell good."

"Will you actually eat any of it?" His question was probably rude, but also genuine. She nibbled. She didn't eat.

Erin made a rueful face. "Yes. It just…doesn't always seem to be worth the effort. You know?" She took a biscuit and handed him the basket. "Help yourself."

She'd set out generous-sized bowls as well as small plates for the biscuits. He dished up a hefty serving for himself and watched as she took less. It seemed to be a reasonable amount, considering she must weigh half of what he did.

"This is nice of you," he said finally, long-ago lessons taught by his mother rising from the depths.

Erin seemed to concentrate on the food in front of her. "It's okay if you don't want to eat here. I kind of put you on the spot today. I just…" She shrugged. "I get lonely, I guess. I thought you might, too. Sometimes I look out the window and see the light above the garage and think it's silly that we're making separate meals."

Get lonely? She had no idea. Having her right in front of him made things worse, increasing his sense of aloneness. It would be hell, being conscious of her every shifting expression, every breath she drew, the tinge of color in her cheeks and the fragility of her too-slender body—when his history felt like an invisible force field that would scald his hand if he tried to reach across it.

After a pause, he said, "Most people are afraid of me. Even when they don't know I'm an ex-con, they watch me when I go by as if they expect me to attack."

Exasperation flashed in her eyes when they met his. "That's ridiculous. I've never been afraid of you."

He wasn't sure he wanted to hear the answer, but he had to ask. "Why?"

She blinked a couple of times, as if he'd taken her aback. "I don't know," she said finally. Her forehead puckered. "I'm not afraid of much. Or

maybe anything." She talked slowly. "I think…
that instinct has been burned out of me. But
I wouldn't have been afraid of you, anyway.
Somebody with bad intentions wouldn't have
reminded me that he'd just gotten out of prison.
Besides, you don't have that look."

He ignored the last bit. She didn't know what
she was talking about. The only way to survive
in the pen was to respond to challenges with
quick, vicious strikes. That "do unto others"
saying? In there, you did unto others what you
feared they'd do unto you.

What really caught his attention was the middle part of her speech.

"Burned out of you?"

She shook her head, as if shedding water. "It
doesn't matter. We all have quirks."

True, but an unwillingness to protect yourself? That had to be unnatural.

"What you did for Mr. Zatloka was nice,"
she said.

"Mr.…? Oh. The neighbor." He filed away the
name. "He looked like he'd have a heart attack
by the time he was done, or just topple over."

Erin laughed. "I had the same thought. But
I knew if I offered to help, his male ego would
be bruised."

Cole smiled. "Probably."

Damn, this meal was good. The meat all but

melted in his mouth, as did the biscuits. He reached for another one.

Erin hadn't put a lot away, but she was eating at least. "Have some more," she said, nudging the bowl toward him.

"Did you grow up here?" he asked.

"No, but my dad did. It's funny thinking of him living here as a little boy."

"Where are your parents?" Apparently, he hadn't entirely forgotten how to make conversation.

"Dead. Breast cancer for Mom six years ago, small-plane crash for Dad a couple of years later. He was taking lessons, and there was a mechanical failure." Clearly, she didn't want to expand. But she did raise her eyebrows. "What about your parents?"

"My mother died when I was ten." One of his worst memories, despite everything that came after. "Sudden, splitting headache. Aneurysm, as it turned out."

"Can't those be familial?" She sounded worried.

"That's what the doctor said. My sister and I were tested, but we didn't have whatever weakness they were looking for."

Erin nodded. "Your dad?"

"He's alive."

He split and buttered a biscuit, hoping she got the message. *No more questions.*

"And...your sister?"

"Dani. We stay in touch." He hesitated. "Her husband isn't so sure about me."

"Oh." She squished a potato with her fork. "I'm sorry."

Cole searched for something to say. "The house looks good."

Appearing grateful for the rescue, Erin said, "I wish Nanna could see it." Another crinkle of her nose. "Except I don't think it's ever been painted any color but white. Maybe she's rolling over in her grave."

"I doubt it. She wouldn't have left it to you if she didn't love you. And the trim color reminds me of your hair."

"My hair?" She gaped at him.

A little panicked, he said what he was thinking, anyway. "It's sort of...peach-colored. With gold and a red that's more of a russet."

She kept gaping. Feeling heat in his cheeks, Cole couldn't meet her eyes. Way to let her know how much time he'd spent studying her to come up with a description like that!

Yeah, and so poetic.

"I... Um, thank you?" When he failed to respond, she said, "So the house and I are coordinated?"

"Yeah." Hoarse again. "Something like that."

Both ate in silence for a few minutes.

"Where'd you grow up?" she asked at length.

"Seattle. You?"

"Salem, Oregon. Dad taught at Willamette University. Physics, of all things. I never liked any of the science classes I had to take. Mom illustrated children's books." She smiled, her eyes momentarily losing focus. "I have copies of the books she illustrated in a box somewhere." With a one-shoulder shrug, she returned to the here and now. "I didn't inherit any artistic ability whatsoever. Or musical. Dad played the piano. I took lessons for six very long years before Mom and Dad gave up."

"I played the guitar." He didn't know why he was telling her this, but his dreams of rock stardom were another good memory, along with playing football. "Had a band. A friend's mother let us practice in their basement. We played at some parties, got a few gigs at small clubs around Seattle, but I don't think we'd have made it even locally in the music scene. After we graduated from high school, two of us stuck with it for another year, bringing in replacement band members, but it wasn't as much fun."

Amusement lit her face. "Did you sing?"

"Howled, more like."

She had a rich, full laugh. "Did you prance around the stage?"

"God forbid. I sulked and brooded and let my hair hang over my face."

"You do brooding well."

"What?"

"You do." Studying him, she said, "That wasn't an insult."

"I'm quiet. I don't brood." Yeah, he did.

"Okay, you just *look* like you're thinking deep, dark, dangerous thoughts."

Exasperated, he gave up.

He both wanted and didn't want to ask what else she had for him to do once they'd finished painting the house. Originally, she'd talked about having him take care of the overgrown yard, but he could level it in a day with a weed whacker. Then what?

Apprehension sat heavy in him, as if he'd eaten too much. He stared down at what was left in his bowl.

"I could start working on the apartment in the evenings," he said.

She frowned. "You shouldn't have to work twelve-hour days."

"I can get a lot done in an hour or two."

"Well…" Erin set down her fork. "I don't know. What should come first?"

"The outside stairs. Although once I start, I'll have to work straight through."

"I should've realized they were rotten, too."

He nodded. "Not sure I'd want to haul something heavy like a new shower stall or bathroom cabinet up those stairs right now."

"Okay. When we're done with the paint job, I'll buy the lumber for you to do that next. And I'll pay you." She narrowed her eyes at him until he closed his mouth, ending his protest. "That's not the apartment. It's part of the garage, and a safety issue."

They talked about the rest. She thought he should gut the bathroom, although he could do it over time. "I can get some reasonably priced stock cabinets for the kitchen area, too. And a new sink and faucets. Probably a new refrigerator."

"Or two?"

Ignoring that, she added, "Plus new flooring."

"You know, it's pretty comfortable the way it is." Paradise. "You can rent it out without doing that much."

"I could charge more if it's not so run-down. And it would be a selling point if I end up putting the house on the market."

Cole nodded. Not his decision. And the longer it took, the longer he could stay.

"I'd still like to tackle the yard before I end

up stuck in the house like Sleeping Beauty," she said.

Relief lightened his mood. It might not be a big job, but at least she meant to keep him on a little longer. Of course, his first thought was that he'd gladly kiss her awake. All he said was, "Blackberries climbing in your bedroom window?"

"Something like that."

Shortly afterward, he offered to help her clean up. When she refused, he thanked her for dinner and left, pretending he didn't see the disappointment she wasn't successful at hiding.

Walking back down the driveway, he pondered the fact that eating with her had been… good. More comfortable than he'd expected, if he ignored the hum of near-painful physical attraction. Unfortunately, he couldn't picture her jumping him, even though once in a while he thought he saw her sneak a look at his body. Unless he was delusional, he wasn't the only one pondering what it would be like between them.

He had talked more than he had in years, too, he reflected, although he was less sure *that* was good. He couldn't start spouting off to just anyone.

Cole came close to laughing. He'd become accustomed to living in his head. He doubted that would change. Tonight…well, something creaky had loosened, that was all.

Finding out Erin had lost her entire family didn't surprise him. That kind of sadness he couldn't miss. If her grandmother was Mr. Zatloka's age, though, her death wasn't exactly a tragedy. His mom would have said, *To everything its season.* No, something else was going on with Erin. The untimely deaths of her parents, of course, but he sensed there was more.

He didn't see himself asking.

ERIN'S HEADLIGHTS SPEARED the dark, empty, two-lane highway in front of her. She'd told herself she was going for a drive, nothing more. It wasn't as if she stomped the gas pedal to the floor every time she went out. Sometimes… sometimes, just being out here was enough.

Her Jeep Grand Cherokee wasn't anywhere near as big as the van the college had owned, but tonight she could almost hear voices, laughter. They were with her, and yet they weren't.

They're waiting.

Were they angry? Why them and not her? She would have given her life in a second to save even one of the girls or Charlotte, all so much younger, so much more hopeful. If she died now, tonight, it wouldn't bring any of them back. Erin *knew* that. She did. And yet, the darkness felt like the veil separating her from them.

Her speed climbed.

Did you somehow miss me last time?

WAITING FOR ERIN'S front door to open behind him and for her to join him, Cole unwrapped his sandwich and popped the top on a soda. This had become habit—sitting together on her front porch, talking in a lazy way, planning the afternoon, while they ate their lunches. He didn't have to feel grateful to her for providing his food. He could at least pretend they were on an equal footing.

He liked the sometimes quirky but always analytical way her brain worked, her take on books they'd both read, current headlines, modern technology. As long as the discussion remained impersonal, he could enjoy their conversations, so different from any he'd ever had. He and his dad had never talked easily, and the friends he'd acquired by his late teens were interested in drugs, guns, girls and where to get money.

Today, she didn't reappear immediately, so he started eating. He'd finished his sandwich before he figured out that she didn't intend to join him. Had he done or said something wrong? Was she sick?

Thinking about it, he realized she'd been quiet this morning, her movements slower than usual and dark circles under her eyes. He'd lain awake and rigid for over an hour after hearing her drive away at two in the morning. Wherever she went, it wasn't making her happy. This was the third time she'd gone out in the middle of the night since he'd moved into the apartment, and she always seemed withdrawn the next day. This was the first time she'd avoided him during their break, though.

He'd been hungry when he began eating, but he didn't even open the sandwich bag filled with store-bought cookies he'd intended for dessert. His stomach was too knotted up.

Cole took what was left of his lunch back upstairs to the apartment, leaving it on the counter and using the john. She still hadn't come out when he returned. *Not my business*, he told himself, and moved the extension ladder a few feet before grabbing the paint can and brush, and climbing up. Worried about Erin falling that far, he had insisted on painting the eaves.

He moved the ladder twice more without hearing a peep from her before his resolve broke. Cole wiped his hands on a rag and marched up onto the porch and rang the doorbell.

He waited, but heard nothing. His worry intensified. He hammered on the door, waited again. Finally, he reached for the knob, relieved to find she hadn't locked up. He'd never imagined walking in uninvited, but that was what he did.

The quiet inside the house made it feel uninhabited, even a little eerie.

"Erin?" he called.

Still no response.

He took a few more steps, glancing into rooms that didn't look used, and raised his voice. "Erin? Where are you?"

This time, he heard a mumbled sound from upstairs. He bounded up, sure she'd hurt herself. Knocked herself out?

Two doors in the hall stood open. The first was a bathroom. The second… He stopped, only peripherally aware of the old-fashioned wallpaper and heavy, dark furniture. His gaze had gone straight to Erin, who must have been lying on the still-made bed. Now she was sitting up, looking dazed.

"Cole?"

"Are you all right?"

She blinked owlishly. "I think I must have fallen asleep."

So soundly she hadn't heard the doorbell.

"Damn it!" Frustration and worry exploded from him. "You've been like the walking dead all morning! What's that about?"

Something changed in her expression, and her eyes dilated. It was a minute before she said in an odd tone, "So it shows, huh?"

It *shows*? Real fear hit him then. Was she dying? Maybe of cancer, and she knew she didn't have long? That might explain some of her behavior, not to mention her lack of appetite, and why she wasn't afraid of him. Was the house some kind of final project?

He didn't even realize he'd crossed the room until he was inches from her. Eyes boring into hers, he said, "Tell me."

Her chin came up. "Don't look at me like that."

"Like what?"

"You're baring your teeth."

Crap. He was. Cole made himself take a couple of deep breaths, scrubbed the heels of his hands over his face and sat on the side of the bed without asking permission first. "I'm sorry," he muttered. "You scared me."

"What?" She swiveled on the bed to face him, sitting with her legs crossed. "Why?"

"I rang the bell and then pounded on the door. You must have slept right through both. I thought—" He broke off. "I don't know, that you'd fallen and hit your head or something. And now you're giving me this shit about being the walking dead?"

"You said it, not me," she snapped.

"I didn't mean it literally."

"I…didn't, either. Not exactly."

"What's that supposed to mean?"

"Nothing." She looked away from him. "Just…there are days…"

"And nights."

Startled, she did meet his eyes. "What do you— Oh. Me going out."

She hadn't taken offense yet at him for butting in, so he asked, "Where do you go?"

"I told you. I just drive around."

If that was the entire truth, her gaze wouldn't have shied away.

"Waste of gas."

Her lashes fluttered. "Not my biggest worry."

"Can I go with you some night?"

"No!"

Seeing her expression of horror, he instinctively retreated. With a nod, he stood, backing away. "I need to get to work."

"Cole?"

Pretending he hadn't heard her, he walked out of the room.

SHE DIDN'T EVEN hear his footsteps in the hall or on the stairs. Erin only knew he'd gone outside when she heard the front door opening and closing.

She'd come so close to telling him. Not about how she taunted death. No, about the accident. Funny, since she'd been so relieved to get away from everyone who knew about it. Would Cole tiptoe around her once *he* knew, like her friends and colleagues had?

Swinging her feet over the edge of the bed, she realized she still wore her paint-spattered canvas tennis shoes. In this house, nobody put shoes on the furniture or, heaven forbid, on Nanna's nice bedspread.

"Sorry, Nanna," she murmured.

Would Cole understand anything she felt? Most of her friends had zilch experience of really bad things happening. Lucky people. If they'd ever seen anyone dead, it was probably an elderly grandparent passing away—and wasn't that a euphemism—with family gathered around. What she'd heard and seen would be beyond their comprehension. Cole, though... Even if he hadn't, well, killed anyone, he might have seen awful stuff happening while he was in prison, mightn't he?

She grimaced as she made herself head for the bathroom.

Why would that help him understand? Even if he'd seen men knifed or beaten, they would have been, if not strangers, at least nobody he'd cared about that much.

And unless he wielded the knife himself or battered someone bloody with his own fists, he wasn't responsible. It wasn't *his* fault.

No, better to keep her confusion and misery to herself. Cole was the one who'd drawn the line separating them. Feeling lonelier than she'd realized, she'd tried to erase it, or at least ignore it. But despite the way he'd opened up at least a little during dinner last night, he'd made it clear that the line was still there.

Catching sight of herself in the mirror on the medicine cabinet, she froze. Wow, she hadn't looked this bad in a while. Weeks. Since before she'd hired Cole. No wonder he'd seemed shaken.

She leaned closer, tipping her head one way and then the other. Last night had not been good. She'd regressed. She wanted to lie to herself and believe she had no idea why, but she couldn't.

It was because of him. She felt things for him that were foolish and hopeless and not helpful to her state of mind.

She was still studying the bruises beneath her eyes and the paint she'd managed to get in her hair when a surprising thought surfaced.

Cole had come searching for her. He'd worried about her. No, he said she'd *scared* him. He'd demanded she tell him what was wrong.

If anybody had stepped over the line, it wasn't

her. And sure, maybe his initial fear was that he'd find her dead and, as an ex-con, he'd be in big trouble. But that didn't explain why he'd stayed worried once he realized she'd only been asleep.

Right now, all they had was each other. That probably made it inevitable they'd start to care. Didn't mean it wasn't temporary, she reminded herself. Even so, she felt a warmth that was at odds with last night's devastating awareness of how alone she was.

Cole would hate knowing what she did when she went out driving. At least it mattered to one person if she didn't come back some night. Erin wondered if that would make any difference.

CHAPTER SIX

COLE TURNED HIS head sharply at a burst of laughter coming from behind him. With an effort, he dialed back his tension once he saw the group of teenagers. The pizza parlor had his nerves on edge.

He hadn't realized this was Friday until they arrived to find the parking lot nearly full. The booths inside were, too, and they'd had to stand in line to order. While he waited to get his fountain drink, a kid had backed right into him, spilling his own and babbling apologies. The jumble of voices was loud, movement constant, numbers being called over an intercom adding to the sensory overload.

Getting a pizza had been his idea, a way of making up for hurting Erin's feelings last night, if he had. She'd readily agreed, then suggested that, instead of having it delivered, they eat out. He had cautiously said yes, and still hadn't decided if he was sorry or not. It made him uneasy to know this was the closest to a date he'd had since he was convicted. And yeah, he also liked knowing that almost everyone here would see them as a couple—and that she was, hands down, the most beautiful woman in the whole place. Not his, but for this interval, he could enjoy the illusion.

When he wasn't shrinking from the racket or resisting the instinct to lash out the next time someone bumped him…

At least they'd managed to claim a corner booth. Ironic, when he'd read that cops liked to have their backs to the wall in a place like this, too. Who knew he'd have something in common with anyone wearing a badge?

"So," Erin said, "you must have had a driver's license."

A couple of kids ran by. He hoped she didn't see that he was twitching.

"Sure."

"Is there any reason you can't get a license again?"

Why had she brought this up? "You mean, legally? No."

The two boys tore by them a second time. Erin rolled her eyes. "I guess they're running laps."

"Looks like it," Cole said tersely.

"What I'm thinking," she went on, "is that you could apply for a learner's permit so you can practice without getting a ticket. Then you could take the test in my car."

She had his full attention. "You'd let me do that?"

"Why not? Having your license might help you get a job somewhere that expects you to make deliveries, for example. And you'd be all set once you can afford to buy a car."

In what decade would that be? But the idea of having a driver's license aroused what even he knew was hope. It would be another step toward feeling like a human being. He'd have a real ID. And it would help when he opened a bank account. He hadn't looked at prices, but a couple thousand dollars might buy a piece-of-junk car, mightn't it? A goal he'd hardly been able to imagine was beginning to seem possible as his stash of money grew.

He waged a quick battle between his dislike of accepting favors and his realization that he'd never get anywhere if he *didn't* accept them. And this one…it wouldn't cost her much other than some time and a few gallons of gas. Unless he wrecked her Cherokee, of course.

"Yeah," he said finally. "That would be good, if you're willing."

"Definitely. I'm—" She cocked her head. "Isn't that our number?"

He slid out of the booth, despite his reluctance

JANICE KAY JOHNSON   107

to walk through the dimly lit restaurant, smile at some sixteen-year-old employee and make his way back without colliding with someone. Being surrounded like this had the potential for violence where he came from.

The pimply faced boy behind the counter tried to give him the wrong pizza. A young woman grabbed that order, smiling quickly at Cole, and the kid produced the right one.

Cole's body was in battle mode by the time he made it back to the booth. Sweat trickled down his spine and his hands were shaking. They'd gotten plates and silverware before sitting down, thank God. He wasn't sure he could've forced himself to turn around and go back for anything they'd forgotten.

This was why he'd fled Seattle.

Erin noticed, he could tell, but she didn't comment, for which he was grateful.

Once she'd dished herself up a slice of their half-veggie, half-sausage-and-mushroom pie, she said, "I think they're open tomorrow." He must have looked blank because she added, "The DMV. We can stop on our way to the lumberyard. You'll have to get a learner's permit if you want to practice driving before you take the test. If you go for the learner's permit, we should pick up the booklet you have to study to pass the computer test. Maybe you remember all that stuff in the booklet, but I sure don't. You know, how far in advance of a turn you have to signal, and whether it's three hundred or five hundred feet from an oncoming car that you're supposed to dim your high beams at night."

He nodded. He didn't remember those things, but he doubted most drivers actually did. Memorization came easily to him. The thought of getting behind the wheel of a car... Around town, it would be fine. Probably even feel good. The freeway... Cole doubted he was ready for that.

"I think I should go for the permit. It's been a long time since I've driven."

Nobody had warned him how fast the world moved. How hard it was to tamp down his oversensitivity to danger. A flicker seen out of the corner of his eye made him want to whip around. There was no danger in here, but he still struggled to distinguish voices, to watch everyone. He kept an eye on the parking lot outside the window.

He wanted to go home, but took a bite instead.

"Best pizza in town." Erin wiped her mouth with a napkin and reached for her drink.

"It's good."

"Did you take driver's ed?" she asked.

"Yeah." Man, he hadn't appreciated the guts

that instructor must have had. Nerves of steel. Almost smiling, Cole felt his tension ease.

"Me, too." She laughed. "After about two sessions, I figured I had it down pat. My father did not agree."

"Mine was the same." World War III whenever they'd gone out. Cole realized he'd already been turning into a butt. When he struck out the first time he took the driver's test, Dad ramped up the pressure. By the time Cole was allowed to take it again, he wasn't a half-bad driver, thanks to his father.

"The trouble is, you get so cocky." Erin sounded sad, but gave herself a shake. "I'm sure it's like riding a bike. It'll come back."

Yeah, he thought she was right.

"Either tomorrow or Sunday we can go by the high school or middle school," she suggested. "You can get the feel of my Cherokee before we head out onto the road."

He finished another slice. "You're paying me to work."

"By the time we do errands, buy the lumber for the stairs and unload it, you won't want to start, anyway."

That was true. He didn't love the prospect of her watching critically as he relearned to drive, but he had to live with it.

"Did you ever operate heavy equipment?" she asked. "I mean, when you were doing construction?"

"Bulldozer and forklift. That's not really like driving a car."

Conversation drifted. He would've eaten in silence, but he liked listening to her talk. Watching her, too. She had such an expressive face, her eyes changing color with her mood, her lips curving or pouting, her nose often wrinkling. He liked the tiny dimple that formed beside her mouth when she smiled. It was hard not to wonder whether her hair was silky or coarser, how soft that fine skin would feel to his fingertips, whether she ever smiled when she kissed a man. Looking—that felt safe. Whenever he imagined touching her, though, he got aroused, and that was dangerous.

She started talking about the garden her grandmother had tended so lovingly until her health failed.

"My grandfather had a vegetable garden in back." She smiled. "I had no idea that corn and peas taste better when they're *really* fresh."

He nodded.

"That's a lot of work, though. I'd like to restore some of Nanna's flower beds. I've read about old roses. I think I'll look into whether there's a local nursery that sells them."

What made a rose "old" versus "new" he couldn't guess. Right now, he just let her talk.

"I want climbing roses in front of the porch. White and pink. And maybe one on the south side of the house that reaches up to my bedroom." She focused on him. "I could have you build a trellis."

"I can do that." Once he found out what she had in mind. "There's one rose still alive in front. The canes are pretty long, so I think it must be a climber."

Erin nodded. "I'm hoping that's the pink rose I remember. One of her two climbers always got rust or black spot or something. She was constantly spraying it."

"It's probably the one that didn't survive."

She brightened. "That's true."

Eventually, they boxed up what was left of the pizza and slid out of the booth. He stayed vigilant, as if his role was bodyguard, and was very conscious of her walking in front of him.

After they'd climbed into her SUV, she said, "Maybe next time we do this, you can drive home."

Nice thought, although her dashboard looked like a control panel in a spaceship to him. Electronics seemed to have taken over cars, like everything else. And it wasn't as if he'd been driving the latest model before getting arrested.

After graduating from high school, he'd worked six months or so in an auto body shop, then had done construction without staying with any one contractor. Save money? Why would he do that? Cole had taken a lot of pride in the '98 Pontiac Firebird he'd bought on his own, though.

He'd scraped up what cash he could and sold his car in a useless attempt to pay for better legal representation than the public defender assigned to him. But it had been all too obvious that the woman he'd hired didn't believe in Cole's innocence. Hard to convince a jury when your own attorney only went through the motions.

As always, he made himself close a door on his anger. Bitterness would corrode him if he let it loose. Fortunately, shutting it down had become easier since the day Erin had run out of the hardware store to offer him a job.

COLE GAVE HER a quirky grin. "I could crash through the gym wall."

"Don't even think about it."

In fact, he put her Cherokee in Drive and set out sedately to circle the middle school parking lot, do some figure eights and finally brake gently.

He looked so happy, so she said recklessly, "Let's head out on the streets."

"You sure?"

"I'm sure." Although she really ought to check with her agent to find out whether her insurance would cover a driver using a learner's permit. Maybe she needed to add his name. And, while she was at it, she'd transfer her insurance to a local agent.

They drove around for a while, Cole stopping a few times to practice parallel parking, even though she didn't think he'd have to do it in the driver's test.

"Most of downtown has only parallel parking," he reminded her.

He certainly didn't need an instructor, which was fortunate, given that she was completely distracted by her awareness of him. This was an ideal opportunity to study him without embarrassing herself.

Great cheekbones, a strong jaw and those light blue eyes made him male-model handsome. Erin was pretty sure he didn't see himself that way, but it was true. His hair was noticeably growing out. It wasn't as dark as she'd thought it might be. Kind of a nut-brown.

She kept sneaking peeks at his powerful thigh muscles, flexing as he moved his foot from the gas pedal to the brake and back. He wore khaki cargo pants, which suited him, the cotton fabric stretched taut over those muscles. He had a strong neck, too, the lick of a tattoo she'd decided was flames reaching above a T-shirt that also hugged impressive muscles.

Mostly, she loved his forearms and hands. Sinews and veins showed on his arms, and he had thick wrists and big hands to go with his size. They weren't hairy, like some men's. She'd seen him effortlessly rip boards loose with those hands, but also do delicate tasks.

Erin hoped he couldn't tell that she was melting inside just from imagining his hands on her body.

She wasn't the only woman who had that reaction. So far, he either didn't notice other women staring, or pretended he didn't, which she appreciated. Maybe he was so accustomed to women lusting after him, he could shrug it off. Except…had there been any women where he'd been held?

He also looked a lot healthier than he had when she first saw him in the hardware store. His color was better, his face no longer gaunt. Working outside, he'd picked up some sun, too.

"Why don't we stop at the grocery store while we're out?" she suddenly suggested. "I need some veggies."

He flicked a glance at her. "Okay."

She was counting on parting ways inside, as they always had. To her dismay, he picked up a basket and waited politely for her to maneuver a small cart into the store.

When he strolled beside her into the produce department, she said, "Don't you need anything?"

"Not especially, but I'll pick up some fruits and vegetables, too. I don't eat enough of them."

Watching as he gently fingered cantaloupes until he found one to his satisfaction had her mouth going dry and her knees unsteady. When she wrenched her gaze away, she was annoyed to see shoppers eyeing him distrustfully.

She stepped closer and glared at one balding guy who was just standing there, as if he was afraid to turn his back on Cole. What was *his* problem?

It could only be the extremely short hair, Erin decided as they progressed from the fruit section to vegetables. So many people in their twenties and thirties had tattoos now, and the tiny glimpse of one on his neck wouldn't disturb anyone. His size drew attention, too, of course, and there was that sexy saunter. The guarded expression and aloof air might not help—but when he glanced at her and raised his eyebrows, she saw amusement he would never have let her see even a week ago.

"What?"

"You're staring at me."

"Oh." Darned if her cheeks didn't warm. "Sorry. I was thinking."

"About something deep?"

"No, um…" She cast around for an excuse. "Whether to buy romaine or red leaf lettuce. Or maybe one of those mixes in a box."

Something that was almost a smirk told her he didn't believe her.

The romaine looked tattered, so she snatched up a head of frilly red leaf lettuce and stuffed it in a plastic bag before dropping it in her cart.

She could invite him into her bed. But as she grabbed several bell peppers, Erin knew what a mistake that would be. Casual sex had never been for her. She was bound to get attached. Or was it *more* attached? Face it, she couldn't afford to risk being devastated when he moved out, moved on.

Cucumber. Sugar snap peas would be good in her salads, too.

She really, really needed to stick to business.

COLE OFFERED ERIN the car keys when they left the store, but she shook her head and said, "You drive."

The Jeep Cherokee was a lot bigger and heftier than his Firebird, but he liked the feel. Pleased at how comfortable he felt behind the wheel, he decided Erin was right; apparently,

this was one of those things you never forgot
how to do, once you'd learned. He was kind
of sorry to get back to her place, set the emergency brake and turn off the engine. This time,
she did take the keys. She also scooped up her
grocery bags, said good-night and went in her
house without issuing any invitation.

Lying in bed later, hands clasped behind his
head as he gazed at the ceiling, he thought about
their relationship. Keeping it simple was good.
For whatever reason, she was vulnerable right
now, which might make her susceptible. He'd
despise himself if he came on to her. And if they
did have sex, what would happen after?

Between one blink and the next, he imagined
her—*saw* her—sprawled on her bed, naked,
slim and pale and beautiful. Their legs were
tangled, and his much darker hand stroked her.
Slipped between her thighs. Damn it.

Why worry about after? a voice whispered
in his head.

Even thinking that made him a son of a bitch.
Erin had taken a chance on him. She wasn't
a woman he could dismiss the minute he was
done with her.

He shifted uncomfortably, frustrated as he'd
been from the minute he set eyes on her. He
should be looking elsewhere, but how could he
bring a woman to this apartment? Hell, without

his own car, he couldn't take that hypothetical woman anywhere. She'd have to do the driving. Here, where his bedroom window looked out at Erin's, wasn't an option. The idea felt distasteful.

Plus, available women were likely to be found at a bar or tavern, and places like that made him especially uneasy. The minute he walked into one, everybody in the place would turn to stare at him. With his luck, there'd be a couple of the kind of assholes who'd instantly see him as a challenge. He could not afford a fight.

Was this what the rest of his life would be like? Always knowing he didn't dare take risks? He wanted to believe he could quit thinking this way once he was released from parole, but maybe not. Cops would never get over assuming the worst about him, he knew that.

His mouth tightened at the thought. His dreams of freedom had never taken into account the suspicion he faced everywhere he went. Somehow, people could tell on sight that he was an ex-con. He didn't get it, but he couldn't miss the stares.

What chilled him was wondering what he would have done if he hadn't caught Erin's eye. Would somebody else eventually have given him a chance and hired him? Did that only happen if you had family or friends to recommend you? Would he have gotten desperate enough to knock on his father's door?

God, he hoped not. What Dani had said—about Dad finally believing that he'd been wrongly convicted—enraged Cole. If that was true, why hadn't he written? Visited his innocent son? Had he expected Cole to come begging for a job or money?

At a soft sound outside, Cole stiffened. After a minute, he relaxed. Erin would have started the engine by now if she was going anywhere.

At least he'd been distracted from brooding about his father. Erin, though… Why wouldn't she tell him where she went? Why did her eyes evade his even while she was saying as much as she did?

Thinking about tearing out the rotten steps proved more conducive to sleep.

At one point, he awakened abruptly, as he'd often done in his cell, thinking he'd heard a scream. But when there was no repetition, he decided it had been part of a dream he didn't remember, and didn't *want* to remember. He'd thought he heard screams other nights, too, but he was likely having flashbacks.

Strangely, this was the second night in a row that he'd jerked awake. Unsettled, he got out of bed and looked out his windows, but the night was quiet and especially dark. The moon must be covered by clouds.

The next time he opened his eyes, it was morning. He listened for rain but didn't hear any on the roof. Except for that one interlude, he'd slept straight through, which meant Erin hadn't gone anywhere last night.

Today might be the Lord's Day, but he was eager to get started, anyway. Once he'd had a hasty breakfast, he glanced out the window. Gray skies persuaded him to add a sweatshirt on top of the navy blue tee.

Hauling up the garage door reminded him to suggest Erin buy that automatic opener for him to install. She didn't have the muscle to lift this damn door on a regular basis.

He came out of the garage, wearing work gloves and carrying a crowbar and hammer, to find her waiting for him. In contrast to yesterday morning, she looked as if she might actually have slept.

"Do you need help?" she asked.

"Are you good with a circular saw?"

"Dad taught me how to use one, but it's been a long time."

Cole shook his head. "Then thank you, but no."

"Are you starting at the bottom?"

"Yep. I'll tear out and replace steps as I go."

"You know we need to paint the garage, too, right?"

He hadn't thought about why they had unopened paint cans left over, but he should have. He turned to assess the building. "Yeah. I guess we do."

"I figured we should wait until you replace anything that's rotting."

Another few days of work. The relief was unsettling. "Once I finish the stairs, I'll check the siding." He glanced upward. "I hope it doesn't rain."

"Me, too." She smiled. "Since you don't need me, I'll get to work digging out the front flower beds."

"You want me to scythe the yard first?"

"Don't waste your time. I'll rent a weed whacker when you're ready to do the yard. I'd buy one, except I doubt I'll need it long-term."

They separated to their respective labors, but Cole was in a position to keep an eye on her.

He'd have to ask her about old roses, he mused as he wrenched up a semirotted board with the crowbar he'd restored using steel wool and oil. Now that the house was painted, it did seem to cry out for flowers.

His hands went still as memories stirred of

his mother, who had been a gardener. After she died, her flower beds were taken over by weeds. The next year, Dad planted them with grass seed. Now Cole saw it as symbolic. Despite everything, he still loved his father, who wasn't a bad man. But the reality was, Mom had taken all the softness and color in their lives with her when she died.

Typical Dad, he apparently enjoyed trimming the boxwood hedge around their small yard near Green Lake, and seemed obsessed where the lawn was concerned. It had to be emerald green, cut to an exact length and weed free.

"Is something wrong?"

Startled, he looked down to see that Erin stood a few feet away, peering up at him. He'd been so damned lost in the past he hadn't even seen her coming.

"No." He hesitated. "Just thinking."

"What about?"

As always, his instinct was to repel her curiosity. But what was the harm in her knowing?

He told her how the flowers disappeared from their yard after his mother died, to be replaced by the order and straight lines his father preferred.

He smiled crookedly when he said, "There was this house down the block that might have been a rental, or maybe the owner didn't care about his yard. The lawn was always shaggy, but it was the dandelions that really ticked Dad off."

"The seeds do have a way of spreading."

"Yeah." Kneeling on the raw wood of the step he'd just replaced, he found himself grinning. "I was twelve or thirteen, I don't remember. I asked Dad why he didn't sneak over there some night and spread weed-control fertilizer. He glared at me and said, 'You ever hear of trespassing?'"

Erin laughed. "Did he do it?"

"I don't know." His smile faded. "I don't remember those dandelions much after that." He shrugged. "We'd started butting heads by then, and he gave up on making me do yard work."

She was quiet for a minute, and he thought about going back to work. Then she asked, "Did he visit you while you were in prison?"

He clenched his jaw. "No."

Her consternation showed. "I'm sorry. I shouldn't have asked."

He gazed toward the house instead of at her.

"Do you miss him?" Her voice was very soft.

His esophagus burned. He couldn't answer. Couldn't say "yes." His father had written him off. End of story.

After a moment, Erin nodded in acceptance of an answer that didn't have to be spoken aloud, and turned to go back to the shovel she'd left leaning against the porch. He still didn't move.

What would Dad say if he heard his son's voice on the phone?

Did it matter? Cole asked himself impatiently. It would be healthier not to waste another thought on his father. From long practice, he shoved any regret down deep. He needed to get his butt in gear. Erin wasn't paying him to stare into space.

Twenty minutes later, he was in the garage and had just set the saw aside when he heard the ringtone on Erin's cell phone. Her very occasional calls weren't his business, he told himself, gathering the two-by-fours he'd cut to length for the next several steps. But the minute he left the garage, he saw that Erin was looking toward him as she talked. He immediately knew why.

Had to be Ramirez, checking up on him. Cole's good mood evaporated. Ice formed, killing everything he'd let himself feel. Maybe the reminder was good.

Deliberately turning away from Erin, he climbed the steps, knelt and laid out the first board.

CHAPTER SEVEN

ERIN FINISHED TYING her athletic shoes and then reached automatically for her hooded sweatshirt. It wasn't until she was zipping it up that she had a sick feeling. *I wore one just like it that day.* She looked down at herself. Wow. Athletic shoes. Check. Jeans. Check. How could she not have known she'd been unconsciously replicating the same outfit? As if the dead wouldn't recognize her if she was bare-legged and wearing a tank top?

After a minute, she sighed, but she didn't remove the sweatshirt. It was still too chilly out at night. Good justification.

Closing the front door behind herself, she all but tiptoed across the yard to her Cherokee. Cole's bedroom window was dark. Thank goodness he hadn't heard the scream that had torn her from the nightmare.

Tonight, after easing open the driver's-side door and getting in, she decided not to close it until she reached the street.

Cole had completely withdrawn during the

past couple of days. Apparently, he didn't like her talking to his parole officer. As if *he* hadn't asked *her* to talk to the guy in the first place! Was she supposed to ignore all future calls from Ramirez? *The hell with Cole*, she thought bitterly as she started the engine.

She released the emergency brake and shifted into Reverse, turning her head to look over her shoulder. In that instant, a dark shape loomed outside the passenger window. Erin screamed as someone tried to open the door and then fell backward when it proved to be locked.

Operating on instinct, she pressed the gas pedal and the SUV leaped back. Feet pounded outside. Before she could move forward, Cole had run around the Jeep and appeared at her door.

"Stop!"

Shaken and furious, she stepped on the gas. He hung on to the door, so she couldn't slam it closed, and ran beside her. She'd gone twenty feet, almost to the street, before she braked.

"What are you doing?" she yelled. "I could've knocked you down and run over you!"

"Let me go with you." The roof light illuminated his face, set in implacable lines.

Feeling the tremor in her hands, she clung to the steering wheel. "You can't come."

"Why?"

"Because you can't, that's all."

"Then you're not going." Voice grim, he reached in front of her and managed to shift into Park.

If her hands hadn't been shaking, she would've shifted right back. "This is none of your business."

"Erin, whatever you're doing is hurting you. I don't like seeing you the next day so exhausted that you look like you have two shiners."

The walking dead.

What if she were to take him, just this once? Drive around. Bore him to death.

But then what was the point of going at all? And if she didn't bore him… No.

"If you get out of the way, I'll back up and park. I'll stay home, just to make you happy."

"Leave it here. Or let me park it."

The need to vent some of her anguish had swelled inside her for days, as if she were a bottle and the cork had to be popped. Feeling a sudden, hot rush of temper shocked her.

"It's *my* car, *my* driveway." Hating the venom she was spouting, she couldn't stop herself. "You work for me. That's all. So back off!"

His expression altered, as it always did when something threatened his pride. For a second, Erin thought he'd nod in that stiff way of his and walk away. She could drive off, and he'd never say another word about it.

But…for him, coming out here and trying to prevent her from leaving was extraordinary. Interfering, making demands on her, had to be way outside his comfort zone.

To her astonishment, he stayed where he was. Defying his pride, he hadn't backed down.

"Fine." She climbed out, stumbling when her feet touched the pavement. She felt weirdly awkward, her hands and feet not quite under her control.

Without a word, he took her place and moved the Cherokee back to its spot in front of the garage, this time with the nose pointing out rather than in.

I could have made a smoother getaway if I'd parked like that yesterday.

Only she hadn't parked it, had she? Despite her simmering annoyance with Cole, she'd let him drive whenever they needed something at the hardware store or lumberyard.

By the time she plodded the short distance, he was out of the car waiting for her, her purse in his hands. The keys weren't in sight. Had he pocketed them? she wondered resentfully.

He handed over the purse when she reached him. "For what it's worth, I'm keeping the keys until morning."

"I have an extra set," she mumbled.

"I figured."

Neither had taken a step.

"You going to let me in the house?" Cole said after a minute.

"Why should I?" Except it suddenly occurred to her that he'd have to unlock the front door. She'd had a hidden key until he started to tear apart the porch, when she'd taken it inside and stuck it in a drawer, to be forgotten. Smart.

"Because I want to talk to you."

How a man could sound utterly expressionless and yet relentless at the same time was a mystery, but he managed.

"Fine," she snapped again.

He followed her to the front door, where she pointedly stood aside. When he didn't make a move, she said, "You have my keys."

He let them in. She dropped her purse on a side table and led the way to the kitchen. She wouldn't be going back to sleep after this, so she might as well have a cup of coffee. Or three or four. Why not?

As she measured out coffee, from the corner of her eye she saw Cole hesitate, then set the key chain on the table. Instead of sitting, he stood in the middle of the kitchen, feet planted just far enough apart to make him appear ready to spring.

Trying to ignore him, Erin added water and set the machine to brew, then leaned against the counter, facing him. She crossed her arms in a gesture of self-defense.

"Were you planning to wait all night for me to come out?"

"I wasn't outside until I saw your bedroom light go on."

"I don't understand. You were watching?"

"I told you. I sleep light."

"Cole, it's nice that you worry, but this is something really personal. I can't take anyone else with me." Considering her turmoil, she was surprised at how pleasant and regretful she sounded.

"Why?" he asked again. Unless it was her imagination, he'd leaned forward slightly.

Her agitation rose under the pressure. Would he never let up? "I can't tell you. Don't keep asking."

"Why?"

Tears burned her eyes.

"Is there anyone you'd take along?"

She glared at him. "No!"

The coffee machine beeped. She ignored it. Cole never looked away, his intensity making her want to shrink back.

"Tell me."

"Why?"

"I don't like having to wonder. I don't like seeing what your little trips do to you."

"It's not the trips," she blurted.

"I didn't think so." He didn't move, but seemed to…settle. Satisfied because he'd gotten part of the answer? "I'll keep my mouth shut if you let me come. I just got out of prison, remember? You can't be into anything that would shock me."

"It's not like that." Erin fought to keep herself from rocking. She wasn't sure she could stand this for another minute. She had to make him go away.

He leaned forward, his icy blue eyes drilling into hers. "Then what *is* it like?" he asked, implacable. "Why can't I come?"

"Because I might kill you!" she yelled.

HE'D BEEN WRONG. She *could* shock him. She had.

And damn, Erin was clutching herself as if she'd fly apart if she let go. The sheen in her eyes had to be tears.

He closed the distance between them without conscious thought. "Erin." He almost choked on her name. She kept staring at him, eyes brimming with both tears and despair. Gently, he gripped her shoulders and tugged her forward. "Erin."

She didn't fight his hold, even let herself lean toward him, but her body remained rigid. Tentative, he wrapped his arms around her and cradled the back of her head. "I'm sorry," he whispered. "I pushed too hard." Whether he'd done the right thing or the wrong thing, he didn't know.

Damp warmth on the front of his T-shirt alarmed him, but her body didn't shake with sobs, and she didn't make a sound. Holding her, he wondered if she even knew she was crying. "It's okay," he murmured. "It's okay. God, I'm sorry."

Except he wasn't. He still needed an answer, even if he didn't entirely understand what he was doing here. Ever since she'd taken him in, her unexplained disappearances at night had bothered him. They had something to do with the grief and pain she barely masked. And no, whatever was going on with her wasn't his business—but she'd stepped up to help him. How could he do less?

He couldn't resist the pleasure of having her in his arms, either. He rubbed his cheek against hair that was both silky and springy, and breathed in her scent. Of their own volition, or so it seemed, his hands stroked soothingly over her back. He could feel the fine tension in her and the delicacy of her vertebrae and shoulder blades.

When she didn't move, he finally, reluctantly, steered her to the table and eased her down on a chair. However unwilling he was to release her, he did, but pulled up a second chair. He sat facing her, and their knees touched. Then he handed her a napkin from the holder on the table.

Head bent, she only clutched it for a minute, but finally let out a huge sigh that had her shoulders sagging. She mopped her face and blew her nose firmly before she lifted her head again.

Her eyes were red and puffy, her creamy redhead's skin blotchy. Her lower lip trembled. "Why does it *matter* to you?"

"I don't know," he lied, not giving her time to call him on it. "How could you have killed me? Do you practice shooting?" The idea of her target shooting in the middle of the night—in the dark? by flashlight?—boggled his mind.

"No." Her voice was so soft he barely heard it. "I…speed."

"Why?"

Her defiant, bloodshot eyes met his. "I go out at night when hardly anyone else is on the highway and I drive as fast as the Cherokee will go."

Chilled, he asked, "How fast?"

"A hundred miles an hour. More."

He whispered an imprecation. "You're trying to kill yourself." But that couldn't be right. All she'd have to do was swerve off the road into a big Douglas fir and she'd be dead.

"I…" Once again, her gaze slid away. "Not exactly."

He'd heard that before. "Then what?"

"I won't choose to die, but—" She stopped, her lips pressed together.

"If it happens, you won't mind," Cole said slowly, scared shitless. Traveling at that high speed, it would take the tiniest of errors. An instant of distraction. An animal running across the road, a momentary loss of control.

"Only…sometimes."

"I don't get it." But then he remembered the "walking dead" thing, when he'd feared she had a fatal disease. It sounded like she did, in a way. Mental illness? Or something more insidious? Now she looked at him as if she desperately needed that connection. "It's…" She fidgeted for a moment. "I guess there's no reason not to tell you."

"There isn't." Some instinct had him reaching for her hand. He hadn't held a woman's hand in so long he couldn't remember the last time, but this felt right. So right, he shoved the feeling to the back of his mind.

"I was a college professor. Small, liberal arts college in California. I taught history. Revolutionary War, Civil War and Reconstruction. Up through the nineteenth century."

College professor. That meant graduate degrees. She was even further out of his league than he'd imagined. But since he'd never believed she'd see him as an equal, he ignored that as she kept talking.

"I coached women's softball and volleyball, too. I'd played in high school and college." Her eyes, big and haunted, searched his.

He nodded, although he still didn't understand anything.

Seemingly reassured, she said, "We had an away game. I was driving. We always took this extralong van the college owned. Most of the team went, and my assistant coach. Charlotte was only twenty-three."

Had. Was. The ominous verb tenses confirmed that this story wasn't going anywhere good.

Cole's fingers tightened on her cool, slender hand.

"I glanced in the rearview mirror because I thought one of the girls had taken off her seat belt. If I hadn't, I might have been able to react in time. This huge semitruck roared across the median. I swerved and the van rocked and...and fought me. After that, all I remember is hearing screams."

God. His throat tightened. "How many girls did you have with you?"

"Ten. And Charlotte." Erin never looked

away. "They died. All of them. Even the truck driver. Later, I was told the police think he had a heart attack."

"Nobody to blame," Cole murmured.

"Nobody?" She made an inarticulate sound. "Of course there is. I was the driver. Responsible."

"You're not the one who crossed the median."

"I should have seen in time. Braked, sped up, *something*."

"If you hadn't looked in the mirror, you'd have had…what? A split second longer to react?"

"That might be all it would've taken," she argued.

"I don't believe that. Shit happens so fast when you're driving. Even if you'd seen it sooner, how well could you have judged the truck's speed? Or whether *it* would brake or swerve? And you can't tell me that kind of van is very maneuverable. Had you ever had to change lanes fast or stop suddenly before?"

Seeing her uncomprehending stare, he knew he was wasting his breath. She'd stalled on the certainty that, as the driver, she and only she was responsible.

"Erin?"

She blinked a couple of times and finally focused again on his face.

"Were you hurt?"

"I had a concussion. Broken collarbone and arm and ribs." Apparently without noticing, she touched each place on her body, all on the left side. "I was in the hospital for a few days. It was nothing. Not compared to—" She started breathing too fast.

Nothing? he thought incredulously. She meant she wasn't dead.

"Were you charged? Did anybody blame you?"

Her forehead wrinkled with what looked like perplexity. "I wasn't charged with anything. But I'm sure some of the parents blamed me. They trusted me to take care of their daughters, and I didn't."

He'd known guys in prison who were stuck, kind of like this, but in reverse. Phil Mumford didn't think he'd gotten any justice. It wasn't his fault. He'd just gone along for the ride. None of it was his idea, so why should *he* get the same prison term as his two buddies? Or Ronnie Ferrell. Cole must've heard him say the same thing a hundred times. *If I'd just jumped out and run, those cops never would have caught me. I should've just jumped out and run. I'd'a got away for sure. If I'd just jumped out...* Cole wasn't the only one who avoided both Ronnie and Mumford. He never bothered to say the obvious. Every single inmate should have done something different. If they had, they wouldn't be there.

Yeah, Erin's problem was the flip side of Ronnie's or Mumford's. She was so damn determined to *accept* responsibility for all those deaths that she never let herself hear people say, *It wasn't your fault.* He even understood. Cole had read about soldiers who were the only survivors out of their entire platoons. They spent the rest of their lives asking, *Why me?* Imagining all the accusing eyes...

Survivor guilt. He knew the term.

He became aware that Erin held herself as if she was waiting for something from him. Reassurance? Cole seriously doubted that. Plenty of people must have already tried. Judgment, then? Condemnation? Probably.

"Have you had any counseling?" Ah, the irony of his suggesting it, when he'd balked at attending any counseling sessions when he was in the pen. "I mean, a chance to talk about this?"

"At first." Erin shrugged dismissively. "It didn't do any good. How could it?"

"If you're suicidal, you *need* help."

"I'm not! I told you—"

"You're playing word games," he said flatly. "And you know it."

She kept staring at him, her eyes luminous

with gold and green and a hint of earthy brown he hadn't noticed before.

He huffed out his breath. "That's why you weren't scared of me, isn't it? You figured if I slit your throat, hey, that's just another way of making it happen." Hammered by what he'd realized, Cole dropped her hand and straightened. "Is that why you hired me? Did you *hope* I was a killer?"

"No!" She scraped her chair back. "I'm not that far gone."

"Sure you are."

"I'm not." She said it softly. "Most of the time, I'm not. I just…feel this pressure building." She pressed the heel of her hand to her breastbone. "It's as if they're all waiting for me. I can almost see them. Hear them."

Cole swore and let his head fall back. "You really don't know how illogical you're being."

"What do you mean?"

Pinning her with his gaze again, he asked, "Were you close to those girls? Did they care about you?"

She bit her lip. "Yes. They…came to me with problems. I think they really trusted me."

Which made their deaths even harder for Erin. But he said, "You make it sound like they're baiting you. Like they *want* you to die.

If you'd died and only one of them had survived, wouldn't you be glad for her—if you could know?"

"Yes, but that's different. The accident wasn't their fault. It was mine." She'd circled right back, her mental tape in a loop.

"And so they're vengeful, unable to move on unless you die horribly so they can take you with them?"

Shock transformed her face. "No! It's not like that! It's…" She lowered her gaze to her hands lying on her lap. "It's…just so unfair. So strange. I should have died, too. The van was—" She shuddered. "There was no way I should've made it out with such minor injuries. I keep thinking it was a mistake, that I was *meant* to die. Out of all of us, why did *I* walk away? I'm not special." She lifted her head again, her expression beseeching. "I'd have died for any of them. I wish I could."

"But you can't." That rough-gentle voice didn't sound like his, but man, the ache in his chest wasn't familiar, either. "You can't bring any of them back. Your death wouldn't change a thing except sadden the people who care about you. You can't tell me you don't have friends, even if you've been dodging them."

She opened her mouth. Closed it, because he was right.

"The one good thing that came out of it," he went on, "was your survival. I'll bet those girls told their parents about you. How cool you were. How you understood them. Gave the best advice."

Erin had gone completely still. He couldn't tell if she was really hearing him.

"People kept saying I should live for my girls," she whispered. "What could be more pointless?"

"Dying for them."

She flinched, and he felt brutal, but he had to say it. Keep saying it, if she gave him the chance.

Her eyes stayed dry, but the devastation he saw on her face made him wonder if he'd hurt her more than he'd helped her. He felt a sudden, desperate need to escape. He had his own problems. Who was he to try to solve hers? Everything he'd said was probably wrong.

Erin scrubbed at her eyes with closed fists, for an instant looking like a child. But when she lowered her hands, she offered him a twisted smile. "Thank you. I think maybe I needed to tell someone. I'm not sure why, since I could hardly wait to get away from everyone who did know about the accident. They just didn't seem to understand. I couldn't decide which was worse, the idea that I should feel *lucky*—" she said that with loathing "—or that God saved me for a reason. What reason? To remember, over and over? To suffer? Or am I supposed to be looking around for a chance to save someone, to make up for my failure?"

As if a puzzle piece had slotted into place, he understood. "That's what you're doing, isn't it? You're saving me."

Her eyes widened at whatever she heard in his voice. "You didn't need saving. Just…a chance."

Why he should feel so damn humiliated, Cole didn't know. It wasn't as if he hadn't realized he was a pity project for her. But he'd been stupid enough to forget.

He shoved back the chair and stood. "Yeah, you've done that."

"Cole, you've become a friend." She rose slowly. "Is it wrong to want to help?"

A friend? Compared to her, he was like a drooling baby, trying to pull himself up on the furniture. Even if she *was* screwed up. It wasn't possible for them to have anything like a genuine friendship.

Just as he was turning away without answering, she asked suddenly, "Why did you try so hard to stop me tonight? And insist I tell you what was wrong?"

He shrugged. "I don't like owing anyone. Call

it payback." Not letting himself see the new hurt he'd caused, he walked out. He'd finish painting the garage tomorrow, and then maybe she'd be done with him.

CHAPTER EIGHT

ERIN LIFTED THE last flat of perennials from the back of her Cherokee. In the three days since her breakdown in front of Cole, she'd continued digging out the flower beds by the porch, extending to each corner of the house. She had spent this morning at a nursery, choosing perennials, several roses and a couple of low shrubs.

Before she left, she'd asked Cole if he needed anything. He paused in the act of pouring gas into the rented weed whacker to glance up with apparent indifference.

"No." Pause. "Thank you for asking."

Terse and civil. That summed up their communications since that night. They'd obviously hurt each other's feelings. He'd certainly made clear that he thought the idea of even being friends was ludicrous.

So be it, she thought, not acknowledging the hovering depression. Nothing new there. For whatever reason, she hadn't felt compelled to steal away in the night since he'd caught her. Why bother? She was beginning to believe she *couldn't* be killed. Some people would say she'd proved that by hiring a hard-faced, tattooed ex-con who had no references, and all but taken him into her home.

The buzz of the weed whacker drifted around the side of the house. The front yard was down to stubble, although even an optimist wouldn't call it a lawn. She'd thought about digging up the whole thing, but decided to try using a weed-control fertilizer to encourage the grass and kill everything else.

The sound of the weed whacker stopped just as she was setting down the flat of lavender and delphiniums by one of the cleared beds. The thud of feet coming fast made her straighten.

"Call 911," Cole snapped, and ran by.

Erin spun to see him tear down the driveway. What— Oh, dear God. The crumpled figure on the sidewalk across the street had to be Mr. Zatloka. A lawn mower sat idle beside him.

Running after Cole, she did as he'd asked.

"An elderly neighbor has collapsed…No, I didn't see it happen." She crossed the street. "I don't know— Wait. It looks like he hit his head when he fell." She held the phone away. "Is he breathing?"

"Yes." Cole's relief was obvious. "Pulse is fast."

She repeated what he'd said to the dispatcher. "Please hurry."

The front door of the house opened, an elderly woman appearing. Tiny and hunched, she clung to the iron railing that framed the two concrete steps. "Roy?"

Erin hurried over to her. "I'm sorry, Mrs. Zatloka. He either fell or collapsed, we don't know. Cole saw him on the ground. I've already called 911." She squeezed the woman's arthritic hand. "I think I hear a siren."

She helped Mrs. Zatloka down the steps and across the lawn to where Cole knelt at their elderly neighbor's side. Mr. Zatloka had a huge bump on his head that was oozing blood, but not so much that they needed to stanch it.

"It might be his heart," his wife said tremulously. "He's on so many pills it's hard to keep track of them."

"Do you have a list of his medications?" Erin asked. "The medics and emergency room doctor will want one."

"Yes. Oh, my." She looked back toward the house. "I carry it in my purse. I always go with Roy to his appointments. He doesn't hear very well, you know."

Erin had noticed. "Is your purse somewhere I can find it?"

"Would you? It's by the phone in the kitchen."

She ran again. Thank heaven the purse was

exactly where Mrs. Zatloka said it was. Erin grabbed a chair, too, and carried it out.

Cole rose at the sight of her and came to take the chair. "Good idea," he murmured. Erin watched as he set it down on the sidewalk, spoke quietly to Mrs. Zatloka and put an arm around her as she sat. The old woman's hands shook when she accepted the purse.

The ambulance came around the corner and down the block. When Cole lifted an arm, it lumbered to a stop at the curb, the siren cutting off just before two blue-uniformed medics leaped out.

Erin watched as Mrs. Zatloka fumbled with her purse. She itched to take it from her, but most women—including her—were funny about their purses. At last the old woman produced a many-times folded piece of paper that appeared to be a computer printout with written additions and deletions.

When she handed it over, the medics already had an oxygen mask over Mr. Zatloka's face and a collar around his neck. One was unloading a stretcher. They paused to study the list, loaded him and the driver ran around the back to jump in. The other medic, a woman, came over to ask if Mrs. Zatloka was okay.

"Can't I go with him?" she asked, struggling to stand up.

"I'm afraid not," the medic said gently, glancing at Erin.

"We'll take you," she said. "We don't want to hold them up."

Half an hour later, the three of them perched on the edges of their seats in the ER waiting room. Getting here hadn't been speedy. Erin had to race back into the house to grab Mrs. Zatloka's walker while Cole fetched the car. She was incredibly grateful that he'd been willing to come along. He had been astonishingly kind, teasing the frail woman as he picked her up and set her in the front seat of the Cherokee. He'd lifted her out, too, once Erin braked in front of the ER. While she went to find a parking spot, he had hovered at Mrs. Zatloka's side as she tottered in using her walker. When Erin made it back, it was a relief to see that he'd persuaded the poor woman to sit in a wheelchair.

Time dragged. Erin found herself staring at the wall clock, frustrated at how slowly the numbers moved. Wishing she could reach for Cole's big hand, instead she clasped Mrs. Zatloka's small, knobby one. She was glad she had when she felt the elderly woman latch on to her. Mrs. Z had to be terrified.

It seemed an eternity before they were summoned into the back. When Erin rose, Cole hesitated, but then did the same. The nurse chattered on the way back, giving them a piece of good news. Mr. Zatloka had regained consciousness.

They arrived to find a young doctor leaving the cubicle. He turned and came back in.

"Your husband has had an MRI," he told Mrs. Zatloka. "We think he's fine, but we're going to admit him for the night, to be on the safe side. Our best guess is he either tripped and hit his head, or had an episode of low blood pressure."

"Just clumsy," he growled from the bed. "Bunch of nonsense."

Cole's mouth twitched as Erin hid her smile. She saw the doctor doing the same.

"I assume you don't drive?" he asked Mrs. Zatloka, who shook her head.

"Roy does all the driving."

Erin had seen them in their great boat of a car that had to date to the eighties. It moved almost as slowly as Mrs. Zatloka walked.

"We're neighbors. We'll be glad to pick him up when he's released," Erin volunteered.

They all accompanied him to his assigned room. Cole and Erin remained in the hall to allow husband and wife a few minutes of privacy.

"I told him I'd mow," Cole muttered. "Why the hell didn't he call?"

"Pride." She was careful not to look at him. "It's apparently a big deal with men."

Silence.

Finally, he said, "That a shot aimed at me?"

"Maybe."

After another pause, he said, "I guess you're entitled."

She forced herself to look at him. "Is it so bad that I felt sorry for you that day at the hardware store?"

"No." He moved his shoulders in a way that betrayed an uneasiness unusual for him. "I wish I'd met you some other way, that's all."

Was he saying he would have approached her if he'd already had a job when they met? The possibility made her pulse speed. They stared at each other, Erin finding it hard to draw a full breath.

"I shouldn't have said what I did," he added, his voice rough. "About payback. I do owe you, but leaning on you like that..." Either to avoid her eyes, or because of his constant vigilance, his gaze followed an orderly passing with a trolley that rattled. "I don't like seeing you hurting yourself. Didn't seem like you have anyone else to call you on it, so..." Another jerk of his powerful shoulders.

Erin swallowed the lump in her throat. "You gave me stuff to think about. So...thank you."

His surprise was evident, but they were interrupted by Mrs. Zatloka calling them.

COLE MOWED THE Zatlokas' lawn as soon as they got the old lady in the house. She had admitted to often napping, but decided to watch her soaps instead.

Erin returned to her gardening, promising to bring dinner to Mrs. Zatloka. Fortunately, she had homemade spaghetti sauce in the freezer, and had bought French bread the last time she was at the store. *To feed Cole*, she realized now. *Wishful thinking.*

She set out the roses and shrubs first, still in their pots, followed by perennials. Somewhere she'd read that they looked best in "drifts," giving the impression they'd spread on their own, she supposed.

Studying the results, she saw an awful lot of bare soil in between puny plants. When she heard footsteps, she turned. Wiping sweat from his forehead with his forearm, Cole stopped at her side and studied her effort.

"Looks good."

"I don't know," she said doubtfully. "I guess I can buy some annuals to fill in the gaps."

"Things'll grow faster than you expect." What might have been a smile lifted his mouth. "Think about grass. And blackberries."

Erin made a face. "You have a point."

"I'll get back to work."

"I wonder if Mr. Zatloka will be willing to give up maintaining the yard on his own after this."

"I don't know." Cole frowned. "Place could use some work. Is their money tight?"

"I have no idea. A lot of the houses in the neighborhood are getting shabby. The owners are all elderly."

"They're living on Medicare?"

"Maybe. But Nanna and Grandpa had investments and his retirement income. She could have hired help. She just didn't." Erin sighed. "Maybe she didn't notice that the place was deteriorating. It could be the same with the others."

He grunted, but more as if he was thinking than rejecting what she'd said. "Mrs. Zatloka will be in a wheelchair soon. Even with the walker, she'd do better if they had a ramp."

"That's true." Which gave her an idea. She hesitated, then decided not to say anything.

"I'll build it for them if they can buy the lumber," he said.

"That's nice of you." She tried for matter-of-fact. "Will you join us for dinner?"

A struggle showed on his face. "I don't want to make her uncomfortable."

Erin gaped at him. "For heaven's sake! I'm pretty sure she thinks you walk on water. I know she kept looking to *you*, not me."

Was that embarrassment burnishing his angular cheeks?

"Yeah, I'll have dinner with you," he muttered, and left her, going around the house and out of sight. A moment later, the buzz of the small engine began again.

You can run, but you can't hide, she thought, feeling...exhilarated.

MR. ZATLOKA CAME home the next day, complaining nonstop about how ridiculous it had been to call an ambulance or for that foolish doctor to think he needed something as fancy and expensive as an MRI.

That tiny dimple showed in Erin's cheek as she suppressed a smile.

"We didn't know what had happened," Cole said mildly, getting out of the Cherokee in the driveway to help the old guy down from the back seat.

"And keeping me overnight!" Mr. Zatloka exclaimed. "It's just greed, that's what it is. Do you know what they *charge* for a hospital bed these days?"

"No idea," Cole admitted. He didn't like to think these bills were going to put an old couple like this in a hole financially.

The neighbor scowled. "Well, *we* won't be

paying for it, but I see what things cost. It's greed, that's all."

Erin laughed. "You know better than that, Mr. Zatloka. It's not the bed or clean sheets you're paying for. It's the building and all that high-tech stuff that beeps, and the nurses and doctors and aides. Dieticians and a kitchen and meals delivered three times a day. They took good care of you, didn't they?"

"I suppose," he said grudgingly. Looking at his yard, he said, "You mowed for me again."

"And didn't mind doing it," Cole agreed.

From the front seat, Erin said, "We were wondering if you should have a ramp from the house. I worry about Mrs. Zatloka."

The old man was nodding. "I been thinking about it. The wife says she's fine, doesn't need anything like that, but walking is getting harder for her. Just wasn't sure whether I needed to call a decking company or what."

Cole frowned at Erin. She frowned back, looking annoyed, but shut her mouth.

Mr. Zatloka turned watery, faded eyes on Cole. "I've seen what you're doing over there for Ms. Parrish. Looks like you can do just about anything. Any chance you could build a ramp?"

"I can. If you'll buy the lumber, I'll be happy to—"

"No, no! 'Course we'll pay you. You just

let me know when you're free to take on another job."

Cole glanced at Erin, then said, "I can do it anytime, Mr. Zatloka. I'm still doing bits and pieces for Ms. Parrish, but I'll fit this job in."

They briefly discussed details. Cole agreed to measure and make up a materials list this afternoon, and Erin offered to pick up what was needed from the lumberyard rather than have them deliver. Then Cole walked the man to his front door, greeted Mrs. Zatloka and returned to hop into the passenger seat.

He expected her to gloat because he'd been hired to work for someone else, but instead, even as Erin turned to look over her shoulder as she backed out of the driveway, she said, "I've never asked if they have kids. I feel so guilty. I wish I'd visited Nanna more often, seen how much she needed. I just never thought."

"Did she care whether the front porch got replaced or not?"

"She sure would have if she'd fallen through a rotten board and broken her leg."

Cole shook his head. "But she didn't."

"Well, no, but…" Erin had the grace to laugh. "I have a guilt complex, okay?"

Laughter was an improvement over her usual despair. He'd take it.

Not until they'd reached the house did he say, "You have a computer?"

"Sure, a laptop. Why? Do you need to use it?"

"Yeah, if you don't mind." He couldn't help sounding stiff. "I'm hoping I can find some instructions for the ramp. I'm not sure about the slope."

"If it's too steep, a wheelchair or walker might get out of control."

"Right." He cringed at the idea of Mrs. Zatloka's walker running away from her.

"Come on in," she suggested. "I'll get it for you."

She made coffee, too, as he sat at the kitchen table with the skinny little laptop that wasn't even plugged in. She must have wireless. Electronics intimidated him more than anything else in this changed world.

He now knew how to get online and type in a search query, although his fingers felt too big for the keyboard. A ton of answers popped up immediately. He'd barely started reading when Erin set a notebook and pen within reach.

One foot for each inch of rise. Huh. Fortunately, the Zatlokas' concrete stoop wasn't more than twenty-four to thirty inches high. Handrails—yeah, they'd need those. He found suggestions about the ideal width for the ramp, which was good because Mrs. Zatloka didn't yet own a wheelchair. He'd seen some pretty fancy ones a lot wider than the basic edition available as a loaner at the hospital. The ramp should be built to accommodate a wheelchair of that size.

He could build it using poured concrete, and studied those directions, but he decided to go with wood so it could be torn out more easily. A young family probably wouldn't want one. Mom and Dad wouldn't love catching a kid using the ramp as a skateboard park.

He looked up to realize he was alone. Taking advantage of Erin's absence, he typed in a query about extralong passenger vans, and was dismayed by what he read. There were plenty of warnings about the relative instability and difficult handling of twelve-person and larger vans. Had Erin ever checked into it?

Finally, he closed the internet.

He found her outside, watering her new plants. Somehow, she'd managed to soak one leg of her jeans. She was cleaner than she'd been yesterday, digging in the dirt, but wisps of pale hair had escaped her braid and curled around her face, and in the sunlight her freckles were a lot more apparent than they were indoors. Cole wished he didn't have these moments when he was especially struck by how beautiful she was, and how that long, leggy body turned him on.

"Ah, you want me to shut down the computer?"

She looked up. "No, it'll go into sleep mode. I'll probably go online later. Did you find what you need?"

"Yeah, I think so." The job was going to be more complicated and take longer than he'd envisioned, but he felt kind of buzzed. It was lucky he'd always been good at math. The stuff about the van—he could talk to her about it when the timing seemed right. "I'm going over there now. I can't do any calculations until I have measurements."

He managed to subdue his physical reaction to Erin before he crossed the street. Wouldn't want to shock the old guy.

Speaking of Mr. Zatloka, he came out to watch and hold the other end of the tape measure. Cole suggested building the ramp from the back stoop rather than the front, and Mr. Zatloka agreed. He didn't look dismayed when Cole told him the job would probably take several weeks, explaining about the gradient and the landing he planned to put halfway. He thought by tomorrow he might be ready to order what he needed.

Walking back across the street, Cole felt exhilarated. This was a real job and—aside from her original hint—Erin hadn't gotten it for him.

Two days later, Erin and Cole picked up the first load of lumber for the ramp project, and she bought paint for another couple of rooms in her house, as well as more stripper so she could start on the molding downstairs.

When Cole saw that in her hand, he said, "You know, you'll want to have the floors refinished."

Her shoulders slumped. "They'll look worse once I've redone everything else, won't they?"

"Yep." He seemed cheerful today, a mood she hadn't associated with him before.

"I'll have to move all the furniture out." The idea was enough to make her feel overwhelmed.

"You'll need to move out, too," he said. "The stuff they use stinks, and the fumes probably aren't good for you."

"Ugh." She slid her credit card through the reader. "I'll do a Scarlett O'Hara on this one."

He looked inquiring as the clerk laughed.

"'After all, tomorrow is another day.' Quote from *Gone with the Wind.*"

Cole didn't say anything, only picked up the paint cans. As they crossed the parking lot, she glanced at him.

His throat worked. "I spent years knowing nothing would be any different tomorrow."

"I'm sorry." She touched his arm. If he noticed, he didn't react.

They drove into the loading zone then, and he got out to help while she stayed put. The lumber and concrete blocks they were picking up today would form the underpinnings. They'd have to come back when he needed material for the ramp itself and the railings.

When he got in behind the wheel again, she said, "You need to drive on the highway and the freeway. Once you've done that, there's no reason you can't get your license."

Lines deepened on his face, but after a moment he nodded. "You're right. I think I'm okay to do that now."

He was okay to do a lot now, she thought. So, all right, she could feel him slipping away. It was her problem that she desperately wished she didn't have to lose him. In retrospect, she could see that she should've kept him at a distance. As it was, he'd become her best and only friend. No, it was more than that; she *wanted* him, too, in a way she didn't think she'd ever wanted a man. Maybe it was just his dangerous vibe. A typical, stupid, female response to a man any woman should steer clear of.

The trouble was, he wasn't anything like she'd expected. Withdrawn, yes, but he was also patient, kind, smart and proud.

She suspected that pride was what had kept him going all these years; it would also keep him from laying a hand on her or asking for anything but the most minor favors.

Well, she was bound to see less of him now that he was working across the street. She could wean herself away from her dependence on a man who was probably eager to stand on his own feet, needing no help from her.

At this low point in her reflections, he stopped to back into the Zatlokas' driveway, then turned off the engine and raised the hatch door.

He didn't argue when she got out to help him unload, which was a blessing since Mr. Zatloka popped out and insisted on doing the same. Seeing him trying to lift a concrete block was enough to make Erin lunge forward. Fortunately, Cole took the block from his hands and said, "You mind looking behind the front seat? I think that's where I stuck the bags with screws and other hardware."

Damn it, there he went, being both tactful and kind again. Because he respected another man's pride. She couldn't imagine him ever putting someone else down to make himself feel better.

Her heart sped up as she acknowledged what she already knew.

CHAPTER NINE

ERIN HAD JUST pried open a can of paint the next morning when she heard a car in the driveway. Who on earth could it be? Somebody using her driveway to turn around? Certainly, nobody had dropped in for a visit since she'd moved to West Fork. She'd hoped that by judiciously responding to friends' and her aunt's emails, she'd head them off from tracking her down. Outside, she heard a car door slam. She straightened and went toward the front of the house.

A dark-haired man in a rumpled suit had climbed out of the blue sedan and was looking at the house. With a sinking feeling, Erin suspected she knew who he was.

She opened the front door and went out on the porch. "Can I help you?"

"Would you be Ms. Parrish?"

"I am."

He mounted the steps. "I'm Enrique Ramirez, Cole Meacham's parole officer. I should have visited before now, but I've been swamped."

"How do you do?" she said politely, accepting

his handshake. Cole would *hate* having the man show up here. Had he known parole officers did this? Seeing no option, she invited him in and offered him coffee, which he accepted with apparent pleasure. Just sugar, he said.

"Is Mr. Meacham here?" he asked.

Pouring from the carafe, she said, "He's at a neighbors'. I still have some small jobs for him to do, but he's currently building a wheelchair ramp for the elderly people across the street."

"A wheelchair ramp?" He looked startled. "Has he ever done anything like that before?"

"I don't think so, but he studied plans online and says he's good at math." She grimaced as she put a mug on the table in front of him, sitting down with her own. "Which I'm not, so I didn't totally understand his calculations. The ramp can't be too steep, for obvious reasons. His father is a contractor. Cole worked for him at one time and had some construction jobs later, too." He'd barely mentioned those, but she had the impression he'd been trying to get out from under his father's thumb.

"I see." After dumping a couple of teaspoons of sugar in his coffee and stirring, he studied her from tired brown eyes. Gray threaded the dark hair, and the beginnings of seams in his face put him in his forties or early fifties. "Is he still living here?"

"Yes, as I told you, in the apartment over the garage."

"You've had no problems with him?"

"None at all," she said firmly. "He's done wonders with this house. The front and back porches were rotting, and so was some of the siding. The staircase up to the apartment was rotting, too. My grandmother had really let things go. Cole's done all the work on the exterior, including the paint job on both the house and the garage. His latest job was whacking the weeds and blackberries down."

"And personally?"

Offended on Cole's behalf by all these questions, Erin did understand that the man had to do his job. Would he leave without seeing Cole? She wished.

"He's polite, a hard worker, patient and kind. I wouldn't have offered him a place to stay if he hadn't been. He started mowing the neighbors' lawn across the street without asking for pay. Mr. Zatloka looks about ninety, and was still trying to do it himself. In fact, Cole was willing to build the ramp for nothing if the Zatlokas would cover the materials, but they insisted on paying him."

A shrewdness and skepticism in his eyes made her uneasy. Did he suspect she was falling for Cole, and therefore didn't believe what she was saying? Her annoyance was tinged with embarrassment, because, of course, Mr. Ramirez was right. She was falling—*had* fallen—for Cole, although she didn't think she'd have been willing to lie for him. No, if she'd had to lie, he wouldn't be the man she thought he was.

So she stubbornly kept her mouth shut instead of continuing to babble.

"Has he made friends? Found a girlfriend?" His pause had the same delicate quality as his earlier question. "Or is he sticking close by?"

"You'll have to ask him about friends and women. I don't know. I don't keep track of him. I've seen him head out in the evening sometimes. Mostly to the library, I think. I often see him coming or going with an armful of books."

"Are you aware he has no driver's license?"

"Yes. He has a permit now and is about to take the test to get a license. He's a good driver."

He kept asking questions, trying, she thought, to trip her up, but since she was answering honestly, there wasn't a thing he could do. The temptation to ask him what Cole had done to end up with such a long prison term was huge, but she wouldn't let herself. Either Cole would tell her, or he wouldn't.

At last the parole officer finished his coffee, thanked her for her time and asked where he could find "Mr. Meacham." Walking him to the door, she said, "The neighbors don't know he's an ex-con, Mr. Ramirez. I hope you can avoid telling them."

This glance was sharp. "You don't think they should have known before they employed him?"

"No, I don't. They're quite elderly, and probably easily frightened. If I thought he was a danger to them in any way, I wouldn't have recommended him—or at least would've made sure they knew. As it is, he's something of a hero to them. Mr. Zatloka collapsed in his yard a few days ago. Cole is the one who noticed him. He ran over to see if he could provide first aid. Once the ambulance arrived, we both accompanied Mrs. Zatloka to the hospital. Her difficulty in getting around was why the idea of a ramp came up."

"I see." That seemed to be his go-to, noncommittal remark. "Again, thank you. I may stop by from time to time."

"You're welcome to leave the car here while you talk to him, if you'd like."

"I appreciate that."

Erin stayed on the porch longer than she should have, watching him go down her driveway and cross the street. A knot had formed in her stomach. A mere call from Mr. Ramirez had been enough to cause Cole to retreat for days. What effect would an in-person appearance have?

She hoped the parole officer understood how destructive it would be if Cole lost a job that had him so engaged.

KNEELING ON THE lawn behind the house, Cole set aside the drill and reached for the screw and his screwdriver. At this stage, he was being extracareful, measuring and then measuring again before cutting or putting anything in place.

Hearing someone behind him, he turned his head, expecting Mr. Zatloka. When he saw Ramirez, he stiffened. Son of a bitch. What if he'd already introduced himself to Mr. Zatloka? Or intended to?

"Ramirez," he said flatly.

"Cole." He nodded. "Ms. Parrish told me about your project. I was curious to see it."

The back door opened, and Cole gripped the handle of the screwdriver so hard his knuckles ached. He had trouble loosening his jaw enough to speak. "Mr. Zatloka."

"Oh, I thought it might be Erin here." The old man peered at Cole's parole officer.

Ramirez stepped forward and offered his hand. "Enrique Ramirez. I was just talking to, er, Erin, and she mentioned what Cole was up to over here. I hope you don't mind. I'm being nosy."

Zatloka beamed. "We've been admiring Cole's work on Erin's house and are real happy he could take on this job, too." Clutching the iron railing beside the concrete stoop, he said, "My wife uses a walker now, and that with difficulty. We have to plan for the future."

"Erin's house looks really good," Ramirez agreed, a hint of surprise in his voice. "I didn't see the 'before,' but I gather it wasn't in great shape."

"No, her grandmother and my Laureen were friends. Once she was widowed, I'd have liked to help more, but I'm getting to an age when keeping up one house and yard is about all I can handle."

Getting to an age? Under other circumstances, Cole might have been amused.

"Perfectly understandable," Ramirez said. "Well, I just stopped by to say hello." He smiled at Cole. "Any chance you'd take a minute and walk me back to my car?"

"Sure." Like he had a choice, he thought bleakly. Had Erin known what she was doing, sending the guy over here? He stood, realized he still gripped the screwdriver like a weapon and hastily bent over to set it beside the drill. Then he nodded at Mr. Zatloka. "Be right back."

The two men walked around the house, down

the driveway and across the street. Only then did Ramirez say, "Ms. Parrish gave a good report on you."

A report. The knowledge that she could screw him over royally with a *bad* report ate at his stomach like acid. She was his employer and his landlady, damn it. Apparently, he needed the reminder.

He had to say something. "I was lucky when she hired me."

"If you don't mind my asking, how did that happen?"

Cole did mind him asking, but Ramirez could grind him under his heel if he felt so inclined. He hadn't been this aware of how little power he held since he'd walked out of prison.

"I was applying for a job at the hardware store in town. The minute the manager saw I'd been convicted of a crime, he tossed my application. She heard what was said and followed me outside. I guess she hadn't seen any notices for handymen, and preferred that route to hiring a contractor."

"Pretty gutsy of her." Ramirez sounded thoughtful.

Not able to argue, Cole gritted his teeth again.

"She's been giving you a chance to drive, too, she says."

"She has. I need a little practice on the freeway, but then I'm ready to take the test." He hesitated. "I hope having a license will help with job applications."

"You planning to stick to construction?"

He shrugged. "It's all I know."

Ramirez studied him. "According to what I read, you have a knack for small-engine repair and even automobile repair."

"Both are necessary on a job site, but I'd rather not be stuck on my back under a car all day. There's more variety in construction."

"I assume Ms. Parrish will give you a recommendation when you finish everything she needs you to do."

"I haven't asked, but I assume so."

"You plan to stay in this apartment?" The parole officer nodded toward the garage.

"If I can get a job here in town." The idea of leaving, not being able to see Erin… Not something he wanted to think about. "I promised to do some work on it in lieu of rent, and I've barely started."

"You been in touch with family?"

He hesitated again. "No, beyond letting my sister know I wasn't coming to her place." Guilt bit hard. She'd supported him all along. She was the only one who had. "I keep meaning to buy a phone, but I haven't yet," he concluded, ashamed.

"Might want to do that. You have any other plans?"

God, he wanted to get this man off his back. Out of his life. Would it help to sound ambitious?

"Once I have a car and I can afford to, I'd like to take some college classes."

Ramirez's bushy eyebrows rose. "You have a start already."

He did have some credits. He'd have had a lot more if Washington state taxpayers hadn't decided not to fund education for prison inmates. "I want to get a four-year degree eventually."

"In what field?" The guy leaned a hip against his car. He sounded curious versus demanding.

Cole shoved his hands in his jeans pockets. "Don't know yet." That wasn't quite true, but was he willing to admit to something that might prove to be out of his reach? But Erin had been teaching him not to be quite so closemouthed. Gruffly, he said, "Engineering."

The eyebrows rose even higher this time. "I seem to remember you having high test scores, particularly in math."

Despite letting his grades sink his senior year of high school, Cole knew he might still have been able to get academic as well as athletic scholarships if he hadn't had his head up his ass.

"I'd better get back to work," he said.

Ramirez nodded and surprised Cole by holding out his hand. "I'll be calling, and I'll probably stop by again, but I've got to say, I'm really pleased with how you're doing. You look a hell of a lot better than the first time we met, and you have people in your corner. I don't usually say this so early on, but I think you're going to make it, Cole."

"Thank you for not telling Mr. Zatloka about my background."

"Didn't seem any need. You keep up the good work, son."

They shook hands and Ramirez got into his car.

Cole started down the driveway, making himself nod when the car came even with him. He was glad to have an excuse not to see Erin for a while. This supervisory visit brought up a lot of conflicted feelings. He needed to think about those emotions, come to terms with them. But he wasn't as angry as he'd expected to be. In fact, among all the negative shit he was feeling, there was a small warm spot. It had something to do with saying aloud where he wanted to go with his life, but also with Ramirez sounding up front when he said what he had. *I think you're going to make it, Cole.*

Damn straight, he was.

He needed to call his sister. Say *Hi*, say *I'm doing okay.* Tonight, even if it meant borrowing Erin's phone.

ERIN CAUGHT HERSELF glancing out the window way more often than she should have as she watched for Cole to come home. It truly was a coincidence, though, that she'd gone out to get something from the Jeep when she turned her head to see him striding up the driveway.

Would he think she'd been lying in wait for him?

Weren't you?

"Hi. Um, I left some paint samples in the car."

His expression remained impassive. No telling whether he was mad, depressed, had been fired or had put Ramirez's visit out of his mind.

Oh, to heck with it. "I was wondering if you'd join me for dinner. The house smells like fresh paint, but if you don't mind that…"

His answer hung in the balance. She could almost see the gears spinning. Finally, he said, "Thanks. Let me get cleaned up first."

"Okay. Good." She was about to race for the house to accelerate meal preparations, but then she remembered those paint samples. She did want to make a decision tonight.

Five minutes later, he showed up, for once not

knocking. The first she knew, he'd opened the door and called, "Erin?"

"In the kitchen." When she heard his footsteps, she said, "It's spaghetti again. I hope you liked it."

"It was great. Anything I can do?"

He always asked. She had him pour drinks and get the garlic bread out of the oven while she dumped the spaghetti into a colander and dodged the steam that leaped up.

Not until they sat down did she say, "So, how'd it go with Ramirez?"

He gave her another of his unreadable looks from those cool blue eyes. "Okay." Pause as he ladled sauce over his spaghetti. "Probably thanks to you."

Which he no doubt loved. She shrugged, as if unaware of how he must feel about her involvement, and said, "I told him the truth. You've done a great job. You're a nice man. You haven't held any wild parties."

"Did you ask him not to tell the Zatlokas I'm an ex-con?"

"Yes." And what was wrong with that?

He nodded and started eating.

Erin didn't even pick up her fork.

After a minute, he paused with a bite halfway to his mouth. "You want to know what he said?"

"Yes!" She subsided. "Well, if it was important. I mean, was he satisfied?"

Some expression flickered in his eyes. "Yeah. He seemed...pleased."

"He should be!"

Cole's face relaxed almost into a smile. "Did you chew him out for doubting me?"

"You're making fun of me."

He gave a quiet chuckle. "Yeah, a little."

"Oh." His smile made her skin feel tight and tingly. And warm, too, which undoubtedly meant she was blushing.

"Thank you." He was suddenly serious. "I mean that."

Her cheeks were downright hot now. "You're welcome. You've done amazing things around here." Hating the huskiness in her voice, she said, "I feel lucky to have found you."

He shook his head in automatic repudiation, but didn't actually argue. Instead, they looked at each other, neither taking a bite. The air felt electric, and his eyes were a brighter blue than usual. All she heard was the rush of her heartbeat.

What if I asked... There was so much she wanted to ask him, but she knew she couldn't. She didn't always understand male pride, but she did know that he had to make the choice to come to her, and that would happen only if he overcame the obstacles he kept tripping over.

She wasn't sure who looked away first. Maybe they both did at the same moment. They resumed eating but in silence, until she couldn't stand it for another minute.

"How is the ramp coming along?"

"Good. I think my plan will work." The corners of his mouth twitched. "It might be easier if the old guy wasn't hanging over my shoulder all the time. He's obviously overdue for some excitement in his life."

She wrinkled her nose. "Wasn't collapsing and getting taken off to the hospital in an ambulance enough excitement?"

"Not the fun kind. He wants to hold boards for me when I saw. If I stop to calculate, he ponders right along with me."

Erin laughed. "He'll probably tell the neighbors he did half the work."

Cole actually smiled again. "He's okay."

They talked about how far she'd gotten with the paint job, and he mentioned a book he'd just finished that she had loved. He had more doubts about the central argument, so they had the kind of debate she loved. The kind she'd once encouraged in her classroom and enjoyed with friends. Since he'd relaxed and was, for him, chatty, she asked what else he'd been reading, and was surprised anew by the range of subjects that interested him. They'd already talked about *The Good Soldiers*, a powerful look at one unit in the Iraq war. Now he mentioned *Five Days at Memorial*, about the horror in the aftermath of Hurricane Katrina, and he had just begun *All the Single Ladies*, about unmarried women and the trend toward independence.

Erin blinked at that one, coming from him.

"The world's changed," he said seriously.

"You feel like Rip Van Winkle." She'd known that, on one level, without realizing how profoundly those ten lost years had impacted him.

A nerve ticked in his cheek, and she wondered if he'd answer. But he started talking, slowly at first, then more naturally.

"Incarcerated, you watch some television, and you can get books and magazines from the library. Sports are the most popular on TV. The selection of books isn't all that current. Even if it was…reading about something isn't the same as experiencing it." He went quiet.

He'd never said this much before. The fact that he had…felt like an odd kind of gift. *Trust*.

But then he surprised her even more by going on. "I took a bus from Walla Walla to downtown Seattle. I was just about paralyzed when I stood on the sidewalk and watched all those cars jockeying to get in the right lane, lights

and movement everywhere, people shouting—"
He shuddered, although Erin wasn't sure he
knew he had. "Things I wouldn't have given a
thought to ten years ago made me feel as if I'd
been skinned and all my nerves were exposed.
I needed someplace slower."

"To dip your foot in the water."

"Instead of cannonballing in? Yeah, you could
say that."

"Were you at all tempted to go home while
you were in Seattle?"

His lashes veiled his eyes. "No."

That was all. *No.* Erin wished she hadn't
asked. He'd already told her his father hadn't
once visited him. Why would Cole want to go
home?

Because we all do, she thought sadly. Selling the house where she'd grown up, after her
father's death, had been so hard. Driving away
the last time, seeing it in the rearview mirror
just before she turned the corner, knowing she'd
never be back... Even the memory cramped her
heart. And how much more painful would that
have been if her father still lived in the house—
but she knew he'd never welcome her again?
She wondered if his father was still in Cole's
childhood home.

If Cole's dad ever showed up on her doorstep,
she thought she might punch him.

CHAPTER TEN

THE FOLLOWING MONDAY, when Erin got home from Lowe's with a bathroom vanity, molded counter and sink and miscellaneous plumbing parts in the rear of her Cherokee, Cole trotted across the street to meet her. He must have been watching for her.

Just like I always do for him. Yeah, but probably for a different reason, she thought resignedly. As usual, he looked really good in cargo pants and a gray T-shirt. His hair was merely short now, his arms, neck and face tanned. His body wouldn't be, since he had yet to strip off his shirt when working outside. Or inside, for that matter, at least that she'd seen. How many tattoos did he have? Was he afraid they'd label him as an ex-con?

Today was actually warm, the sun out, trees, daffodils and early tulips blooming everywhere. Hard to believe it was already May. The buds on a couple of Nanna's big rhododendrons promised a colorful show.

When she met Cole at the rear of the SUV,

he said, "Let me call Ryan." He pulled his new cell phone out of his pocket. "He offered to help carry the heavy stuff. I don't want you trying."

"Do I know Ryan?" she asked, disconcerted.

"He's your neighbor, the one on the corner." The call was obviously answered, because he said a few words, then stowed the phone, looking satisfied. "He's on his way."

Wanting to do something, Erin grabbed the new faucet assemblies for both the shower and bathroom sink and carried them upstairs to the apartment. By the time she'd returned, Cole and a stranger were sliding the vanity wrapped in cardboard and plastic from the back. Erin got out of the way.

Cole introduced her to Ryan Sager, who was probably in his early thirties, maybe five foot nine or ten but stocky, with plenty of muscles, a friendly face and russet hair.

"Hey," he said, "I've seen you passing. Another redhead."

Erin laughed, even though she was chagrined to realize she'd never noticed him. Apparently, she was wearing blinders. "I pretend I'm blonde."

"I tell my wife my hair is brown." He grimaced. "It almost works until my beard starts to grow in."

"Copper red?"

He rubbed his jaw. "Unfortunately."

They both laughed.

Then he reminded Cole to call as soon as Erin got back from Lowe's with the shower stall, and headed back up the street.

"How did you meet him?" Erin asked, watching him go.

"Oh, I saw him trying to unload a sofa from the back of his pickup truck a few days ago. His wife was supposed to take the other end. I helped get it in the house." Cole grinned. "*She* was sure happy to see me."

Remembering her aching muscles after hefting sheets of plywood above her head, Erin said, "She has my sympathies."

An hour later, watching Cole and Ryan muscle the old, cracked shower stall down the stairs, Erin thought about how she'd deliberately isolated herself, when so many of the neighbors had been Nanna's friends. They were people who cared about her, for her grandmother's sake. Meanwhile, Cole, deeply reserved, readily extended a helping hand to complete strangers. She'd do better, she vowed. Time to do some visiting. And maybe, just maybe, she could drum up some more work for him.

For his sake, she told herself, *not for mine…* But lying to herself didn't work very well.

After the two men plunked the old shower stall down in the driveway, Cole studied it. "I thought about taking an ax to this. Maybe I still should. We can get it in the garbage container little by little, instead of making a dump run."

"I should've kept that Dumpster for longer."

"Maybe. But I can break down the cabinets, even burn them, and the old sinks will go in the can." He shrugged, then joined Ryan, who was already untying the ropes holding the new shower stall on the roof of the Cherokee.

Watching Cole and Ryan wrestling the bulky thing up the stairs, turning the corner and miraculously getting it through the door, Erin heard some serious profanities. Muffled voices continued to come from inside the apartment. It was quite a while before they reappeared. She guessed they'd unwrapped it and set it in place in the bathroom.

"Did it fit okay?" she asked the minute Cole emerged.

"Perfect," he said, looking surprised that she'd doubt him.

He shook Ryan's hand and thanked him, Ryan saying, "Michelle wants to meet you, Erin. She'll probably drop by one of these days."

"That would be nice," she said, meaning it. "You have kids, right?"

"Eight-year-old boy, five-year-old girl. Michelle talks about going back to work once Gracie starts kindergarten this fall."

He was already backing away, so she didn't ask what his wife had done before choosing to stay home with the kids. When he reached the sidewalk and turned out of sight, she asked Cole about Ryan.

"Do men discuss things like what you do for a living?"

"Sometimes. Ryan is a real estate appraiser, if that's what you wanted to know."

She nodded, almost asking if he'd told the other man his own history, but glad she'd kept her mouth closed when Cole said, "Listen, unless you have something planned, I thought I'd make dinner tonight. Uh, if you don't mind breakfast."

"Breakfast?"

"I bought a waffle iron at a garage sale last weekend. I've been wanting to try it."

She laughed. "What if it doesn't work?"

"It heats up." His rare grin flashed. "If the waffle sticks to it, we'll have pancakes."

"Works for me. Thank you."

"I owe you a few dozen meals," he said. "I wanted to ask you a favor, too."

"Really? What?" He didn't usually sound so casual about asking her for anything.

"I wondered if I could drive on I-5 tomorrow." They'd talked about it, but hadn't done it yet.

"Definitely. If you feel confident, you could take the test next week."

"That's what I was thinking."

"Sounds good," she said, smiling enough to satisfy him.

They agreed on six o'clock for dinner, and he went across the street to get a few more hours of work in. Erin wondered if the Zatlokas were paying him the same she had, or more. How much did he have stashed away? He hadn't mentioned opening a bank account, but might have by now. Earlier, he'd talked about buying a bike to extend his ability to get around, but he never had. He must be saving for a car instead. That would give him real independence.

The thought made her glad and sad at the same time. His confidence grew by the day, while she was still trapped in her grief.

COLE'S PHONE RANG that evening, only a minute after Erin left following dinner and some lazy conversation over coffee. Dani, he saw, and answered immediately.

"Hey."

"So, I was thinking," his sister said. "Could I take you out to lunch someday if I drive down?"

"I'd like that," he said. He didn't bother pointing out that she'd be making a two-hour round-trip drive. She'd driven across the state to see him a dozen times during his incarceration. She wouldn't say much, but he knew her husband, Jerry, hadn't been very happy about it. Cole cleared his throat. "You visiting me in Walla Walla. I don't think I ever said—" *knew* he'd never said "—how much I appreciated that."

"I was the only person who ever came, wasn't I?"

"Yeah."

"Not even Lexa?"

He shifted uncomfortably, glad Dani couldn't see him. "I told her I didn't want her to."

Funny, he hadn't thought about Alexa in years. She'd been his girlfriend before his arrest. She had stayed at his side, even though she considered him foolish for insisting he was innocent, for turning down plea bargains that would've had him out of prison in three or four years instead of ten. He'd gradually come to realize she took for granted that he was guilty, whatever he said to the contrary, and that she really didn't care.

That was the moment he had fully understood how low he'd sunk.

"You told me not to come, too," his sister said tartly.

That made him smile. "I know."

"I never liked her, anyway."

He laughed. "Looking back, I'm not sure I did, either."

"Hmph."

When Dani didn't say anything else immediately, he tensed.

"Dad asked about you."

"I'm supposed to care?" Cole knew he sounded hard.

"You'd been doing some bad shit. Is it so surprising that he didn't know where you'd draw the line?"

"Or if I would?" He shook his head, even though she couldn't see that, either. "*You* knew better." Although sometimes he'd wondered if she really did, or just loved him enough to lie to him. Thinking one person believed in him—he couldn't afford to let go of that.

"Of course I did," Dani said impatiently, "but you and I were still talking regularly. All he knew was that you'd gone to the dark side."

If he was going to be reasonable, Cole would've had to admit she was right. His clashes with his dad had been angry, the possibility of violence hovering. But Cole had never so much as struck out at his father, and couldn't forgive him for believing he was capable of killing a man.

No, not a man—a boy, at least from Cole's perspective now. The kid, who still had lingering acne, had just turned twenty-one and been

working at the convenience store for a month.
Cole had only been a year older. There'd probably been terror in the guy's eyes when he saw
the gun pointed at him. Cole didn't know, because he wasn't there. The photos of the vic-
tim exhibited at the trial had haunted him. How
could anyone who knew him think he'd pulled
that trigger? Especially the man who'd raised
him?

Yeah, but if he'd stayed with the same group
of friends, gotten deeper into drugs, needing
money to feed an addiction, might he have become someone who *would* have done exactly
that? Wondering had caused him some bleak
hours.

"You mind if I give him your phone number?" his sister asked.

"I'd rather you didn't."

"Okay," she said after a minute. "I guess I
understand."

"When do you think you can come?"

She said she'd call next week, once she knew
the kids' schedules.

By then, he thought, laying the phone on
the 1950s-vintage end table, he might have his
driver's license. He'd open a bank account, too.
Get a debit card, like everyone else had. One
evening, Erin had shown him how she paid her
bills online. He could do that—once he had

bills. And, oh, yeah, a computer. Which he would, in the not-too-distant future. It wouldn't be long until he'd done the basic work to update this apartment. Then he'd either have to pay rent or move on.

ERIN FINISHED THE page in her book—and realized she didn't remember anything she'd read on this page, or the last several.

This was Tuesday—D-day, so to speak.

The Department of Motor Vehicles wasn't nearly as crowded as she'd expected this morning, meaning she was one of only about a dozen people sitting in the waiting area. Cole hadn't seemed nervous about taking the test, although it was never easy to tell, because he excelled at hiding his emotions. In fact, during the drive here, he'd talked about how the work on the bathroom was going. He was currently without a toilet until he laid the vinyl flooring this afternoon. He planned to wait to install new molding and to paint until he was ready to do the entire apartment.

Which meant it was time she chose some cabinets for the kitchen area.

The door behind her opened, and she turned to see a man enter, Cole behind him. He flashed her a grin. She smiled in return.

Once he'd had his photo taken and accepted

a temporary license, which he placed carefully in his wallet, he was ready to leave.

The minute they were outside, Erin asked, "It went okay, then?"

"No problem at all." He was quiet until they'd crossed the parking lot. "Not like the first time I took the test." He offered her the keys, but she shook her head and went around to the passenger side.

Once in the car, she said, "Did you really screw up?"

"Yeah." He started the engine. "I ran a red light."

"No!"

"Yup. We came straight back to the DMV." He chuckled. "Man, I was so cocky. I couldn't take the test again for—I don't remember. Weeks. I had to make an excuse to my friends for why I hadn't done it yet. No way was I going to tell them I'd flunked. Dealing with Dad was bad enough. In his book, nerves weren't an acceptable excuse."

Erin laughed, too.

"Being a DMV examiner has got to be as scary as teaching driver's ed," Cole remarked. "Although today we never did go out on either Highway 9 or the freeway."

"Self-preservation."

He laughed, the sound still a little rusty, but coming so much more readily than it had before.

"Any errands?" he asked, and she told him no.

When they got back, she said, "I have you on my insurance for the moment, so you're welcome to borrow the car. Just let me know."

Without moving from behind the wheel, he studied her, furrows in his forehead. "You mean that."

"Of course I do."

He gave a little shrug. "Then maybe I'll go to the bank right now. Set up an account. I didn't want you to have to sit there and wait."

"Feel free." Erin smiled, hopped out and walked toward the house, wishing he *had* wanted her there, waiting for him.

BEHIND THE WHEEL, unsupervised, Cole would have liked to feel pure triumph, the way he had when he was seventeen and finally able to drive on his own for the first time. Then, he'd felt like the king of the road. Totally cool. Girls would turn their heads, take him seriously. The guys he hung out with would, too.

Increasingly, he was discovering that nothing was as simple anymore. Maybe he would've already known that if he hadn't spent the last ten years in cold storage. Blink of the eye, you wake up to find yourself in the future. Except coming from cold storage, presumably you'd be unchanged, and that wasn't true for Cole. The shock of the arrest, the greater shock of the conviction. Figuring out how to defend himself in prison, to acquire allies even as he learned never to trust anyone at all. Hopelessness, mixed with the stubbornness that kept him confined those extra years because he still refused to say "I did it, and I'm sorry" to a parole board.

Now, there was Erin. Plus the debt he owed her, along with the disturbing realization that he *did* trust her. She might hurt herself but never him, and not because she'd made him into some kind of project. If he'd ever believed that, he no longer did.

It did feel good to open the checking and savings accounts. The banker who helped him didn't look at him askance once.

When he got back, he rang Erin's doorbell and handed over the keys. She smiled, said, "Hope it wasn't a hassle," and closed the door without inviting him to dinner.

He ate alone that evening, uneasiness heavy in his stomach. There'd been something off with her today. And just now? She'd said the right things, her lips had curved, but her eyes had been blank.

Tonight, he thought. She hadn't gone out in a while, but she would tonight. Cole wanted to stop her again, but what good would that do? He wouldn't always be here to protect her from herself.

But he wouldn't sleep tonight until she was home, safe.

ERIN LINGERED OVER her coffee in the morning until she felt certain Cole would have left to work at the Zatlokas'. She pushed herself to her feet, feeling as slow and old as Nanna must have in her latter years.

Well, she wasn't going back to bed, which meant she had to do something useful. She needed to paint the ceilings upstairs, but it made her dizzy even to think about that, so she'd do the walls in one of the extra bedrooms instead. She just had to get her supplies and the right can of paint from the garage.

She opened the front door, started across the porch…and saw Cole standing at the bottom of the steps. His feet were planted apart, his arms were crossed and his expression was both formidable and furious.

Erin froze.

His eyebrows climbed as he surveyed her. "You look like something the cat dragged in," he said scathingly.

Part of her was startled to hear such an old-fashioned insult coming from him. The rest of her… She peeked down at herself, as much to hide her flushed cheeks as anything. Paint-spattered jeans and shirt. Ragged, also paint-smeared canvas tennis shoes.

She shrugged. "Seems appropriate."

"You know what I'm talking about."

"You heard me leave," she blurted.

"And come home," Cole bit off. "Two hours later."

He made it sound like a sin. And maybe tempting fate the way she did *was* wrong.

Suddenly shaky, she stumbled to a seat on the top step. "You didn't try to stop me."

"I can't stop you forever."

Because he wouldn't be here. She was the one who should've been mad. What was with him, pretending to be scared for her, to *care*, when he had no intention of hanging around? Only… things had changed last night. She didn't have anyone else to tell.

"I almost hit something last night," she said in a thin voice.

"What?" He mounted the stairs two at a time, and was suddenly there, sitting a step below her so their faces were on a level. He took her hand. "Tell me."

"It was… I don't know for sure." She shuddered at the memory. "For a minute, I thought it was a person. Someone crossing the highway, or walking down it. I even thought—" She swallowed.

"That it might be a ghost."

She met his eyes, aware of the desperation in her own. "Except I know it wasn't. I think…I think it was a cow or maybe a horse. There are some farms along there."

He nodded, waiting.

"Of course I swerved."

"Because you don't want to risk anyone else."

Erin bobbed her head. "A couple of other times, I've had near misses. The kind where I almost lost control and went off the road. You know? I don't think I felt anything at all."

"This time, you did."

Despite his earlier anger, all she saw in those blue eyes now was compassion. Even the hard line of his mouth had softened. Had he guessed what she was going to say?

"I was terrified." She felt pathetic, holding on to his hand as if she'd go tumbling down the steps if she let go. "Like any normal person would be."

"Because you *are* normal." He tugged her closer, encouraging her to lean forward and rest her head on his shoulder. Still, she held on to that big, warm hand. "You've been healing, Erin. Maybe I've been your redemption. Maybe coming to a place that feels like home has you remembering happy times. Working on this place, seeing it come to life again."

She wasn't so sure about anything he'd said, except…she hadn't wanted to die last night. There'd been no relief, no thinking, *Finally.* Only sheer terror, fast reflexes and luck. That animal—too big to be a deer—had lumbered in panic back the way it had come at the same moment she swerved over the yellow line. If it had kept coming— Remembering made her heart pound.

"I knew you'd go out," he whispered, his mouth brushing her hair. "I can always tell. You…withdraw."

She nodded against the reassuring strength of his shoulder. "I can feel it coming on."

His fingers slipped into her hair, his hand cupping the back of her head. "Will you go again?"

"I…don't know," Erin said honestly.

His steady breathing stopped, reason for her to lift her head to see his face. Worry seemed to deepen the lines, aging him. But he sighed and said, "I guess that's better than hearing you say yes."

"Maybe…" No, she wasn't ready to say this yet. It would sound like a promise she might not keep. But she was serious.

Maybe he's right and I should make an appointment to talk to someone. Maybe I will.

Cole hadn't released her. His arm was looped around her shoulders. His gaze had dropped to her mouth, and the temptation to lean forward scant inches and press her lips to his was hard to resist. Or to lay her hand on his angular cheek, feel the texture of his freshly shaved jaw.

His eyes had darkened, narrowed, and she knew he was thinking the same. Hoping, *she* quit breathing now.

Abruptly, he straightened, letting her go. Rose to his feet. "What's your plan for today?" he asked from high above, as if nothing had happened.

Probably it hadn't. Humiliation warmed her cheeks as she realized any response on his part must have been in her imagination.

"Paint one of the bedrooms. Then I'll see. How are you progressing?" she asked.

"Good. Come take a look later."

"I might," she said. "Unless you think I'd scare the neighbors."

"Scare the— Oh." He smiled. "I guess that was rude."

"Nanna used to say it. About something the cat dragged in."

"My mother did, too." Sadness flickered in his eyes. "She'd have said it a lot if she could have seen me my last few years at home. Staggering in wasted."

"Except those years might have been different if she'd still been alive," she pointed out, pushing herself to her feet. Still creaky.

"Yeah. I hadn't thought about it, but I think you're right. She softened Dad." He half smiled. "And she made me want to live up to her standards."

"What about your sister?"

"Dani spent a lot of time furious at both of us. Hey, she's driving down on Saturday to see me. I'd like you to meet her."

Warmed, Erin said, "Just let me know when." She stood. "Now we'd better both get to work."

"Yeah." For a moment, he didn't move.

Once again, Erin had the sense of standing on the edge. If he reached for her...

Instead, he rolled his shoulders as if to loosen stiffness and turned to go. "See you at lunch?"

She waved. He broke into a trot, as he usually did. Erin was a lot slower when she headed for the garage.

CHAPTER ELEVEN

COLE GROANED AND slapped his second pillow over his face, no closer to falling asleep than he'd been two hours ago. Last night, he'd lost sleep worrying. Tonight…

He growled an obscenity and rolled onto his side, bunching both pillows beneath his head. He kept seeing Erin's bewilderment as she whispered, *I was terrified. Like any normal person.* But bewilderment wasn't all he saw. In that moment when his arm had been around her, when they did nothing but look at each other, he'd been completely absorbed. He always thought she was beautiful, but with only inches separating them, he'd been painfully aware of her lips, her fine-textured skin, lashes darker than the red-gold flame of her hair. He had ached to touch her, to feel that skin beneath his fingertips, to trace her eyebrows and the curve of her cheeks. To rub his thumb over her lips, even if he couldn't allow himself to kiss her.

He lay rigid, staring toward his window, thinking about her in bed not that far away.

What if he *had* surrendered to temptation? She'd wanted him to, he knew she had. Would giving in have been so wrong? Did she know why he hadn't?

Usually he ignored the inner voice determined to taunt him, but this time he couldn't. His answer was too important.

Because it would be a shitty thing to do, that's why. He wanted to be better than that. *Honor* was a word he'd added to his vocabulary over the ten years he'd spent thinking about mistakes, and about who he wanted to be.

He owed Erin too much to take advantage of her current fragility. If that sounded stupid, so be it. If he was positive all she wanted was sexual release, that would be different. Damn, he wished he did think that, because there was nothing in this whole world he wanted more than her. Too bad she was more messed up than he was, which was saying something.

And sure, he was probably afraid of feeling too much for her. He was a guy; he could enjoy sex without emotional entanglement, but not when it came to Erin. Unfortunately, he knew that anything they started would inevitably hit a brick wall. Someday, if she didn't succeed in killing herself first, she'd wake up and wonder what she'd seen in an uneducated ex-con not good for much but lifting heavy loads. It humiliated him to think of how she'd have to introduce him to friends or her former colleagues.

She felt...diminished right now. That was the only reason she looked at him the way she did. The only reason she leaned on him.

If he let himself fall all the way for her, he'd be the one who ended up feeling worthless—and, if he was going to make it, he couldn't afford anything that brought him down.

He got up to take a leak, considered reading or even turning on the TV, but decided to have another try at knocking himself out. Tomorrow would suck if he didn't get five or six hours of shut-eye.

Back in bed, he disciplined his thoughts. He'd have to find out if Zatloka wanted him to paint the railing. Might tie it into the house better. He needed some groceries. He could borrow the car, or ask Erin if she wanted to go, too. Seeing Dani in a few days—

A scream from the house sent his heartbeat into overdrive. He shot to a sitting position just as he heard a second scream. God, what if somebody had broken into the house?

Cole bolted out of bed, taking only enough time to pull on the pants he'd left hanging over a chair. Thank God Erin had given him keys a couple of weeks ago, so he could replace electrical outlets whether she was around or not.

Listening, hearing nothing, he located his key chain, tore down the steps and ran, barefoot, up the driveway.

ERIN HUDDLED IN a ball, shaking. The nightmare had been the worst ever. She knew that much, even if fragments were all that lingered. Even those were already blurring with what she'd really seen that day.

And then she heard her front door open and slam shut, and someone thundering up the stairs. She felt a split second of panic before Cole shouted, "Erin?"

"I'm here," she tried to say, but when she rolled over, she could see him crossing the room. "What—"

"Can I turn the lamp on?" He didn't wait for an answer.

Erin closed her eyes against the sudden light, but afterimages flared behind her eyelids.

The mattress compressed as he sank down on the edge of the bed. The next thing she felt was his warm hand cupping her cheek. "You're crying." He sounded shocked.

"Crying?" What was he talking about? She didn't cry in her sleep. Yet, when she lifted her own hand to her face, she found her cheek wet. "I am," she whispered.

He made a gruff sound. "You scared the shit

out of me. You sounded like someone was attacking you."

Through blurry eyes, she saw him bending over her, his face creased with worry. He stroked her cheek, then rose to his feet.

"I'll get something for you to mop up with."

Why was she crying tonight, when she hadn't cried before, after her nightmares? Shocked, she knew tears still fell.

Cole came back with a wad of toilet paper. With him sitting on the edge of the bed again, watching, she dried her cheeks and blew her nose.

"I can't believe I woke you up," she mumbled.

"I hadn't fallen asleep yet."

"Oh." She blinked until the numbers on her bedside clock came into focus—2:17.

He took the wet tissue from her hands and stood, going briefly into the bathroom. "You want to tell me about it?" he asked as he walked back toward the bed.

That was the moment she realized he was shirtless. That his chest and shoulders were as spectacular as she'd imagined. His khakis hung low on his hips, letting her see the line of brown hair that disappeared beneath the waistband. He was barefoot, too, which she found as disconcerting as seeing him without a shirt.

"Your tattoo." A clawed hand of some kind reached over his shoulder. "Can I see it?"

Between one step and the next, he went still. After a hesitation, he turned so she could see his back.

Unsurprisingly, it was a dragon climbing his back, hooking a front paw over his shoulder. The flame shooting from its mouth crept up his neck.

"It's beautiful," she said. "Whoever did it is an artist." The dragon was sinuous, seeming to move whenever Cole shrugged.

"Guy in prison. It…seemed like the thing to do." He turned so that she could see only the claws and flame again.

She wanted to ask if it was associated with a gang, but kept her mouth shut. "I thought prison tattoos tended to be crude."

He shook his head. "Depends on the tattooist. What most guys want is symbolic. Teardrops." He touched beneath one eye. "Barbed wire, gang or biker identification. A shackle with a broken chain." He looked down at her. "Will you be able to get back to sleep?"

"Sure."

She must have said it too hastily, because he sat on the edge of the bed again, his frown apparent. "You're a lousy liar, you know."

"I'm not—"

"You are," he said. "Tell me about your nightmare."

He'd go if she said it wasn't any of his business, but he'd come racing to the rescue after hearing what must have been a bloodcurdling scream. Or…

"I had my window open."

"What?" He looked in that direction, nodded. "Mine was open, too."

So maybe her scream hadn't been any louder than usual. Still, he sat there waiting.

Drawing her knees tighter to her chest, she said, "It was mostly the same thing. Except worse. In the real world, I…regained consciousness before the bodies were removed. I saw some of them." A shudder rattled her. Even her teeth chattered.

Cole swore and, to her shock, pulled back the covers, swung his legs up onto the bed and laid down on his side, facing her. As stiff as her body was, he drew her down onto her side, pillowing her head on his taut bicep. "I'm sorry," he murmured.

Self-consciousness, not to mention awareness of *him*, scattered her thoughts. Even as she longed to put her hand on his chest, feel his heartbeat, she reminded herself why he was here. *Not* because he wanted to make love with her. He'd made that clear.

The nightmare.

And…it might be easier to talk if he couldn't see her face. She knew exactly why she needed to hide.

"Tonight—" Erin swallowed "—their eyes were open. They were staring at me."

"God." His arms tightened around her. "Was there more?"

"I'm not sure," she said uncertainly. "There was something else, but I can't remember." Rising goose bumps told her she didn't *want* to remember.

"Tell me they didn't talk."

Another, more intense shudder gripped her.

"I shouldn't have said that." One of his hands moved up and down her back, over her thin T-shirt. "Have you tried sleeping pills?"

"At first." She was talking to his throat. "They made the nightmares more vivid."

Cole swore. "Are you having them every night?"

She shook her head.

"You never said when it happened."

"October."

"Seven months, then. You know the nightmares will get farther and farther apart."

"So everyone says."

He kept quiet after that, just held her. Usually

by now she'd be out of bed, probably dressed, and downstairs making coffee. All that adrenaline made lounging in bed after a nightmare a physical impossibility. But…in the shelter of his arms, her tension gradually eased. Her fists unclenched. She pulled away enough to straighten her legs, so her knees were no longer poking him in the belly.

The really hard belly, rippling with muscles.

This shiver had nothing to do with the nightmare, but Cole tightened his arms in a way meant to comfort.

And it did. Despite her physical reaction to him, despite the shadow of the horror that had awakened her, this felt like being enclosed in a cocoon. His embrace, the heat of his body, the gentle rise and fall of his chest and the whisper of his breath on her hair combined to make her feel safe.

But…tears must still be leaking. Her eyes stung.

He rubbed his chin on top of her head. "Let yourself cry," he said, voice low and husky. "I'll bet you haven't done that very much, have you?"

No. She'd been too afraid of breaking beyond any possibility of putting herself back together. But maybe, with him holding her, she could grieve without fear.

At the mere thought, a sob ripped from her throat.

THE WOMAN IN his arms cried and pounded his chest with a fist while her whole body quaked. Her body seemed determined to tear itself apart. All Cole could do was hold on.

At one point, he realized he was trying to rock her, and he knew he'd been murmuring something soothing—probably trite bullshit.

He doubted Erin heard a word, anyway. She sobbed, at first irregularly, then with clockwork precision. He found himself timing his own breaths to sync with hers. Not that she'd notice, tumbled as she was by a tidal wave of emotion. And, damn it, he was afraid his own face was wet.

Cole hadn't cried since his father had grimly paid his bail and brought him home. Alone in his room that night, he'd let go. By morning, he'd convinced himself that the arrest was such an obvious mistake he didn't have anything to worry about.

After he was convicted and led from the courtroom in shackles, he'd gone numb. To survive, he'd had to become cold, all the way through.

He'd be embarrassed by his tears now if he thought Erin would notice them. Because he knew she wouldn't, he didn't try to shut himself down. Maybe this was something he needed to do.

Her grief had triggered his. He hoped he cried mostly for her, but it had to be a little for himself, too. For things he couldn't go back and change, and for a future that would forever be affected by his screwed-up past.

Her sobs gradually lessened and she relaxed slowly until she went limp, looking as wrung out as he felt. He shouldn't stay, but he didn't want to move too soon and wake her up. He could close his eyes… Yeah, he'd wait until she was sound asleep…

STIRRING, ERIN BECAME grumpily aware that her bladder was making demands. Warm, comfier than she could remember being in ages, she tried really hard to ignore it. She didn't *want* to wake up.

But she had to. A headache began making itself felt, too. Ugh. This ache felt like a sinus infection, her head stuffed full of cotton wool. She should get up, pee and take some ibuprofen. Yes, but that meant moving, and she couldn't bear to. The steady heartbeat beneath her ear was too comforting, and she hadn't been so relaxed in forever.

Abruptly, she snapped to full wakefulness. She wasn't alone in bed. In fact, she practically lay on top of Cole. She had to have, well, climbed on him during the night. Oh, dear God, had they…?

No. The memory crept out of the muddle in her head.

He'd come bursting into the house, and she cried on him and even beaten him with her fists. After all that, he'd probably been afraid to leave her alone.

The thought made her cringe.

Now she *really* needed the bathroom. Pretending to stay asleep until he woke up and left wasn't an option.

At her very first movement, his muscles went rock-hard beneath her. She lifted her head to see his eyes open, sharp, unfriendly. But then he blinked a couple of times and only looked confused.

"Erin?" His head rolled on the pillow. "Damn. I didn't mean to fall asleep here."

That caused a little burn in her chest.

Wondering whether her hair was sticking out every which way, she forced a smile. "It's okay. You coming over here and letting me weep all over you was so…nice. I think this is the first time I've ever fallen back asleep after one of my nightmares."

His expression softened. "I'm glad I did stay, then."

"Um…" Feeling awkward, she shifted herself

off him, swung her feet to the floor and made an undignified beeline for the bathroom.

When she came out, he was sitting on the edge of the bed, running a hand over his hair as if the spiky texture irritated him.

"If you need the bathroom..." she said politely.

"No." He rotated his shoulders and stood. "I need to take a shower and get to work. I'll, uh, see you at lunch?"

Erin managed another smile. "Sure."

Not until she heard the front door close behind him did she gather her clothes and head back into the bathroom, where she spent an embarrassing length of time gazing at herself in the mirror. Threadbare T-shirt, flannel boxer shorts, puffy eyes and hair flattened on one side did not add up to an inspiring sight.

She made a few faces at herself before deciding he'd probably seen her looking worse. Paint-spattered and sweaty, or zombie-like, take your pick, couldn't have been all that appealing, either.

At least she'd really slept. And she knew how his muscles felt, flexing beneath her hand. She knew his smell, his husky, nighttime voice.

She knew what a good man he was. Just... not hers.

ONCE ERIN HAD slapped a second coat of paint on the bedroom walls, she showered and started baking. Yesterday evening, she'd sat down with Nanna's box of recipes and chosen several favorites. Ginger and molasses cookies—who didn't love them?—pumpkin bread and lemon scones.

She'd begin with the cookies today, since she'd noticed a jar of molasses in the pantry. A shopping trip would be required before she could tackle the other recipes.

The cookies smelled so good baking her mouth watered by the time she took the first sheet out of the oven. Once she got the next batch in, she gobbled two of the cookies with embarrassing haste before sliding the rest onto waxed paper spread on a cutting board.

Erin had discovered an entire cupboard filled with miscellaneous plastic storage containers. Astonishingly, every single one was matched with a lid. She used those for the cookies she was going to give away.

If Cole hadn't specifically mentioned lunch, she might have avoided it, but she felt compelled to make a pretense at normalcy. And really, she'd miss the half hour they spent together most days, talking quietly.

When she heard him coming up the steps,

she went out, carrying not only her sandwich and pop, but also a plastic container of cookies.

Not allowing herself to analyze his expression, she said, "I've been baking up a storm. These are for you."

His surprise always gave her a funny feeling in her chest. He didn't expect anything good, even a gift of cookies.

"All of them?" he said. "Aren't you eating any?"

Erin made a face. "Already did. And don't worry, I saved some for myself. I used Nanna's recipe." And tripled it. "I'd forgotten how sinfully delicious these are."

While he ate his sandwich, he said, "I thought you were going to paint again today."

"I did both." She managed a pert smile. "Thanks to my extrawarm pillow, I slept better than usual."

He chuckled. Whether that was any more genuine than her smile, Erin couldn't tell.

He finished his own sandwich, then ate three cookies before groaning and putting the lid back on the container. "I won't be able to bend over if I don't stop."

Now that she knew what his stomach looked like under his T-shirt—washboard-hard, rippling with muscle—a snort came naturally. "Yeah, right."

He smiled, thanked her and took his container of cookies up to his apartment before going back across the street.

Erin waited until he was out of sight to "go calling," a Nanna way of saying she was going to drop in on neighbors.

"YOUR GRANDMOTHER'S PLACE looks fine. Just fine. Josephine would be real pleased if she could see it," Del Wagner told her. "You've done a heck of a job."

Perfect setup. She smiled over her coffee cup. "I wish I could claim credit, but I think most of it goes to the guy renting the apartment from me. Cole Meacham. He did the majority of the work. In fact, he's building a wheelchair ramp for the Zatlokas right now."

"Nice fella," Del said with a nod. "Insisted on pulling my garbage can to the street a couple of weeks ago."

Someday, she'd have to march into the hardware store in town and tell that manager what an idiot he'd been.

"Cole is like that," she agreed. "He's the one who found Mr. Zatloka after he collapsed."

Del then got distracted telling her about his wife's stroke, which had led months later to her death, but eventually asked, "You think this Cole fella is interested in any more jobs?"

After assuring him that she believed Cole would be finished at the Zatlokas' any day and likely open to taking on another job, Erin began the slow process of extricating herself from this elderly neighbor's house. She really hoped he'd talk to Cole—for his own sake as well as Cole's. She'd climbed his front porch steps gingerly, not liking the way they felt underfoot. His porch wasn't as high as hers, but she could withstand a fall better than a man his age. A broken hip might well mean the end of his independence.

She'd intended to go to the Cooks' next, but after drinking a cup of coffee at each of four neighbors' houses, she desperately needed a stop at home. Nanna would have disapproved of her asking to use anyone's bathroom.

Once she was home, she decided she'd done enough for one day. Except maybe she'd go introduce herself to Ryan's wife. Mikayla...no. Michelle. It was only polite to offer cookies as a thank-you for Ryan's help, right?

Plump, pretty and a good five inches shorter than Erin, Michelle seemed almost as happy to invite her in as Del Wagner had been.

"A grown-up!" she exclaimed. "I've been playing the Disney Princess Enchanted Cupcake Party game. I kid you not," she added, seeing Erin's expression. "Your turn will come."

That stung a bit, since she had trouble imagining herself with a family, but she laughed, as expected.

Five-year-old Gracie didn't seem to mind Mommy quitting midgame, not when she was allowed to watch a movie while her mother visited with the neighbor.

"She looks like you," Erin said, awed by the sparkly pink-and-purple getup the little girl wore.

"Except for the red hair."

"Which she couldn't possibly have gotten from her dad, since he has brown hair," Erin said with a straight face.

Michelle laughed. "He tried that on you, huh?"

"I told him I'm a blonde."

"Instead of a strawberry blonde?" The other woman gave an exaggerated scowl. "Argh, Gracie's favorite doll is Strawberry Shortcake. I must have cakes on the brain."

"And what did I do but bring you goodies." Erin held out the container with the result of her morning's labor. "At least I didn't bake cupcakes."

Michelle giggled. "I'd have eaten those, too. Give me anything sweet. And these look divine."

Over coffee and cookies—Erin managed to restrict herself to only one more—the two women talked. Michelle had taught sixth grade until her son was born, and she and Ryan decided she'd stay home until their children started school themselves. "It's been a luxury," she said, "but I have to admit I'm looking forward to getting back in the classroom. I've taught third through sixth grades, but my favorite was the sixth grade. They're children one minute, budding teenagers the next. Awkward, excited, silly." She smiled. "Here I am, going on and on. Ryan didn't say what you do for a living."

"At the moment, nothing," Erin admitted, then hesitated. Since coming to West Fork, she had yet to tell a single person other than Cole what had happened. She and Michelle had the potential for real friendship—but not if she lied now. She drew a deep breath. "I was a college professor. I taught history and coached women's volleyball and softball."

"You must have a PhD."

"I do. But…I don't know if I can ever go back." She swallowed. "You see, I was driving my volleyball team to a match when…something happened."

By the time she finished, Erin was crying and apologizing all at once. "I'm so sorry! I thought I could tell you without falling apart." She started to stand. "I should go." Apparently, she hadn't secured last night's floodgates when she closed them.

"No." Michelle's hand on her arm stopped her. "Please don't."

Erin slowly sank back onto the kitchen chair. She sniffled and wiped at her cheeks with the back of her hand until Michelle held out a napkin.

"This will work better."

"Thank you." She blew her nose hard, mopped up and finally crushed the paper napkin. "I'm a mess."

"And no wonder," Michelle said. "It's only been—what?—seven months? And look what you've accomplished on your grandmother's house! Has the work been therapeutic?"

"It has. I suppose that's what I had in mind. Plus—" she grimaced "—I wanted to go home, and this was the closest thing I had. I just wish Nanna was still alive."

She ended up telling Michelle about losing her parents, too, after which the other woman said thoughtfully, "When you've suffered that much loss, being handed more must've hit you even harder than it otherwise would have."

Erin stared at her. That had never occurred to her, but…it sounded right. She'd isolated herself in her grieving when she hadn't needed to. She'd spent holidays with Nanna, but never let herself understand that Nanna, too, had lost her family. First her only child, then her husband. All she'd had left was Erin, who wished now that they'd talked more. But that hadn't been Nanna's way. She…accepted, instead of bewailing. *Like I've been doing.*

"That's…possible," she said. She cleared her throat. "Have you ever thought of becoming a school counselor? You seem to have a knack."

Michelle grinned. "If you're going to spend all day in the company of preteens, you have to be prepared for a lot of angst and drama."

Seeing the humor in it, Erin had to laugh. "I'm giving you a reminder of what you'll face this fall."

The other woman shrugged. "Assuming anyone hires me. I've got a bunch of applications out there, but I'm still waiting."

Half an hour later, Erin walked home, feeling cleansed. Having a friend again would be good, and instinct said that, despite her having broken down in tears, Michelle wouldn't fuss over her emotional state the way college friends had. She was refreshingly different.

I hope.

CHAPTER TWELVE

"I WOULD'VE BEEN fine with Erin joining us." Dani studied Cole with eyes as blue as his.

They had ended up at the same pizza parlor where he and Erin had eaten the one night, and from which they'd ordered takeout several other times. There were more upscale restaurants in West Fork, but Dani had readily agreed that pizza sounded good. If she'd guessed he was happier going somewhere he knew so he could feel reasonably comfortable, she didn't say so.

"It's been a while since you and I have seen each other," he said.

"I feel bad we didn't include Erin. Maybe next time?"

"I probably won't still be living at her place by the time we get together again." Saying that casually was hard.

His sister's surprise didn't help. "That apartment's great. Why would you want to move?" She frowned. "Or is your landlady a problem?"

Erin was a problem, all right, but not in the way Dani meant.

He shook his head. "Not like that."

"Like what?"

"My needing to leave doesn't have anything to do with Erin. I...like her." Long practice let him sound unemotional, kept him from any physical tells. "I was lucky to meet up with her. But I don't like having to feel grateful."

"She *wants* you to?"

He smiled a little at his sister's indignation. She and Erin had a few things in common, it occurred to him. "No. It's not her. It's me. I want to know I can make it without charity."

"You did some amazing work on her house."

After introducing her to Erin, he'd given Dani a tour of the exterior as well as his apartment before they left for lunch.

"Yeah, it looks good, doesn't it?"

Hearing their number, he went to get the pizza.

He should've known that Dani would be in pit bull mode. He'd barely slid into the booth when she demanded, "What was charitable about her hiring you? With everything you're doing in the apartment, she has to be gaining as much as you are."

Cole put a slice of pizza on his plate, giving himself an instant to think. He wished the subject hadn't arisen. The truth was, if he and Erin hadn't become friends, he might not feel the way he did. Objectively, they'd made an even trade. He'd worked his butt off for her, refusing every time she tried to up his pay.

"It's the extras," he tried to explain, without quite telling his sister the truth. "Her helping me get my driver's license, letting me borrow her SUV." She baked him goodies. No, he wasn't going to tell his sister that. "I think she's waging a campaign in the neighborhood to get me jobs. She's suddenly visiting everyone up and down the block, taking cookies and scones."

Dani could read him better than anyone else. Nothing new about that. In this case, it wasn't a bad thing, because after some serious scrutiny, she stopped pressing him. Instead, as they started eating, she asked if he had any plans, and he told her some of what he'd said to Ramirez.

She suggested he move to Bellingham. "Housing isn't expensive, especially during the summer when most students go home. And we have both a community college and Western."

The thought had occurred to him, but if he left West Fork, he knew he'd never see Erin again. Even thinking about that made him feel as if his chest had been split open. But if he stayed in town, seeing her in passing might be painful, too. At least he could be sure she was okay, though. Another thing he couldn't say to his sister.

And it wasn't as if he'd see that much of Dani, given her husband's attitude.

"I'll think about it," he said, but could tell she knew he didn't mean it.

She whipped out pictures of her kids to show him, which hurt in a different way. A niece and nephew he'd never met. Might not meet for years, if ever. Cole knew that, if he asked, Dani would bring the kids with her next time, but he didn't want to be the cause of a blowup with Jerry.

So he said admiring things, and only grinned as she talked about their excellence. *Her* kids were ahead of most of their peers in every way, from schoolwork to dance and baseball.

"Both brilliant and talented," he teased. "With you as a mother, how could they help it?"

She sniffed. "They couldn't."

They managed some casual conversation until they were driving back to his place. *Erin's place*, he corrected himself. Damn.

A few blocks away, Dani said, "I talked to Dad last night."

He groaned. Of course she had to go there.

She turned her head long enough to narrow her eyes at him. "I'm just telling you."

"Nagging."

"I am not!"

"Are, too."

Her spine straightened as she went into her "I am above your pettiness" mode. "Can we have a little maturity here?"

He gave her a crooked grin. "If you promise not to mention Dad again."

"Oh, fine." She pulled into the driveway and braked. "It's just that—"

He kissed her cheek and opened the door. "Thanks for the visit, Dani."

She rolled her eyes. "Jerry will come around."

"Since his wife's a bulldozer?"

His sister stuck out her tongue. Cole was laughing as he slammed the door.

THE NEXT MORNING, Cole was putting primer on the ramp railing when he heard someone approaching from behind. He went completely still, making sure he was balanced on his feet to move fast. Even as he prepared to fight, he reminded himself that things were different out here. He straightened and turned fast.

He didn't know this old guy's name, but did recognize him. He was a lot bigger than Mr. Zatloka, raw-boned, moving as if every joint hurt.

Tamping down the minispike of adrenaline, Cole nodded. "Came to see the wheelchair ramp?"

The guy said, "I don't need one of these yet, but I do need a new front porch. Got the same problem Ms. Parrish did."

"Rotting?"

"The steps, anyway. She suggested you might be almost done here…"

"I am." He really hated that she was out drumming up business for him, even if her intentions were good. And yes, every small job helped him build a bigger financial cushion, gave him more experience and the possibility of another reference. All of that didn't seem to prevent the small slap of humiliation.

"I'm Del Wagner," the guy said. "You helped me with my garbage can a couple of weeks ago."

"I remember. Tell you what, while this dries, I'll come down to take a look." Turning down an opportunity would be stupid.

Wagner thanked him and plodded back around the corner of the house. Every step seemed to be an effort.

It took Cole another half hour to finish applying the primer. He'd give it two or three hours, then put on the first coat of paint. The balusters were to be white, the top rail black, like some of the trim on the house.

He wiped his hands with a rag, grabbed a tape measure and screwdriver and walked down the block. This house looked to be about the same age as Erin's, although smaller. The detached garage didn't have a second story. At first glance, Del Wagner had maintained his home decently, but Cole didn't have to poke at the steps to see that they did need replacing. A few boards on the porch did, too. He could see where the roof above the porch had leaked, soaking some supports.

Once Mr. Wagner had come out, Cole also checked the back porch and the siding.

He learned that the house had last been painted two years ago. He gave Wagner the bad news about the porches, and agreed that he could do this job next. Like the Zatlokas, Wagner offered fifteen dollars an hour, still cut-rate from what Cole had learned, but more than satisfactory.

He'd resolved to report his income. Nothing under the table for him. Everything he did would be scrutinized in a way most people didn't have to worry about.

With a notebook page listing the measurements jammed in his pocket, he decided to take his lunch break and walked back to Erin's. The awkwardness between them since she woke up and discovered he'd spent the night, uninvited, in her bed tempted Cole to eat in his apartment, but he couldn't bring himself to hurt her feelings if she came out and he wasn't there. It was a nice day, too; he'd just as soon sit outside with the sun on his face.

The truth was, he didn't want to miss a minute he could spend with her, either.

WHEN COLE SAW the slices of pumpkin bread that Erin had brought out on a plate, his eyebrows rose. "Trying to fatten me up?"

"Actually—" she inspected him, head to toe "—there *is* a little more substance to you than there used to be. I remember thinking you looked too lean the first time I saw you."

"Prison food is lousy." He settled in his usual spot at the top of the steps, on the right side. "If you can afford it, you can buy snack food at what we called 'the store.'" He unwrapped his sandwich, as much to give himself a minute as anything, Erin thought. "After I got out, I had to conserve money. I'd probably lost some weight by the time we met."

Conserve money, she suspected, was an understatement of monumental proportions.

"Truthfully, I've been in this baking frenzy. I don't know why."

"Mr. Wagner told me you'd taken him some of those cookies."

Her face brightened. "Oh, did he talk to you? I was hoping he would. His porch steps are squishy, and all I could think was how risky a fall would be for a man that age."

He gave her an indecipherable look, but only nodded. "I'm going to replace both porches for him." The corner of his mouth twitched. "He's not having any of those gaudy colors, though.

His Emmie always said a white house is dignified, and he won't insult her memory by getting fancy."

Erin laughed. "I can just hear him. Oh, dear. Have I shocked all the neighbors?"

"Mrs. Zatloka likes the colors you painted the house. Even the pink." He grinned. "Mister is dubious."

"Ryan's wife *loves* the colors. She's thinking about shades of teal when they paint their house next year."

"The old folks won't recognize their neighborhood."

Nanna wouldn't have minded. Erin was sure of that. She sneaked a look at Cole, who picked up a slice of the bread. "I hope you like raisins. And walnuts."

"There's not much I don't like. I just don't want you feeling like you have to do all this for me."

She pulled her knees up and wrapped her arms around them. She shouldn't feel prickly, but she did. "If you want a loaf, you're welcome to it. If not, I won't be insulted. I'm planning to give away a couple more. I've resolved to get to know the neighbors. I was ashamed when I met Ryan and realized how I've been hibernating."

"A few of *them* can use fattening up," he said with a sidelong smirk.

She laughed, as he'd no doubt intended, then let the silence ride for a few minutes. The fact that he'd readily mentioned prison food encouraged her to ask questions.

"In prison. Was it violent, the way the news makes it sound?"

The look he sent her wasn't encouraging. But after a minute, he said, "It can be." Pause. "Except when tensions between gangs are especially high, the worst is when you're new. You have to…establish yourself as someone it's not worth messing with." He looked out over the yard. "I was lucky, being a big guy. I was also young, stupid and stunned, but I took up weight lifting right away, bulked up."

"Were you in fights?"

Another quick glance. "Yeah."

Erin rested her chin on her knees. "Did you ever see anything really awful?" Lord. Was this what she'd been working her way around to? Did she need to know whether he could understand what *she'd* seen, experienced?

This time the silence went on so long she thought he wasn't going to answer. But he did, his voice rough. "Hard not to. Once I saw a guy get knifed in the shower."

She pressed her hand to her mouth.

"I knew dead when I saw it. I kept walking, got dressed and was out of there before his body was reported." His tone was unemotional, yet tinged with darkness. "When they asked, I said I'd left a couple minutes earlier than I really did. Didn't see a thing."

"Because if you'd identified the killer—" She could hardly whisper.

"I'd have been dead, too," he said flatly. Not giving her a chance to say anything else, he surged to his feet, walked down the steps and went up to his apartment.

Erin didn't move for at least five minutes, but he didn't reappear. She carried the wrapped loaf of pumpkin bread back into the house.

RAMIREZ CALLED TWO days later.

Despite Cole's mixed feelings about how he'd gotten his latest job, he was glad to be able to say, "Yeah, I'm still working." In fact, he'd been on his knees pulling up rotten boards when the phone rang. "Another neighbor."

Yes, he'd gotten a driver's license. No to a car. He wasn't about to buy anything that wasn't halfway reliable. He had to explain that he couldn't even apply for a job with a contractor until he had the ability to get to job sites.

"You're good at working on cars, though," Ramirez countered.

"Don't have the tools for anything complicated," he said briefly.

They pretty much left it at that, Ramirez just reminding him that he had to report any change of address.

Cole had checked out Craigslist and seen a few vehicles worth looking at. He didn't let himself forget the cost of insurance and gas. If he had a job, he might quality for a car loan of a few thousand dollars that would extend the possibilities, but he doubted he could get a job without already having transportation. So—cheap car, upgrade later if necessary.

Assuming anyone would hire him, of course. He'd forever face the stigma of the felony conviction. He'd only been working something like six weeks. Whether that was enough to make a difference, he had no idea. The coward in him wanted to keep taking temporary projects, put off handing applications to strangers who'd drop them in the trash the minute they saw the checked box at the bottom. But it had to be done eventually. Would another month of this kind of work help? Two more months?

Construction was busier in spring and summer. It was already past the middle of May. Waiting too long to start applying wouldn't be smart. Not many people would hire him to do this kind of small job once the rains started in the fall, either.

Still kneeling on Wagner's porch, Cole felt

cold despite the sun on his back. Once he got the new kitchen cabinets and sink installed in his apartment, he'd be left with painting the walls and replacing some of the molding. A matter of another week or two, if he worked hard.

Only when he heard the front door opening did he toss the rotten board onto the grass and apply the crowbar to the next.

"THANKS FOR OFFERING to help," Cole said, taking a last swallow of coffee. "Ryan saw where I was at and came over to give me a hand with any heavy lifting."

It was time to start clearing the table, but Erin didn't want to give any signal that would have Cole excusing himself and leaving. After at least a week of seeming cool toward her, tonight he was friendly and relaxed. She just wished she knew why he'd been so distant all week. Had it been her questions?

"Well, he does have more impressive muscles than I do." She flexed her puny bicep for the pleasure of seeing him laugh.

The change she'd seen in him was astonishing. He *did* laugh these days, and smiled often. He openly took pride in his work, and seemed to enjoy watching her garden take shape as much as she did. He'd offered to build an arbor over the walkway where it parted from the driveway, so she could plant more climbing roses. Before she could even open her mouth, he'd narrowed his eyes and told her not to say a word about pay. She could buy the lumber; that was it.

The labor and skill, she understood, was his way of saying thank you. So she'd only smiled and nodded. He had promised to build it as soon as he finished Del Wagner's porch.

He stretched. "I think I'll head up to the library. Nice that it isn't getting dark so early."

"You're welcome to take the car."

"Thanks, but I enjoy walking."

"You must be a speed reader." Unless he was lying about his destination, he went to the library several nights a week.

"A lot of the time I just use the computer."

She frowned. "You don't sound as if you had much exposure at Walla Walla."

"I didn't. Partly my fault. They offer some classes, like programming. The one I regret not taking was Computer-Aided Design. That would've been handy for planning small projects." He shrugged. "Once I get a computer."

"You know you're welcome—"

"I'll ask if I really need it."

His terse response told her not to push it. "You couldn't email?" she said, almost at random.

Cole shook his head. "Recently they've let

some inmates buy a low-cost tablet that allows email. I wasn't interested."

Nobody to email. He didn't have to say it.

"Dani…"

"Yeah." His expression eased. "She would've liked that."

Erin nodded. She'd been careful to ensure that they didn't feel obliged to invite her for lunch last week, but thought she'd like Cole's sister. Shorter than Erin and small-boned, Dani was still unmistakably related to him. Same hair color, same blue eyes, a chin that looked as if it could be as stubborn as his, and cheekbones that, while considerably more delicate than her brother's, echoed his.

"I took some scones over to the Zatlokas. She told me how happy she is with her ramp."

He raised his eyebrows slightly. "I'm glad to hear that."

"Have you met Lottie Price? Across the street and a few doors down?"

Cole didn't move, but she felt new tension from him, anyway. "Yellow house?"

"That's the one."

"She another senior?"

"A contemporary of Nanna's. They were friends and competitors. Their gardens, you know. Cooking, too." Remembering, Erin smiled. "Lottie would bring over some banana bread and say sweetly, 'I know you fuss over how dry yours always is. I'll be glad to give you my recipe if you like.'"

Cole laughed. "What would your grandmother say?"

"'How kind of you, Lottie. If you find your bread's a bit *soggy*, I'll be glad to share *my* recipe with you.'"

His grin lingering, he said, "Friends, huh?"

"They really were. They just enjoyed sparring." More cautiously, she said, "Lottie asked about you. She's been thinking she needs a wheelchair ramp, too."

"Erin." He sighed. "You need to quit looking for work for me."

"She'd heard about the one you built for the Zatlokas! She asked because I was there, not because I was…was pitching your skills. The neighbors talk, that's all."

"So you set out to visit every single homeowner within a two-block radius—because you've decided to be sociable."

"Yes!" Feeling warmth in her cheeks, Erin couldn't help remembering Cole telling her she was a lousy liar. "Don't you want the work?"

"I need to find my own jobs." Suddenly, he sounded…hard.

She opened her mouth to ask why, then closed

it. She knew. He must believe she didn't think he could find a job on his own.

Swallowing the lump in her throat, Erin looked away and nodded. "I understand. I'm sorry. I just wanted—" She broke off, pushing back her chair and getting up.

"I know what you wanted." There he went, sounding so gentle she couldn't stand it.

Erin grabbed her own dishes and carried them to the counter.

"I'll go talk to this Lottie," he said, his resignation clear. "But that's it."

Back at the table, she reached for the serving bowls. "I heard you," she said stiffly. "You don't have to worry."

Moving with startling swiftness, his hand shot out and closed on her wrist. "Do you know why I don't want any more help from you?"

She lifted her head to meet eyes darker than usual. Stormy. "It's embarrassing."

"I was a mess when we met. Now it's time for me to do the important things myself."

"Fine." Her voice came out barely above a whisper.

His fingers flexed on her arm, and he abruptly stood, knocking his chair aside. He tugged her toward him. "I already wish things were different, that I was more—" He shook off whatever he'd been about to say. "Now you're putting me in debt."

"It's not like that!"

"You really don't get it, do you?" His expression oddly bleak, he released her wrist to put his hands on her shoulders. "Maybe this will give you the idea." He bent his head and kissed her.

CHAPTER THIRTEEN

HER LIPS WERE as soft as he'd imagined. Hazily aware that he was gathering her into his arms, Cole had trouble thinking. The pleasure of finally kissing Erin zapped him as if he'd opened himself to an electrical shock.

Shouldn't have done this.

Too late.

She hadn't moved at all, not to respond, not to pull away. God. She was probably in shock.

Cole began to lift his head just as Erin rose up on tiptoe to press her lips harder to his. She flung her arms around his neck, too. The kiss became clumsy and desperate. He nipped her lower lip: their teeth clanked together. If he'd ever had any skill at this, it had atrophied from disuse. Which didn't seem to matter, because her body was plastered against his, his blood felt thick and hot in his veins, and she was kissing him with as much urgency as he kissed her.

Not one-sided, he thought exultantly. Why he'd started this eluded him. It didn't seem to matter. Nothing did but the sensations bombarding him—her breasts pressed to his chest, her thighs to his, the quivering intensity running through her body and jumping to his. Her taste, the thick silk of her hair, the little sound she was making.

When his tongue touched hers, it was so damn erotic he jolted.

And thought, *What am I doing?*

Somehow, he wrenched himself away. One hand hadn't gotten the message and still squeezed her hip, but at least a few inches separated their bodies.

Erin stared at him, her eyes dazed and heavy-lidded, her lips parted. She blinked, then again, and seemed to realize he wasn't just catching his breath.

"What…what's wrong?"

Wrong? Nothing. Everything.

"We can't do this," he said hoarsely. "I was… trying to explain something here."

Her expression slowly changed.

"I already feel like roadkill under the tires of your fancy new SUV. I'd enjoy—" he managed to stop himself from being too crude "—sex with you. I guess you can tell." He gestured toward his obvious hard-on. "But that's one thing I'm not willing to do for pay."

Still she stared, for another second, then cried

out and leaped back. "That's what you think of me?"

"No." His mouth twisted. "That's what I think of myself. We're not equals. We can't be." Could she hear how desperately he wished it was different? That he could have her without savaging his pride? "I'm sorry. I owe you so much, I can't start anything like this."

She spun away. "Fine. You feel like the hired hand. I get it." She opened the dishwasher and gazed into it as if she had no idea what the damn thing was.

He felt… He didn't even know. His fingernails bit into his palms. "I'll finish what I promised you."

"Fine," she said again, but stayed where she was.

Cole backed up until he bumped into the doorframe. He'd been an asshole when he didn't have to be. He wished he knew what to say to make it all better, to go back fifteen minutes to when they were friends. But so much was churning inside him he couldn't think.

"Thank you for dinner."

The sound she made might have been a laugh.

WHEN SHE WAS sure he was gone, Erin slumped onto a kitchen chair. She labored for breath.

Cole had implied that she'd thrown herself at

him. Attacked him. Like she'd expected him to service her in bed because of everything she'd done for him. But *he* was the one who'd started it. Wasn't he?

A while back, he'd said something snotty about payback. Maybe that was what this had been. *See how scummy you make me feel? Try a little of it, why don't you?* Was humiliation the whole purpose of that kiss?

If so, it had worked. At least she wasn't crying. She was too stunned. Hurting, but also… She didn't even know. Why would he do that? Make her feel so much, then lash out so viciously? Was that his version of "thanks, goodbye"? Maybe she'd been totally naive where he was concerned.

If she was careful, perhaps she could avoid seeing him. For all she cared, he could leave the apartment key on the doorstep when he left.

Did she still owe him any money? Erin didn't think so. She'd stick a note on his apartment door reminding him to return her house key. Not like he'd want to make use of it, she thought painfully. Apparently, *that* was his message.

The agony swelled and receded like ocean waves. It stung like salt water did on raw flesh, too. Ever since she'd brought him home with her, she hadn't felt so alone. She would have sworn a bond had formed. Maybe…maybe she was wrong, and she'd only been using him. If so…she wouldn't apologize. She'd given everything she could in return. Too much, obviously.

Trying for slow, deep breaths, she asked herself what if, come morning, she found out he'd left? A huge hole seemed to open inside her. She reminded herself that he'd promised to finish the work on the apartment. He couldn't do that overnight.

Yes, but it might be better if he did just leave. She really didn't want to see him right now, and saying goodbye would be unimaginably awful. *I'm such a fool*, she thought, the pain cresting. She'd fallen in love with him, and he'd been looking at her with wariness and contempt all along. Pathetic, lonely woman who imagined she could buy him.

She was more than that. She was.

With a whimper, Erin buried her face in her hands. Why had he pretended to care? Tried to prevent her from going out at night? After the nightmare, spent all those hours holding her with such tenderness Erin couldn't imagine.

When she lifted her head at last and managed to focus on the microwave clock, she saw that at least half an hour had passed. The hurt had…not dulled. It had left behind an ache, the way a horrible cough left chest muscles feeling strained.

She was mad, too. At herself, at him, at fate, if there was such a thing. She'd lived for *this*? Maybe tonight she should— No. She wouldn't give him the satisfaction. He'd know *he* was behind her need to ask Death again if she'd really been meant to be spared.

When he's gone. Then I'll do it.

COLE SNAPPED AWAKE on a flood of adrenaline. Had he heard an engine starting up? He lay completely still, listening for any sound. Nothing. He'd imagined it. Or she'd already escaped.

That thought provoked him into getting out of bed and padding to the front window that looked down on the driveway. The dark bulk of the Cherokee was there. Back in his bedroom, he stood staring at the house, also dark. He'd left his window open, in case—

In case what? Erin had another nightmare and needed him? Yeah, think how welcome he'd be.

He kept grappling with what he'd done. He'd dumped on her because...?

It was the only way to keep her from drumming up new jobs for him. Except he'd already asked her not to, and she'd agreed.

He'd needed her to know how much he wanted her. Why?

Feeling as if he'd been ripped open, Cole thought, *I had to push her away before...* He didn't want to finish this explanation, but forced himself. *Before I broke and made love to her. Before I got in so deep I convinced myself pride wasn't worth shit.*

His shoulders slumped. Nice to know he'd hurt *her* to save himself. What happened to all his deep thoughts as he lay in his prison bunk—about honor, about being a man who works hard and takes the high road? About becoming the kind of man who never would have been arrested, far less convicted? A man people would have *believed*?

If he was going to apologize, he had to bare himself. How else could he expect her to understand?

Cole flopped into bed, groaned and laid his arm over his eyes. Tomorrow, no excuses.

There wasn't a lot left of the night. He dozed on and off, jolting awake often enough to leave him with a pounding headache come morning.

He winced at the sight of himself in the new bathroom mirror, big and brightened by the also-new, four-bulb vanity light fixture above. He looked like crap. The sleeplessness showed in eyes that appeared sunken and skin that seemed tinted gray. The hollows beneath his cheekbones would, in his opinion, remind anyone seeing him that the human face overlaid a skull. And damn, he wished his hair would grow out faster.

His hand seemed to have a faint tremor, too, that made him glad he'd finally bought an electric shaver and didn't have to risk drawing blood with the straight razor. When he was done, he rinsed and dried his face before eyeing himself again. Shaving hadn't improved the view. Maybe seeing how bad he looked would soften Erin's anger.

Usually, he tried to have a decent breakfast—eggs and toast, or at least cereal. Today, he used a cup of coffee to wash down a couple of too-dry, powdered sugar donuts. Then he picked up his keys, startled for an instant when he remembered one of them was for Erin's front door.

He'd be returning both of them soon. That knowledge gave him a pang. Being handed the key to the apartment had meant a lot to him. Privacy, independence. Strange that he could've accepted the house key from Erin without marveling at the trust involved. Two keys, two gifts, neither of which he could keep.

Shaking his head, he stuffed them in his pocket, and jogged down the stairs and up to Erin's front door. He rang the doorbell, and heard the chime inside. Followed by...nothing. No lights, no footsteps, no voice.

If she'd had as crappy a night as he had, she might be sleeping in.

He wished he believed that.

He went to the garage to collect what he'd need to install shingles on Del Wagner's porch roof. When he was done, he'd go talk to Lottie Something. Reluctant as he'd felt, Cole had calculated how much money he'd come out of it with and realized he couldn't turn down the job. It would give him a little time to hunt for a five-day-a-week job and a room for rent.

Another gift from Erin, one he might resent, but had needed. And she'd known that.

He'd try to catch her at lunchtime. She couldn't hide forever.

ERIN MANAGED TO ignore the ringing doorbell for the rest of the day. Working on the house would have meant sneaking out to the garage for paint and supplies, so instead she settled at the kitchen table with her laptop to do research. She started by looking for psychologists within a thirty-mile radius who had expertise in working with victims of trauma. She didn't put much stock in online reviews for counselors, but she did note specific comments as she made a list.

From there, she browsed job listings, just as Cole had probably been doing, only for herself. If she didn't start working at least part-time once he left, she thought she might really go nuts. College teaching was out. If not forever, certainly for now. She didn't have elementary or secondary teaching certification, but talking to Michelle had reminded her of all the other jobs available in schools, and this was probably the right time of year to apply for positions open in the fall. She'd be okay working with younger children.

The county-wide public library system seemed to have regular openings, too. Continuing to browse, she discovered that the city of West Fork was looking for people to teach recreation department programs for the summer. Mostly fun stuff, some computer classes, art for all ages— and sports. Her gaze seemed to freeze on the listing for volleyball.

The next thing she knew, she'd opened the school district website. Feeling as if she was slipping surreptitiously into enemy territory, she read about the high school girls' sports programs. They did have both volleyball and softball. The volleyball team had a disastrous record. She couldn't imagine the league was that tough. Probably the team was so bad girls with any athletic ability went out for other sports. Erin couldn't help wondering who coached it. A teacher who wanted the bump in her paycheck? Or someone who'd been guilted into taking it on despite zero experience, because otherwise the girls wouldn't have a chance to play at all?

Could I?

Even the timid question was enough to throw her into a panic. No, no. Never again. Or at least…not yet.

How could she step foot in a gymnasium without being deluged by memories? Wouldn't that be terrific—new volleyball coach midcourt in a catatonic state? Or shouting about ghosts and running for her life?

Back to the public library. She could shelve books, help with research questions, quiet noisy kids and encourage shy ones. Many of the jobs that didn't require a master's degree in information science were part-time, but that was all she wanted for now, anyway. The pay wasn't great, either, but money wasn't an issue yet. Just getting out there, meeting people, feeling useful and involved, was what she needed. Preparing to rejoin the human race.

When the doorbell rang again at seven thirty, she closed her laptop and tried to convince herself she ought to eat something.

Nobody is on the front porch.

A salad? What about a grilled cheese sandwich? Wasn't that the classic comfort food?

He'd see the lights on in here. *So what?* she

thought defiantly, before remembering he had a key. He wouldn't let himself in, would he? He had to know she didn't want to see him, didn't want to talk to him.

Soup. There were a bunch of cans in the pantry. Soup was easy.

Fine. Erin went to the pantry and decided on tomato, even though it didn't sound any more appealing than cream of mushroom or corn chowder or black bean.

She would not use Cole as an excuse to regress to the pitiful creature who'd thought it was an achievement when she succeeded in doing one useful thing a day. No more excuses. No leaning on anyone else. She'd made a start. Cole had helped. Reaching for the can opener, Erin thought, *The rest is up to me.*

She also decided that tomorrow she would let him say his piece.

When the front door opened the next morning, Cole jumped.

Wearing her paint-spattered getup, Erin stood in the opening. "Cole?" Her voice was pleasant, the same one she might use for a stranger on her doorstep.

"Uh, can I come in?" He couldn't seem to stop himself from shifting his weight from foot to foot, even if that did give away his discomfiture. "I'd like to talk to you."

"Of course." She stepped back, closing the door when he was inside. He wouldn't have been surprised if she'd led him to the living room, where she'd take a vacuum salesman if she'd decided to listen to his pitch. Instead, he trailed her to the kitchen. "Coffee?" she asked.

He didn't really want any more, but the offering and accepting felt like a bridge. "Thanks."

She'd had it brewing and only had to pour. A moment later, they were sitting across from each other at the kitchen table, exactly as they'd been before he ruined the best thing that had happened to him in a very long time.

Erin waited, her expression inquiring and completely impersonal.

"I need to apologize," he began.

"I'm pretty sure you already did. I'd just as soon not hear it again." She betrayed not a shred of emotion.

"It took me a while to figure out—" Damn, it was hard to keep going in the face of that cool stare. Refusing to so much as twitch, he said baldly, "I got scared."

A tiny crinkle appeared on Erin's forehead. "Scared of what?"

"Of…letting myself feel too much for you."

The crinkles became a full-blown frown. "I

have never implied in any way that I expected a romance or…or sexual services." The last was as sharp as an open blade. "Why you felt compelled to warn me off—"

"No," he interrupted. "You don't understand. I think…I was pushing you away to keep myself from being too tempted. That was a crappy thing to do."

At least *some* emotion showed on her face, even if it was only bewilderment. "But I've never so much as touched you," she said.

He knew what she meant, but she *had* touched him. She had. He remembered every time she'd laid a fine-boned hand on his forearm, every brush of her body in passing. He especially remembered how it felt to hold her for most of the night.

Cole's gut knotted. Feeling sick, he knew he had to be completely honest.

He flashed back to something that had happened his first month in the pen. He'd been showering with the usual group of other men. Having ducked his head under the hot stream, he made the foolish mistake of relaxing his awareness. Not until he lifted his head and shook the water from his face did he realize the others had silently left the shower room, leaving water running to cover their retreat. In a terrifying instant, he'd understood that they had been *ordered* to leave him alone. Before he could so much as spin around, deliberate footsteps sounded on the tile floor behind him. Naked, with nothing in reach that could be turned into a weapon, he had been completely vulnerable.

He'd survived with no more than an ugly scar, but the memory still had the power to turn his stomach inside out. Then, he'd had no choice but to face his fears. Now, he could run away—or face them again.

He locked his gaze on hers, knowing how much she might see, but that was part of what he had to do. Less for himself than for her. Leaving her hurt wasn't an option.

"I wanted you the first time I saw you," he admitted. "I thought you were beautiful. Then, when you chased after me even though you knew what I am—" He cleared his throat. "You blew me away. I've…never known anyone like you. You were so determined to save me you'd have given me anything."

Erin made an inarticulate sound that probably started as denial but failed to take shape.

"I wanted to take everything you'd give." He had to suck in a deep breath before he let himself say, "I still do. But only a creep would do that." Cole groaned. "No, I have to say this. I'm not somebody you'd want to keep for good." His shoulders tried to draw up like a turtle pulling back into its shell. *Lay it out*, he told himself. "When you lose interest in me, I could be wrecked."

Something breathtaking lit her face. "What makes you think—"

"I didn't even go to college. You're a professor." When she opened her mouth, presumably to argue, he talked right over her. "We don't have anything in common. I spent ten years in a prison cell while you had a real life. Friends, lovers. I can hardly remember having either. You had to teach me to drive again. I probably know less than little kids about computers or anything electronic. No matter where I go or what I do, I'll never catch up."

"You think knowing how to use apps on a phone is a measure of how worthwhile you are?"

He shook his head. "That's not the point. The point is that I work with my hands—when I can get someone to believe I won't murder them the minute they let down their guard. That's what getting a job will come down to."

Erin was quiet for a minute, and Cole had a sinking feeling. It told him that, despite his intentions, he'd hoped to fail at getting her to see how unequal they were.

"You're a reader," she said, surprising him. "When we talk about books, you understand them as well as I do. Your perspective is different and interesting."

"That's not—"

"Now it's my turn," she said sharply.

Cole nodded, conceding the point, pretending to be relaxed.

"At the rate you're reading, you *will* catch up. I doubt most college grads read as voraciously as you do, or bother to keep educating themselves. And while you work with your hands, you do more than that. I saw you designing the ramp for the Zatlokas."

"You saw me looking it up. There are formulas—"

She poked a finger at him to shut him up. "I have no doubt you could design something a lot more complex than a wheelchair ramp, especially once you get computer literate enough to use CAD software."

Apparently, she'd really listened when he talked about computer-aided design and the class he regretted not taking.

"You're an incredibly hard worker. Generous. You've made friends up and down the block, Cole. Helped people without waiting to be asked. They *trust* you."

"They don't know I'm an ex-con."

"Do you really think they'd change their opinion if I told them now? Mr. Zatloka, whose life you may have saved? Mrs. Z, whose life you've made easier?" Erin shook her head. "You're more than you think you are, Cole." Her smile was sad. "But I also know I'm talking to a deaf man. You have to learn this for yourself."

"You mean, even a college professor can't teach me?"

His rejoinder startled her, and for a fleeting instant awakened complicated emotions she didn't want him to see.

She only shook her head and said tartly, "And what makes you equate sex with hearts and flowers, anyway? We could have shared something in bed that didn't mean commitment or hurt feelings later. We'd both have a memory. It's a lot more likely you'd dump me than the other way around. You've made it clear you're ready to move on. What makes you think I'd try to cling?"

Hadn't she understood what he was saying? *He* would be the one who held on with everything in him, even as she slipped away. Cole already knew his feelings would be hurt. He hurt enough, just thinking about moving out of the apartment, about not seeing her every day, if only for a few minutes while they ate lunch.

But he'd become stuck on what she'd said before that. *We could have shared something in bed that didn't mean commitment or hurt feelings later. We'd both have a memory.*

Cole would give almost anything for that memory. When he was alone, he could take it out and hold it, his one treasured possession.

She seemed to shake herself. "Forget what I said. You're a man. You've probably found women. I'll bet that was the first thing you thought about when you walked out of prison, wasn't it?"

"No."

Her eyes widened. That voice hadn't sounded like him.

"You didn't…" she began tentatively.

"What I thought about was not being watched all the time. Being free to make my own decisions. To go for a walk in the middle of the night if I felt like it, dive into a lake, not see anyone wearing a uniform. I was hopeful and scared." He leaned forward, his voice raw from his intensity. "Do you know what it's like to have no place to go, nobody willing to take you in? To have no goddamn idea where you're going to lay your head, or whether you'll screw up without even knowing what you did and find yourself back inside so fast your head spins?"

"I… No."

Muscles rigid, he said, "All those years, did I think about how it felt, having a soft woman beneath me? Yeah. But during the stretch before I met you, I was too pissing scared to put that on my to-do list."

They stared at each other, her eyes dilated, his… He didn't know.

At last she whispered, "What about since you've been here?"

He shook his head. All he'd been able to see was her. She must have guessed that.

"Then—" Her gaze broke away from his. She appeared to focus on the kitchen window.

Then? Cole's body tensed. Had she been about to ask why they couldn't have that memory? Suddenly, he couldn't think of a single reason making love with this woman would be a bad idea. Down the line, he'd hurt, but at least he'd know she wanted him.

"I was being stupid. When you want something too much…" He had to clear his throat.

Her vivid eyes met his again. "You mean…?"

"Yeah." Did she understand what he was saying? He should make a move…but pride wouldn't let him.

She kept staring at him. He was getting dizzy and realized he'd been holding his breath by the time she finally spoke. "I don't know. The other day…you made me feel really awful."

"I know. I'm sorry," he said huskily. "I… Please."

After one more, breathless moment, Erin got

to her feet, circled the table and laid a hand on his cheek. He saw fear and doubt on her face, but also something that had his heart pounding.

He pulled her onto his lap and captured her mouth with his.

CHAPTER FOURTEEN

ERIN COULDN'T BELIEVE she was doing this. She'd intended to accept his apology with dignity and politely ask for the house key back. Instead, here she was sitting sideways on his hard thighs, her body feeling boneless as she melted against him. Vulnerable, in a way she'd never been during any past relationship.

His kiss was gentle instead of all-in passionate. His lips brushed hers; he nibbled. He rubbed his nose against hers and nuzzled the crook of her neck.

"What are you doing?" she whispered.

"Breathing," he murmured. He lifted his head, disbelief the primary emotion in his blue eyes. Or maybe that wasn't right. Maybe it was wonder. "I can't believe..." His throat worked.

Wonder. No man had ever looked at her as if she was his dream. The way she started to choke up freaked her out and she had to push back. Wait. This was a man who hadn't so much as *kissed* a woman in ten very long years. Of course she was his dream! She could be any woman—

Except she didn't believe that. With his looks and muscles, his pride and instinctive kindness, he could've had sexual partners since he came to West Fork if he chose.

When you want something too much... Me.

He tugged out the elastic that had confined her hair and sifted his fingers through the strands, appearing fascinated.

What if this was a con?

But if that was what he'd intended, he wouldn't have screwed up so badly the first time he kissed her. He could have had her then—she'd pretty much offered herself. Which meant she had to believe him.

Just...savor every minute.

She kissed and nibbled the hard edge of his clean-shaved jaw until she reached his ear. She liked his ears, had studied them entirely too often. Now she nipped his earlobe, then sucked gently.

He jerked, his hands tightening on her waist and thigh. His teeth closed on the side of her neck. When she went still, he applied enough suction for her to imagine his mouth on her breast.

With a tiny whimper, she reached for his T-shirt. Cole cooperated, his gaze never leaving her face as she tugged the soft fabric up. When she didn't move fast enough, he took over and yanked it off, tossing it aside. Her breath caught at the sight of his chest. Powerful muscles slid smoothly beneath the skin. Soft brown hair formed a mat punctuated by a thin line that disappeared beneath the waistband of his cargo pants.

She had to explore. Erin would have thought him unaffected if she didn't feel the shiver and flex of those muscles beneath her fingertips. His stomach was as hard as she'd imagined, and it would have been impossible *not* to notice the hard bar of his erection pressing against her hip.

She must have shivered, too, because he suddenly said, "My turn," and wrenched open her ragged chambray shirt. A few buttons might have gone flying, but Erin didn't care, not with this man looking at her as if he'd never seen anything so beautiful. He slid a fingertip just inside the top of her bra, leaving goose bumps behind. She could see that her nipples had hardened, poking at the thin cotton fabric of her practical athletic bra. Cole didn't seem to notice it wasn't exactly sexy.

"I have to see you," he said suddenly, his voice guttural. When he yanked the bra upward, she raised her arms to help. Moving so fast she was stunned, he had her bent backward over his arm and was studying her with an intent, hungry look, color slashing across his cheekbones. She gripped the back of his neck, her fingers digging in, as his mouth closed over her nipple.

When her hips began to rock, he lifted his head and looked at her, his eyes almost black. "You're sure?"

Nothing could have made her say no. Not now. She ached for him. Her lips formed the word *yes*. Even soundless, it was enough.

He surged to his feet, lifting her in his arms.

"Wait! I can walk."

She saw his teeth and wasn't sure if it was a grin or something else. "You don't weigh anything."

That wasn't true, but despite eating better these days—since Cole had come into her life— she hadn't come close to regaining the weight she'd lost after the accident. No man had ever carried her to bed before and, feminist or no, she found the experience exhilarating.

She wrapped both arms around his neck.

He laughed this time. "Afraid I'll drop you?"

"The thought crossed my mind."

Another laugh, and he started up the stairs. One arm looped under her thighs, the other supporting her back.

"I should have wrapped my legs around your waist."

His gaze flicked to her face. "If you had, I wouldn't have made it."

Mouth suddenly dry, Erin felt a cramp deep in her abdomen. He could have set her down on one of the steps and stripped off her jeans. She wouldn't have minded. She wouldn't mind if he did it now.

She rubbed her cheek against the bulge of his bicep. A rumbling sound came from his chest, but he kept moving.

In her room, he let her fall onto the bed and sank down on top of her, catching some of his weight on his elbows and a knee planted between hers. His kiss was desperate this time, his tongue thrusting into her mouth, even as his hand roved. The sensation of her breasts rubbing against his chest set Erin to moving restlessly as she kissed him back with equal urgency.

He rolled them so that she lay atop him and he could grab her butt, adjusting her hips until the fit was just right. He'd have been inside her if they hadn't both been wearing pants, and suddenly Erin was desperate to get rid of everything separating them. Except…she couldn't stop moving rhythmically against that hard ridge, which felt even better with his hips bucking to meet hers.

She might not have been able to stop—she

was already so close to climaxing—but he flipped them again, his voice harsh when he said, "Enough."

"What?" Dazed, she stared up at him.

"I can't play. I'll lose it. I want to be inside you when I come."

"Please."

Cole growled something and lifted himself off her. On his knees beside her, he unzipped her jeans and peeled them off, taking her panties with them. She should have felt exposed beneath his burning gaze, but instead reveled in the way he looked at her naked body.

Her canvas tennis shoes must have gotten lost. One sock came off with her jeans; the other, he pulled off more slowly. As if he hadn't been desperate a moment ago, he squeezed her feet, seemingly as captivated by them as he'd been by her breasts. Since her feet were a bony size nine, she couldn't imagine why, but she discovered that the feel of his thumb kneading the sensitive ball of her foot sent electric shots of pleasure straight up her legs.

When he wrapped his fingers around her ankle and began caressing his way upward, she protested. "I thought you couldn't play."

He lifted his head. "I don't want to miss anything."

Oh, no. He was going to torture her.

I'll get my chance.

She waited until he was within reach, when she laid her hands back on his chest, teasing his nipples, sliding lower.

Cole groaned.

Just a little farther... Yes!

She squeezed his erection through the canvas fabric of his work pants.

He levitated and swore. Abruptly losing interest in taking his time, he jumped off the bed and stripped. Erin quit breathing as she watched. For an instant, her gaze caught on a scar low on his back, on the right side, then strayed lower. His butt was as muscular as the rest of his body, and the dragon writhed as the muscles in his back flexed. Of course it was breathing fire. Erin felt as if she was, too.

Then he yanked a wallet that must be new out of his pocket and extracted a thin package. Her breath rushed out, causing him to turn and look at her.

"I never thought— I'm not on anything. There's been no reason—"

"I...picked these up a little while ago."

These? Yes, he was tossing another one on her bedside table.

Wait. Had he been thinking about *her* when he bought condoms? Or— *Forget it*, she told herself. She'd been the one to suggest they could make love without any implied commitment. Which meant no jealousy, either.

Or, at least, hiding her jealousy.

And then she focused on his erect penis and forgot everything else. Cole backed away when she reached for the condom. "Not this time. I'm on the edge. I can't let you touch me."

So she only watched while he rolled it on with hands that shook. Seeing that vulnerability squeezed her heart, but she didn't have a chance to dwell on the intensity of what she felt. He had her on her back too fast, him on top of her, separating her thighs.

And then he was there, pushing inside her, filling her. Erin arched off the bed, a cry escaping. Her mind slammed shut. When he paused, she shook her head frantically and tried to pull him deeper.

There was nothing smooth about their joining. If they ever found a rhythm, she didn't notice. As if his control had snapped, he thrust hard, one hand urging her thighs wider. The skin over his cheekbones seemed to be pulled tight, his eyes blazing. She'd never felt anything like this madness. When release hit, it was searing, pleasure that sent liquid fire all the way to the tips of her fingers and her toes. She cried out, "Cole!"

His body stiffened when he followed, his head

thrown back and his teeth bared. For a long moment, he hung above her, a raw sound escaping between clenched teeth. Then he sagged down beside her, most of his weight on one shoulder.

All Erin could think was, *I shouldn't have done this. If I'd known...*

But how could she have, when she'd never felt anything like this before?

IN THE STUNNED AFTERMATH, Cole couldn't seem to move. He knew he should; he must be crushing her. His heart battered his rib cage, and he had to gasp for breath.

At last he found the strength to turn onto his back and stare up at the ceiling. That wasn't sex like any sex *he'd* ever had.

Only because it's been so long.

Uh-huh. Sure.

He should say something, but what? *That was fun, babe? It'll make a really fine memory? So fine I may never be able to enjoy sex with anyone else again?* He didn't remember what he'd said to previous sex partners. Had he said anything at all?

He was making too much of this. He liked Erin. He could love her, if he dared to let himself. Of course, that made sex better. And it'd been his first time in so damn many years he should have expected to go off like a rocket.

Easy explanation. The next time wouldn't be so explosive.

He finally turned his head so he could see her. She was staring up at the ceiling, looking as shell-shocked as he felt.

"You okay?" he asked.

Erin blinked a couple of times. "I…think so."

"That was…really good." To his own ears, he sounded drunk.

He wasn't the only one. Her "Yes" was a mumble.

Cole groped around until he found her hand. He felt better when she returned his clasp.

Good. He wouldn't blame her if she was insulted. Why hadn't he said *staggering*? *Mind-blowing*? *Astounding*?

But she squeezed his hand. "Yes, it was. This was one way to start the day."

He actually laughed. At least, his chest vibrated. If only he could start every day like this.

No, this was temporary. Thinking otherwise wasn't smart. "Damn." Was that a tingle in his feet? He hadn't been sure he could feel them, far less wriggle them. Or stand on them. "Del's going to be wondering where I am."

"Well, this is one place he won't look for you," she said practically.

Cole mulled that over. "I don't know. You don't think the neighbors are suspicious?"

Erin went so still he turned his head again. "I hope not!" she exclaimed a moment later.

Feeling a stab to his gut, he started to sit up. Erin gave a hard tug that had him half rolling to face her instead.

"Quit being so sensitive. I didn't mean that the way you took it. Only that…they're my grandmother's generation. She'd be shaking her head at me right now."

"You so sure about that?" From what Erin had said about her grandmother, he had the impression of a pretty feisty lady. "You don't think she enjoyed sex in her day?"

"Yes, but I doubt she ever had sex with anyone but Grandpa."

"Really? Nobody in—what?—the forties ever had premarital sex?"

"Well, maybe she did with him."

Laughing at her dubious tone, he did sit up. His body had rebooted, thank God. "I'd better go head off Del."

Erin sighed. "I swore I'd paint the last bedroom today. I am so tired of painting."

Cole pointed upward. "Should have done the ceilings first."

"That's a mean thing to say."

The light conversation made it possible for them both to get dressed, for him to give her a quick, hard kiss, say, "See you at lunch?" and leave.

Walking down the driveway, his mood turned bleak. *Mind-blowing?* What he really feared was that making love with Erin could be slotted into the *life-altering* category. Which meant repeating it was dangerous, and even this one memory should be forgotten, not carried everywhere he went.

But he also knew damn well that he'd spend every minute he could in her bed.

SITTING ON THE porch eating lunch with Cole was so much like every other day that Erin felt as if she was having an out-of-body experience. Were those two people she was looking down at faking it? Or had they simply relieved some tension and figured it was all good? What was he thinking? *What am I thinking?*

Thinking wasn't exactly what she was doing. *Feeling* was more like it, and she was better off not acknowledging emotions until he was gone. Whenever that would be.

"I talked to Lottie," he said, as if reading her mind. "I'll put the second coat of paint on Del's porch railings and uprights this afternoon, then start her ramp tomorrow. The lumber should be delivered today."

Erin's relief was huge. He wasn't going right

away. He'd be here for another couple of weeks at least.

The longer he stayed, the more she'd miss him when he did leave.

"She's a character," Erin remarked, reaching for a celery stick. "Don't be surprised if she flirts with you."

His grin looked more genuine than his earlier smiles. "I think she already has. Hard to take seriously."

Lottie had to be ninety. The makeup she applied to her deeply wrinkled face gave her a cartoonish look. A tiny woman, she had a hump worse than Nanna's had been and shuffled along with her walker, stooped over.

"Maybe I should bake her a loaf of banana bread, using Nanna's recipe."

Cole laughed. "She might make *me* tell you it's dry as sawdust."

"Oh, no, I'm sure she'd wait to offer me her recipe, because 'Dear, even your grandmother conceded my banana bread is better.'"

Head thrown back, his laugh deepened. "Consider me forewarned."

Erin chuckled. "She *is* a good cook, so count your blessings if she decides to feed you."

He was quiet for a minute. "I like it when *you* feed me."

It took her a moment to get past the painful contraction of her rib cage. "If you want to come to dinner tonight, I thought I'd make lasagna," she said, careful not to sound too eager, too hopeful.

His frown formed. "You don't have to offer, just because I said that."

Time for a fake smile. "I have to eat, and I've had a craving for lasagna. If you have plans…"

"You know I don't." He crumpled the paper towel that had served as plate and napkin and stood. He bent to kiss her, much as he had that morning, only this time she felt some anger in his touch. But all he said was, "Got to get back to work. See you at six?"

"Six is good."

She watched him detour, as always, to his apartment, but before he could reappear, she retreated into the house.

What had she said to make him angry? Maybe she'd imagined it, but she didn't think so. Well, *she* was angry, too, at his refusal to give them a chance.

And yet, she understood how he felt. He was very much a man, but one who'd lost ten years of his life. Here she was, wishing she could lasso him and keep him penned in this very small and unexciting town that was her refuge. He had every reason to suspect she clung to him for unhealthy reasons, too.

He might even be right.

Any enthusiasm she'd had for starting to paint the ceilings had disappeared. Well, there wasn't any hurry. She could play on the computer a little, look at those job listings again, curl up in the one comfortable chair in the living room and read. Lots of options.

Oh—and check to be sure she actually had the ingredients for lasagna, in case she needed to make a quick run to the store.

WHILE ERIN GOT up to start the coffee after dinner, Cole glanced around the kitchen, thinking how homey the old house felt to him. Concentrating on it was an alternative to focusing on her, the way she moved, her curves. Mentally stripping off her clothes, now that he knew her lithe, slim body.

"What are you thinking?"

Surprised, he saw that she was pulling out her chair. Not so long ago, he'd have known the instant she, or anyone else, approached.

"I like this house," he said, needing a subject that stayed away from the future or what he felt for her. "I guess it feels a little like where I grew up." He didn't say *home*, because it wasn't anymore; home was a place where you were always welcome.

"Is it an older house?" Erin resumed her seat.

As she did, the braid that contained her red-gold hair flopped over her shoulder, momentarily capturing his attention. He loved her hair. And while he'd never thought of collarbones as sexy before, hers were. Delicate.

What had she asked? "Ah, yeah. It's a brick house, not that far from Green Lake."

She nodded. Most people who'd spent any time in the area knew where the lake was in Seattle. If nothing else, they would've visited the nearby Woodland Park Zoo.

"My mother liked old houses. She made Dad refinish the molding downstairs." He smiled at the memory. "Dad wanted to paint instead, but she wasn't having it."

"Good for her. Although…" Erin wrinkled her nose. "Just the idea of stripping all the molding here makes my shoulders ache. I might have to—" She stopped and shook her head.

Hire someone? Was that what she'd been about to say?

His determination to leave had faltered enough for him to think he might kind of enjoy doing the job for her. Stripping and refinishing the floors, too. That would mean her moving out—but she could stay with him in the apartment for that week or two.

Instead of suggesting or promising something he'd probably regret, he told her more about his childhood home, which he seemed to remember had dated to the 1920s. "Brick isn't ideal in earthquake country, but in the older parts of Seattle, the houses are almost all brick, and they've survived a bunch of earthquakes."

Erin nodded. "When I was a kid, I really wanted a brick house. The one I dreamed of had a steeply pitched roof, a front door with an arched top and one of those wings to the side—" she gestured "—with a doorway that leads to the back garden."

"And has an arched top, too."

She laughed at his teasing. "Of course. Those houses had a fairy-tale feel. And it seemed that all the houses I liked had beautiful gardens, too."

No wonder she was working so hard to recreate that ideal, he reflected, doing as well as she could with the material at hand.

"Do you know when this house was built?"

"Later than your parents'. I think the 1930s. If it'd been much later than that, it wouldn't have the details it does."

"Yeah, if I were going to build, I'd meld the good things from houses of this era with modern improvements."

"Like?"

He'd checked out some *Architectural Digest* magazines from the library, and a couple of times when he'd borrowed her Cherokee he'd driven through newer construction on acreage above the river. Mostly, he'd been preparing for his job hunt, wanting to sound well-informed.

"Not wasting so much space in the kitchen," he said immediately.

"You have a point." Even with the table and chairs in here, there was a lot of open floor space.

An island would help, he thought—then shut down that kind of speculation. He wouldn't be remodeling this house.

"Oh!" She leaped up. "I forgot the coffee."

They kept talking, but Cole knew he wasn't the only one aware of growing tension. Had her invitation to dinner implied more? Say, that he could spend the night? Or had this morning been a one-off as far as she was concerned?

If he asked, would he sound like he was begging?

She talked about a book she was reading, a history of the First World War. "I've been lugging it around forever and not getting to it, but today I felt lazy and decided to read for a while."

He could make conversation, too. "That's outside your usual interests," he commented, hoping he sounded semi-intelligent.

"Yes, but somehow my schooling completely skipped the early twentieth century. Well…"

She shrugged. "Actually, the entire twentieth century. But my grandfather fought in World War II, and he told some really horrific stories. I was curious enough to do some reading back then. And Dad was drafted and fought in the Vietnam War." She raised her eyebrows. "What about your father?"

"A little too young."

"Lucky man. Anyway, my high school class in US history never made it to the turn of the century. Too much interesting stuff before that, I guess. So I'm filling in the blanks."

Cole smiled, although he wasn't thinking about either World War. He was thinking he'd almost finished his cup of coffee, and he ought to either offer to help clean the kitchen or make his excuses.

No contest. *Clean the kitchen*, he decided. At least that gave him an excuse to linger.

Taking the last swallow, he pushed back his chair. "You cooked. Why don't you let me clean up?"

Erin jumped to her feet, her protest predictable. "Oh, but you worked today."

Not as many hours as usual, because of the morning interlude. "I'm not tired." *Really* not tired.

"I... Okay." She looked shy. "I'll put the food away if you want to load the dishwasher."

The task didn't take nearly long enough. Meanwhile, Erin covered the casserole dish holding the remaining lasagna with shrink-wrap and stuck it in the refrigerator. She did say, "If you don't mind leftovers, there's enough for tomorrow night, too."

"I could eat that every night for a week and not get tired of it." Cole dried his hands on a paper towel and tossed it in the trash beneath the sink. *Ask? Don't ask?* He hated this hesitancy, this…need that laid him bare. But he couldn't go without knowing.

"Erin."

At the exact same moment, she said, "If you'd like—" After she broke off, they looked at each other. Still seeming shy, she was wringing her hands.

"If I'd like what?" he asked quietly.

"To stay." Color had blossomed in her cheeks, too, not subtle against her redhead's skin. "I don't know how we left it…"

Under a flood of relief, he had to lock his knees to keep from staggering. "There's nothing I want more than to stay."

"Really?"

"Yeah." His voice came out gritty. "Come here." But she didn't have to make a move, because he'd taken the few steps to reach her where she hovered by the refrigerator. He wrapped a hand around her nape beneath the braid. "I thought about you all day."

Her eyes were such an unusual color, made even more vivid by the yearning that echoed his. "I…thought about you, too."

"Good," he said huskily. "Funny thing, but I'm ready for bed."

"Me, too." She'd flattened her hands on his chest, and now her fingers flexed, the bite of her nails sending a shudder of pleasure through him. "Shall we?"

"Oh, yeah." Except he wasn't about to wait until they got upstairs to kiss her.

She obviously felt the same, because her mouth eagerly met his.

CHAPTER FIFTEEN

"THIS WILL BE WONDERFUL." Beaming, Lottie Price stood at the top of the new ramp that, like the one he'd built for the Zatlokas, extended from her back door. "Leaving the house has been such a struggle. The ramp will take me right to the garage!"

On his knees with an electric screwdriver in his hand, Cole had an alarming thought. "You don't still drive, do you?"

"Oh, my, yes! I set my mind to staying in my own house until the day I die, and how could I manage if I couldn't get to the grocery store?"

She brought to mind illustrations he distantly recalled, probably from a children's picture book. A witch with a face like a withered apple, that was Lottie, except she seemed invariably good-humored.

He shuddered at the thought of her behind the wheel of a car, even if he did understand her need for independence. Damn. He'd have to take a peek in the garage to see what she drove. Tiny and crumpled as she was, how could she see out the windshield? Pile pillows on the seat? Then how would she reach the pedals?

"You can get groceries delivered these days," he said mildly. "And I'm sure you have neighbors who'd be glad to shop for you, or take you along when they go to the store."

Her mouth crimped. "But then I'd be indebted."

Cole grinned at her. "Not if you repaid them in baked goods."

She giggled, an astonishing sound coming from a woman so ancient.

He was close to finishing her ramp. The Zatlokas' ramp had taken him over three weeks, Lottie's two and a half. He had the design part down pat, and after all the practice he'd had, he was able to work faster.

He almost wished it hadn't. In the past weeks, he'd been too happy to apply for jobs the way he'd intended, despite the fact that it was June now, but he'd also failed to ask around the neighborhood to find out if anyone else would be interested in hiring him. Apparently, Erin had kept her word and quit soliciting work for him, which left him... He didn't know.

At the sound of a car engine, he swiveled on his heels, his caution automatic. The neighbor's house blocked his sight line until the vehicle was almost in front of Lottie's...and slowing to turn into her driveway.

A patrol car, black-and-white, rack of lights on top. City, not county.

Ice formed in his veins.

He heard the old lady say, "Oh, my! Why would a policeman come *here*?"

Cole set down the drill and rose to his feet. "I'll go ask," he told her, and walked toward the police car. A uniformed officer was just getting out. Over the roof, he looked hard at Cole. As he circled around the front, his hand rested on the butt of his holstered gun in a clear message.

"Would you be Mr. Meacham?" he asked.

"I am." Cole kept his voice low, praying Lottie couldn't hear what was being said.

Likely in his fifties and around Cole's height, the cop carried enough extra pounds to leave his gut hanging over his thick black belt. Gray hair was buzz cut, his face fleshy and his nose red with broken veins. Cole made an automatic assessment. Alcoholic?

"How'd you find me?" Why he'd come looking was a more important question, but Cole hated the idea of this guy talking to Erin.

"Your landlady told me you were working down here." He glanced past Cole. "That the homeowner?"

"Mrs. Price. She's a nice lady who doesn't get around very well anymore."

"Ramp looks good." That sounded grudging. Cole bent his head in acknowledgment.

The hard stare met his again. "We had an armed robbery last night, at the ampm convenience store. Your name came up."

Of course it had. Rage mixed with hopelessness. His voice didn't sound quite right when he said, "I've been employed nonstop since I got to West Fork. I'm making good money. I wouldn't do something like that."

The cop sneered. "You wouldn't have done the time if you hadn't done the crime."

"I did not do the crime," he said steadily, despite knowing how his claim would be received. "I refused to accept a plea that would have shortened my sentence by years, because I wouldn't admit to doing it and express remorse. I didn't do it, and I won't say I did."

"Sure. Now, why don't you just tell me where you were yesterday evening, 'round 11:00 p.m.?"

Cole's thoughts spun. He wanted to keep Erin out of it, but he wasn't willing to get arrested for another crime he hadn't committed. "Did you ask Ms. Parrish that question?"

The cop's expression changed. "You have something going with her?"

Nauseated, he said, "I had dinner at her place. We talked." In bed.

"That what you call it?"

Cole gritted his teeth. "If it was a convenience store, you must have footage from a surveillance camera."

"Guy wore a ski mask."

"And just happened to be built like me."

For the first time, uncertainty showed on the cop's face. He opened his mouth, but didn't say anything.

"How'd he get away?"

"Jumped in his car and peeled rubber."

"I don't have a vehicle of any kind."

"You got yourself a driver's license."

"I did, because Ms. Parrish went along so I could use her Jeep Cherokee for the test." Forestalling the next question, he said, "I do not have a key to her Jeep."

The cop's eyes narrowed, but before he could respond, Lottie spoke from behind Cole. Her voice sharp, she demanded to know what this was about.

The asshole nodded at Cole. "You realize you have an ex-con working for you, ma'am?"

Cole held himself rigid. This was what he'd feared. He should have told people.

Who, then, wouldn't have hired him? He wouldn't have the money in the bank he did now.

"This fine young man?" Lottie snorted. "All

of us in this neighborhood think the world of him. He saved Mr. Zatloka's life, you know."

The guy blinked at her claim, a more-than-slight exaggeration Cole wasn't about to dispute right now.

"Why, he's worked for four of us on this block and done a splendid job. I'd have been housebound in no time if it weren't for him!" She glared at the officer.

"Don't let yourself be fooled by the fact that he knows construction," the cop said. Cole focused on the name tag he wore. Officer Larry Watson.

"Nobody has ever called me a fool, Officer." Lottie's voice had chilled. "Mr. Meacham is quick to lend a helping hand unasked. We don't see many police officers in this neighborhood bothering to find out whether seniors need assistance."

Officer Watson's fleshy cheeks were almost as red as his nose now. "Our job is not—"

"If you don't mind, I'm paying Mr. Meacham for the time you've kept him standing here," she added, somehow looking down her nose even if the cop did tower over her.

Despite the angry flush, he backed up a step. He leveled a scowl at Cole. "You keep your nose clean, son. We're watching you."

Neither Cole nor Lottie moved until Officer

Watson had backed out of the driveway and started down the street.

Cole realized he was clenching his fists. He loosened his fingers with an effort and closed his eyes. "I had no business not telling you." He couldn't look at her. "I knew no one would hire me, but that's not a good excuse."

"You're wrong," she said, the old-age creaks apparent now that she was trying to soften her voice.

Surprise made him turn.

"I've seen the quality of your work. Heard how pleased Del and Roy are. And Erin, of course." Lottie paused. "Does she know your history?"

He choked out a "Yeah."

"I can't imagine she would've recommended you to the rest of us if she'd had any hesitation at all." Now she sounded starchy. "I do not for one minute believe you'd hold up some teenage clerk at a convenience store for a few dollars. Ridiculous!"

"Thank you." Stunned as he was, that was hard to get out, too. Lottie wasn't ordering him off her property. Or looking at him with new doubt.

But what about Erin? She'd let him take her Cherokee out on his own enough times, he could've had the key copied. Had she felt doubt when the cop told her why he wanted to talk to Cole?

His hands had formed fists again, but he willed himself to relax and say, "I should get back to work."

"If you're too shaken…" Lottie's voice trailed off.

"You're a good, kind woman, Mrs. Price." He summoned a smile. "And I'm perfectly capable of finishing what I started."

"Oh, you." She lightly whacked his arm and simpered, a frightening expression. "Why would you be formal now?"

Formal? *Oh.* "Lottie," he corrected himself.

He strode to the backyard as she shuffled after him. Cole took a second to remember where he'd left off, then crouched and reached for the screwdriver with a hand that shook. He had to give himself a minute to feel steady again.

Not once in the remaining hour of his workday did he forget the suspicion—no, *certainty*—he'd seen in the cop's eyes, the outright accusation only because he lived in town and had the conviction on his record. He knew this would happen over and over. This last month…he'd deluded himself.

COLE HAD ESSENTIALLY been living with Erin. He didn't need to ring the doorbell anymore. He walked in. So when she heard the chimes at five thirty, Erin assumed a neighbor was stopping by. When she opened the door, Cole stood waiting, hands shoved in the pockets of his cargo pants, his expression closed tighter than a bank vault.

Surprised, she peered past him. "Was the door locked?"

"Just…thought you might want some warning."

"Warning?" she echoed, before it hit her. This had to do with the cop who'd come by looking for him. Standing back, she said, "Come in. I'm working on dinner."

Behind her, he said, "Me staying might not be a good idea."

Erin stopped and turned. "What are you talking about?"

"You know what happened today."

"The police officer?"

His mouth curled unpleasantly. "Forgot about him, did you?"

"I just thought…that maybe Ramirez asked him to check up on you or something. He seemed pleasant."

He stared, his blue eyes as sharp and yet unreadable as they'd been at the beginning. "There was an armed robbery at the ampm. Who else could have done it but the ex-con lurking in town?"

"Oh, dear God." She fumbled backward for a chair, pulled it out and sank into it. "He really suggested…"

"Oh, yeah." Cole hadn't moved past the kitchen doorway. "He made sure to tell Lottie she'd been foolish enough to hire an ex-con."

Momentarily dizzy, Erin thought she must have turned ghost-white. *My fault.* She'd set him up to have some faith that his past didn't define him. Maybe because he'd been convincing her that she could put her own tragedy behind her. What if they were both wrong?

"What did Lottie say?" was all she could think to ask.

His expression softened. *Soft* wasn't really a word that applied to this man's features, though.

"She told him she was no fool, said I'd saved Mr. Zatloka's life and helped all the seniors in the neighborhood. Good God, I haven't even met most of them!" He shook his head. "Then she got snide and asked why cops didn't take the time to check up on the old folks."

Erin smiled. "That's Lottie."

"Yeah." He leaned a shoulder against the doorframe. "But you know damn well that she started making calls the second she got inside. Everyone will have heard by now."

"Do you really believe they'll change their opinion about you?"

He gave her a scathing look. "Of course they will. The Zatlokas...hard to say. I got to know them. But Del? He's pretty conservative. I don't think he'd answer the door if I stopped by."

Erin didn't know Del Wagner well enough to argue with Cole's opinion.

Hugging herself, she said, "The cop went away. Will he be back?"

Cole sighed and lifted a hand to knead the back of his neck. "Probably not. They have footage from a security camera. The guy wore a ski mask, but I had the impression he isn't as big as I am. I don't have a car, either. Sounds like it was a sedan, not an SUV like yours, or they'd be trying to convince you I took it out last night."

"You couldn't have. And I'd be happy to tell them that." After dinner yesterday evening, he had read while she watched a TV program that didn't interest him. Then...they went up to bed and stayed tangled together all night long. He hadn't once gone back to the apartment; he rarely did anymore. His clothes had gradually migrated to her bedroom, and their loads in the washing machine were mixed.

"No, but sooner or later something like this

will happen when I can't prove where I was. I'm on their radar, and they're waiting for me to screw up." Bitter, he said, "The cops will never believe I'm not the scum they think I am."

"They can't all be that narrow-minded."

He didn't say anything, didn't have to. It didn't matter if not all cops were quick to assume the worst about him. There were enough who would.

"Will you tell me what you were convicted of?"

Cole only looked at her for a minute. Then he asked, "Are you sure you want to know?"

He must have seen that panic had already struck. Finally, she shook her head. Knowing what crime he'd committed might change how she saw him. However cowardly it was to live in a delusion, she'd been happy. Was it so awful to cling to that happiness, just a little longer?

The oven timer dinged and she jumped. She hadn't put on any vegetables yet—but did he even intend to stay? Nonetheless, she got up and took the casserole dish from the oven, bringing it straight to the table where she'd set out a hot pad.

"I haven't made a vegetable or salad or anything, but if you don't mind…"

He gave what seemed to be a resigned nod and came to the table.

They ate in silence for a few minutes, Erin making an effort, although her appetite had deserted her. Cole managed to eat more than she did, but he chewed and swallowed mechanically, his usual pleasure in her cooking gone. He was refueling, that was all.

Plate still half full, Erin laid down her fork. "What are you thinking?" She couldn't make herself come out and say, *You're going to leave, aren't you?*

More slowly, he did the same, aligning his knife and fork on the plate. "This—you and me—isn't going to work. I've been kidding myself." Resignation rang in his voice, but also some anger. Pain, too? She couldn't tell.

"I don't understand," she whispered, even though that wasn't really true. "Why would you be better off on your own? Unless…you plan to go home? Or to your sister's?"

"Neither. And it's not that I'll be better off. *You* will be." When she started to object, he cut her off. "I won't put you in the position of having to provide alibis for me. They'll figure you're lying for me, that you're so desperate you'd take scum like me into your bed."

On a spurt of anger, she asked, "Is that what you think? I'm desperate?"

The slowness of his response told her everything she needed to know. "Of course not."

She stood abruptly, grabbing her plate, and went to the sink. After scraping the casserole she hadn't eaten into the garbage, she rinsed the plate and put it in the dishwasher. Then she faced him, glad of the physical distance she'd opened.

"When?"

"Am I leaving?"

"Yes."

"Not right away. I have a couple more days' work at Lottie's. I'll need to find a place to stay. Apply for jobs." His face particularly expressionless, he said, "Unless you want me to go now."

"Definitely not." She sounded almost brisk. "That would be silly."

"It's time for me to buy a car."

"If you need me to drive you to look at any, let me know."

Cole kept watching her. "Erin, I need to make it on my own. Regain some dignity, if that's possible. If I could—" Wondering if that was torment she saw in his eyes, she waited, but he didn't finish.

If he could, he'd never leave her? Oh, sure.

In another mood, she might have laughed. Face it, she was too damaged for anyone to want to take on, especially a guy with problems of his own. What he'd said was even truer for her. She didn't know who she was anymore.

The sex? He was right; she had been desperate. He was a guy, probably thought, *Why not?*

"Use my computer to look at Craigslist," she suggested. "You can probably get a better deal on a car direct from an owner than in a lot."

"I could go to the library."

"No, that's fine. I have things to do. Let me get the laptop for you."

When she brought it to him a minute later, he hadn't moved. He hadn't eaten another bite, either. Without comment, she set the laptop on the table, to one side.

"Erin?" This voice had been run through a rock tumbler. "It may only be a few days, but… Can I stay with you?"

HE WAS BEGGING. That was what she'd brought him to. But he couldn't help himself. The idea of never kissing her again, never hearing her passionate cries, never losing himself in her body…

She stared at him, not moving, not reacting.

I should have kept my mouth shut.

What, he shouldn't have told her he was moving out until he was packed and ready to throw his duffel in his car? he asked himself incredulously. No. Just…no. This was bad enough. He couldn't leave her thinking everything was fine until the last possible minute.

"You mean, you want to continue sleeping with me."

He winced, unable to tell if her tone was caustic, or just disbelieving. Maybe he was an asshole, wanting to keep having sex until he took off, even though he had pretty much ditched her.

"I want every minute with you I can have," he said, voice thick. "I wish—" He strangled the rest of that sentence, aching because he had to leave her. And yet, that wasn't something he had any right to say.

Erin turned her face away; when she looked back at him, tears shimmered in her eyes.

"I want every minute I can have with you, too," she said, so quietly he barely heard her.

A fireball exploded in his chest. He was on his feet and across the kitchen, pulling her into his arms before he even knew he intended to move. As desperate as he was, he lost the ability to be gentle, to do anything but *take*. He had her up against the refrigerator in seconds, her thigh lifted so he could grind himself against her. If she fought him… But she didn't. In fact, she hooked an arm around his neck so she could hoist herself up, and her other hand slid under his T-shirt so her fingers could dig into his back.

He wanted her shirt off, but he would have to step back to get it over her head and he wasn't willing to do that. Instead, he released her bra clasp, for what good that did when he couldn't have squeezed a hand between them.

He wanted her *now*. Here. But damn, she wore jeans and athletic shoes. He'd have to kneel to strip her.

Condom. *Shit.* He no longer carried any in his wallet. He'd stowed the box of condoms in her bedside drawer. They had to get upstairs.

Cole hadn't carried her since the first time, but he did now. Without protest, Erin wrapped her legs around his waist and kept kissing his jaw, his neck. She nibbled his earlobe, whispered, "Hurry."

In her bedroom, he yanked her shoes off, then her jeans and panties. Pushed her shirt up enough to suckle her breasts even as he fumbled to unzip and free himself. He paused only to scrabble for a condom and put it on before he drove into her hard enough to shove her across the bed.

Too hard.

But she said, *"Yes,"* and clawed at him.

With no tenderness at all, only fierce hunger, he rode her until her body arched and her spasms gripped him. Then he let himself go.

Somehow, he managed to roll over when all the strength left his body. Couldn't crush her.

Please don't let me have hurt her.

CHAPTER SIXTEEN

IN THE NEXT few days, Erin did take Cole to look at several cars he'd found for sale online. Helping him take this step to leave her felt bittersweet, yet she treasured every minute they had together.

After going for a short drive in a 2004 Toyota pickup and taking a long look under the hood, he stood for some time bargaining with the owner. The truck had 130,000 miles on it; the yellow paint bore some scratches and dings and the bed was heavily dented.

He strolled over to where she waited to tell her he was going to buy it.

"That's a lot of miles."

"Runs well, though, and there's no reason it can't go 200,000 miles."

A couple of minutes later, the owner signed and dated the release of ownership part of the title and handed it to him. In turn, he counted out the cash, took the key, and said to Erin, "I'll see you at home."

Twenty minutes later, he parked his acquisition in front of the house beside her Cherokee and got out, smiling.

"I can work on an engine this age if I have to. There's not as much that requires computer diagnostics."

She made a face at him. "If you say so."

As they walked toward the house, he added, "Tomorrow morning, I'll register the sale and get the license." Despite his smile, he didn't sound as satisfied as she'd expected.

Because he knew, as she did, that having his own transportation took him a long way to being ready to start his new life? The one that didn't include her.

She'd come to empathize with the salmon snatched from the river by bald eagles. That was what this dread felt like—the biting grip of talons.

"There's an office right in town," she said, proud of how casual she sounded.

"I've seen it."

He could go tomorrow, because yesterday he'd finished the job for Lottie Price. Erin knew he had asked her for a recommendation, which he'd added to a file folder that already held three other glowing recommendations, including the one she'd written for him. She also knew he'd applied online for several jobs, and had called area contractors to find out if they had openings.

He never said when he got a turndown, but she could tell from his stone face. Each time, she was as mad as she'd been that day at the hardware store, when she saw his stoic acceptance. That she also felt secret relief because he wouldn't be leaving yet wasn't something she let him see.

That night, for the first time since he'd started sleeping with her, Erin had a nightmare. Staring eyes. Hands grasping for her. She knew she'd screamed because her throat felt sore when she awakened, sitting bolt upright in bed. Arms came around her, and she fought until the nightmare images faded.

Swearing as he tugged her down beneath the covers, Cole said, "Damn, that's a shot of adrenaline."

"Bet you won't miss this," she mumbled.

Neither of them said another word after that. With his arms still around her, she did eventually fall asleep again. He was definitely asleep the next time she opened her eyes, the light outside a gray that gradually brightened.

Erin didn't move, needing to hold on to these minutes. His heartbeat, the rise and fall of his powerful chest, the lick of flame reaching up his neck.

She never woke up to find they'd separated during the night. Whenever he changed his position, he obviously rearranged hers, too. And even asleep, she apparently didn't want to lose contact with his big, warm, solid body. She hadn't slept as well in a very long time—until last night.

Tears stung her eyes, but she didn't let them fall in case they woke him up. When she eventually felt him stir, she slipped out of bed. By the time she showered and emerged from the bathroom, he'd gotten dressed and gone downstairs.

He was beating something in a bowl when she reached the kitchen. Scrambled eggs?

"French toast," he said, glancing over his shoulder. "I liked it when you made it, and we have that loaf of sourdough bread."

"Yum."

Aching inside, she couldn't help watching this big, muscular, incredibly sexy man in the kitchen, deftly turning battered toast and transferring it to a plate.

Not until he'd served them both and they'd taken a few bites did he say, "I have an appointment in Marysville this morning to look at a basement apartment. It's not great, but it is cheap and furnished."

Erin nodded without looking up. He must have made that appointment before they went to bed last night.

Cole didn't immediately resume eating. "You okay this morning?"

"Okay?" She finally lifted her head. "Oh, you mean after the nightmare. Sure." She smiled and waved a forkful of French toast. "This is good." It smelled wonderful, even if her taste buds were numb.

"What are you up to this morning?" he asked after a while.

"Don't know. I'll figure it out after I have some coffee."

He nodded, not quite looking at her.

Neither said much after that. Somehow, she wasn't surprised when he decided to shower at the apartment, and left without coming back to the house.

Erin cleaned up the kitchen, getting madder and madder even as her desolation grew. Why hadn't he gone the night he told her he intended to, right after that cop came looking for him? He would've saved her a world of hurt. He shouldn't have taken the job for Lottie Price, she thought, steaming. If he'd left back then, a month ago, she might be well into recovery, instead of feeling as if quicksand was sucking her under.

Looked like she'd parked her pride in the garage and thrown away the key. She'd *let* him use her this week. Wanting to have every minute she could with him before he moved on? Bad decision, even self-destructive. Had the same impulse that impelled her to speed recklessly also pushed her to hurt herself in another way? She couldn't know, but...when he got home, she'd tell him he needed to stay in the apartment until he had someplace to go.

Now, alone, she let the tears stream down her face and thought, *I'm done.*

COLE HAD JUST left the freeway at the northern exit for Marysville when his phone rang. He was so startled he jerked the wheel and came close to climbing the curb. Damn.

He steered into a gas station parking lot and checked the phone. Local number he didn't know. *Please, not a cop.*

"Cole here," he said cautiously.

"My name's Tom Phillips. Got an application you emailed yesterday."

His heart took a hard thud. "Yes, sir." Would the man have called to say, *Why did you waste my time?*

"I'm at a job site in Arlington. Any chance you can run out here so we can talk?"

"Sure, no problem. Where is it?"

"You have GPS?"

"Not in my old truck. But if you give me directions, I'll find it."

Call over, he sat stunned. An interview. A chance.

Maybe the guy hadn't noticed the answer to "Have you been convicted of a crime?"

Nobody ever seemed to miss that.

Cole called the guy about the apartment in Marysville and explained that he had a job interview. He'd call back when he could make it. He could hear the shrug when the owner said, "At this price, it won't last long. Your loss."

That might be true. It was the first real apartment, versus a room for rent, that he'd thought he could afford. On the other hand, from the pictures on Craigslist it looked like a pit. And if he got hired for a real job, one with the kind of wages paid for skilled construction workers, he could afford a step up from that place. Depending on where this Phillips guy had jobs, Marysville might not be ideal, anyway.

Don't get too excited.

Cole sat for another few minutes before he felt calm enough to drive.

Twenty minutes later, he turned past stone gateposts to find paved streets with curbs and sidewalks curving through raw land, logged and then stripped of any vegetation by bulldozers.

Unless each house was going to be on acreage, this would be a monster development. It also couldn't be more than six or seven miles from West Fork.

I could stay. Despite the ache in his chest, he knew better than that.

The minute he parked beside the bones of a house rising from the dirt, a man in a hard hat turned. Cole got out and walked to meet him.

"Mr. Phillips?"

"That's me." Tall and rangy, he had blond hair mixed with gray, deep crinkles beside his eyes and the kind of tan that men who worked outdoors had. The hand he extended revealed some serious nicks and scars.

They shook and studied each other.

"You learn what you claim to know in prison?" Phillips asked bluntly.

Well, at least he hadn't missed that line on the application.

"No, although I did some construction while I was there." He explained about working for his father, whom Phillips hadn't met but knew by reputation. "That's why several contractors took me on later." Cole then elaborated on his recent jobs for Erin and her neighbors.

"Wheelchair ramps, huh? Those can be tricky."

"Planning them was interesting," he agreed.

"Whatever you did to end up behind bars, you planning to do it again?"

Cole considered and discarded making his usual claim to innocence. He settled for "No, sir. I plan to work hard and start fitting in some college classes."

"Okay. You have those recommendations?"

He'd taken to bringing the folder everywhere with him, and handed it over. Phillips flipped through the pages.

"Lottie, huh?"

Cole smiled crookedly. "She's a character. Has to be ninety and still drives, even though her spine is crumbling and she's about so tall." He held his hand waist-high.

Tom Phillips laughed before saying abruptly, "I'm shorthanded. I've had a couple of guys who weren't reliable. I don't tolerate that. You'd better be damn sick if you don't make it to work. I'm willing to give you a try. When can you start?"

Exhilaration rushed through him.

By chance he'd worn his boots instead of the athletic shoes he'd almost put on. "Right now, if you need me."

They briefly discussed pay, when checks were issued, start time and end time and, when Cole asked, what kind of projects Phillips took on and where. He'd be building at least twenty houses in this development, which would keep them busy for a good long while.

"More, if we can stay on schedule."

Cole had to admit he didn't have any tools with him and didn't own a hard hat.

"Didn't expect you to. I've got everything you'll need."

Cole explained that he had to make a quick phone call, then he'd start wherever he was needed. Receiving a brusque nod, he walked back to the truck.

This call to Erin was bittersweet.

"I got a job," he said. "A good one."

HE WENT HOME sweaty and still exhilarated. The work had been easy, nothing he hadn't learned how to do by the time he was sixteen or so. He'd done his best to prove he was strong and tireless, as well as a perfectionist.

As he walked toward his truck at quitting time, Phillips called after him, "I like what I saw. Keep it up."

Cole should have gone to the apartment to shower, but most of his clothes were at Erin's and he was eager to talk to her. Too eager.

And this isn't home, he reminded himself. He had to quit thinking of her house that way.

He walked in, finding her in the kitchen. Something smelled good. She heard him coming and turned from the cutting board, a paring knife in her hand.

"Hey," he said.

"How'd it go?"

"Good." He wanted to say *great*, but couldn't trust that this job would pan out, however hard he worked.

Her smile lit her face. "I'm so glad, Cole. Is the job temporary or...?"

"Long-term, if Phillips is happy with my work. He seemed to be today. Ah, you mind if I go take a shower?"

"No, of course not." Her smile had faded and her expression was grave. "It might be best if you pack up your clothes after the shower, though. I'm happy to feed you dinner until you get moved, but—" Pressing her lips together, she looked away for an instant before she met his eyes again. "I can't keep...pretending everything's fine. I'm sorry, but I just can't."

He almost staggered back from the punch of pain, but long practice at hiding his emotions gave him the ability to simply nod. "I understand." He turned and walked out of the kitchen.

Upstairs, Cole came to a stop in the middle of her bedroom and couldn't take another step. A bellow roared from his chest and caught in his throat. He wanted to punch a wall. Do something violent to vent this anguish. But he couldn't damage her house or anything she owned. And he had to make sure she couldn't hear him. He stood where he was, shaking.

Had to be five minutes before he was able to jerk open a drawer she'd emptied for him and grab some clothes. He turned on the shower as hot as he could bear it and let it pound his neck and the back of his head. *God.* Right this minute, today's triumph didn't mean anything but a source of grief.

He could ask. She might allow him to stay. It was a good apartment; she was an ideal landlady. They could go on the way they'd been before they became lovers. Or even the way they'd been since.

The terrible pain beneath his breastbone told him neither would work. He had to leave, for his sake and hers. Or maybe he was thinking only of himself. He'd get through dinner somehow, carry the clothes and books he had here up to the apartment and then walk to the library. There had to be some local place he could afford to rent. Cole couldn't imagine continuing to see Erin even for a few more days. Sitting down to dinner with her every night would be torture. No, the sooner he could make the split final, the better.

He'd known all along that he had to make something of himself. If he stayed, he'd feel diminished. He'd been broken and she'd put him back together again, for which he would always remain grateful. But if he stayed, they'd both see those cracks in him forever, regardless of how well the glue held.

He'd be saving himself from inevitable grief, too, the gradual understanding that she'd started getting twitchy because he wasn't the kind of man she could see having a lasting relationship with. As she continued healing, became the self-assured woman she'd once been, it would happen. The hurt he felt now was nothing compared to what he knew would come—hearing her faltering explanation of why their relationship wasn't working for her.

No. Better to get it over with now. He hated that he was hurting her, too, but had no doubt that he'd made the right decision for both of them.

He just had to survive the days and weeks until the agony dulled.

OVER DINNER, ERIN coaxed him to tell her more about the job. What he'd actually been hired to do, and the personalities involved. She guessed Cole was willing to talk only because silence was worse.

He'd been accepted readily by the crew he'd be working with, which made him sure the boss hadn't told anybody that the new guy was an ex-con. Phillips, the contractor, seemed like a decent guy. He had high expectations and a temper, but worked side by side with his men. He offered praise along with criticism.

When Cole finished eating, he pushed his plate away, cleared his throat and met her eyes directly. "I've thought about the accident you were in and your problem getting past it. There are a couple of things I've been wanting to say."

Did they have to do this? But seeing his determination, she only nodded.

"I did some research online about the kind of van you were driving that day. Yours seated at least twelve people, right?"

This wasn't at all what she'd expected him to say.

"Yes," Erin agreed. "Actually, I think fourteen or fifteen. We could have gotten two or three more girls in on that trip." Thank God she hadn't.

"What I read is that those extended vans are unstable. People writing reviews expressed the strong opinion that they aren't safe and advise against buying one. From what you've said, I'm not so sure you had any chance to maneuver. It might not have mattered what you were driving. But you need to know the van wouldn't have responded the way a typical car or even SUV would. It's on the college that they bought an unsafe vehicle and didn't warn you of the issues."

Her mouth seemed to be hanging open. She managed to close it. "But—"

"Go online, Erin. Don't take my word for it. See what's being said."

She managed a nod. Was any of that true? There'd been so little time to react that day. *Because I let my attention wander.* But…she'd tried to swerve.

"There's something else." Cole seemed more hesitant now, his voice more ragged. "You haven't gone out at night speeding for weeks."

She hadn't needed to. The nightmares had receded, too…until last night.

"I want you to promise not to do it again. You survived, Erin. I know you're happy at least some of the time. If you feel the pull, fight back." His throat worked. "Please."

The hoarse plea shook her. Confusion swirled as competing needs battled. *Agree*, the hurt in her suggested. *He's leaving. He'll never know.*

Maybe not, but *she* would know. She thought Cole had been honest with her, as she'd tried to be with him. Lying now would feel wrong.

And…what he'd said resonated enough that she suspected he was right. She had stretches of hours now when she didn't think about the girls, when she did feel happiness in the moment, satisfaction at accomplishments, pleasure in other people's company. She wasn't healed…but she might be getting there.

Cole watched her, the hand that lay on the table seeming relaxed. Erin somehow felt sure he wasn't relaxed at all.

"I promise," she said, her own voice small and raw. "I won't deliberately endanger myself." Death would have to work to find her.

He expelled a harsh breath and his shoulders slumped. "Thank you. I want only good for you."

"Sure." She sounded almost careless. "Listen, I'll clean up. You must have things you need to do."

Appearing relieved, he took his cue and said good-night. After hearing the door shut behind him, Erin closed her eyes, the pressure in her chest swelling, and wondered what she'd do if it became unendurable.

IT WASN'T EXACTLY a shock to hear her doorbell the next morning. Erin knew who was here and what he'd say. The temptation was huge to pretend she hadn't heard it. He could leave her a note. A phone message. But that would be more cowardly than she could accept from herself.

When she opened the door, Cole waited on the porch, bracing his feet apart the way he did when he felt on edge. Erin had no doubt he saw the bruising beneath her eyes that told him how her night had gone. He didn't look good, either. Except, of course, he did. His gray T-shirt stretched over powerful muscles. Work boots and cargo pants only emphasized his size and strength.

"Cole." Why hadn't she done something to her hair besides pull it into a tight ponytail that didn't flatter her face? Actually getting dressed would've been an improvement on the flannel pajama bottoms and oversize, many-times-washed T-shirt, too. But really, what difference did it make? She had no secrets from him.

"I found a place to live that's close to where I'll be working," he said. "I wanted to let you know I've vacated the apartment. Here are the keys." He held out his hand.

They dropped one at a time onto her palm. As she curled her fingers around them, they felt heavier than two keys should. Colder. "If you need any of the furniture…"

He shook his head. "I'll manage. I can pick stuff up at a thrift store now that I can haul it."

How could she not have been prepared for this moment? It wasn't like she hadn't seen it coming almost from the first. Holding herself together until he was gone…well, she had to do it.

"I'm…really glad for you, Cole. I want you

to know that. I'd never want to trap you. That wasn't my intention. Seeing you succeed…it's a gift." Her smile probably wobbled, but she hoped he knew it was genuine. "You've come a long way."

"Mostly thanks to you," he said huskily.

"No, it's because you're the man you are." She so didn't want to humiliate herself. "Good luck, Cole."

He stepped forward, kissed her cheek and swung away. He was halfway down the steps he'd built before she could get the door shut.

Erin couldn't watch him leave.

CHAPTER SEVENTEEN

LOOKING OVER THE skeleton of the house that was his current job site, Cole unlocked his truck and tossed his hard hat onto the passenger seat. It felt good to take the thing off and let his scalp feel some air. A breeze—now, that would be even better. Too bad this was July and today's temp had soared into the nineties. Given the typical Pacific Northwest humidity, he'd sweated buckets. If he wanted a breeze, he'd have to find a fan.

Rico Sanchez walked past toward another guy's truck. "See you at Mickey's?" he asked.

"Probably." Cole lifted a hand to a couple of other men, then got in. He grimaced. The cab felt like a preheated oven. His attempt to let the heat escape—by rolling down the windows—hadn't done any noticeable good. Since the air-conditioning was defunct, that was the best he could do.

A popular local tavern, Mickey's was air-conditioned, which right now was its main appeal. Cole had made himself socialize. He even managed to enjoy himself for short stretches of time. Being the odd man out with a crew like this could be uncomfortable. Phillips hadn't been around much this week; he had crews working on four houses at once. But when he did show up, he seemed to watch Cole more closely than any of the other men, probably assessing his ability to work with them, as well as his skills. The month he'd been on the job wouldn't be enough for the boss to let go of a degree of wariness. Cole couldn't blame him; the recidivism rate for ex-cons was high. Still, feeling that extra scrutiny, knowing he had to prove himself, kept him on the razor's edge.

He felt pretty upbeat in general, but he wasn't in the mood to join a crowd tonight. He'd want to flatten his back against a wall and stay where he could see everyone. Too many people around sent prickles down his spine.

At the back of his mind, always, was a question. What would happen when these guys found out about his history, as they inevitably would? Even if they didn't join the jury in condemning him, they'd look at him differently. Fear him, on some level. They wouldn't want their girlfriends or wives around him. Would Phillips get rid of him if the rest of the crew became uncomfortable working with him?

No matter what, *he* stayed conscious of the

gulf between him and everyone else. They didn't know him, and he didn't want them to.

He was surprised his stay at Walla Walla hadn't already been exposed. Had whoever filed his application not even glanced at it? If she had—and he'd seen the bleached-blonde who ran the office in the trailer currently parked here in this development—could she really have resisted the impulse to gossip with the next employee who wandered in? Maybe, because he'd filled out an e-application, Phillips hadn't ever printed it. Cindy, the blonde, might not have access to his computer files. Still, if Cole wasn't outed any other way, he would be the first time a cop came by to accuse him of the latest crime.

While he was living at Erin's, he hadn't fully appreciated what it meant to have a boss and landlady who did know him. Not through-and-through, but close enough. This past month, he'd become quieter, reverting to instinct, which meant double-checking every word before he said it.

Finally preparing to pull away from the curb, he glanced in his rearview mirror. Speak of the devil, a big black pickup was about to pass, the driver none other than Tom Phillips. Seeing Cole, Phillips tapped his horn. Cole waved and started down the street behind him.

He hadn't reached the main road when his

phone rang. Dani, he saw. Smiling, he steered to the curb and answered with "Hey."

"How's it going?" Before he could answer, she raised her voice, but somehow muffled it, too. "No, you cannot go to Damien's to hang out. It's almost dinnertime. No argument."

Cole laughed. "Tough love."

"Sure, I'm going to let my kid go knock on his buddy's door just as Damien's mom is putting dinner on the table. She's thinking, *Oh, God, do I have to invite the kid to stay? Doesn't his own mother ever feed him?*"

Still laughing, he said, "Does Damien ever knock on *your* door at five thirty, looking hopeful?"

"Of course he does. I swear, both of them could eat dinner here, then go down the street and have a second one at Damien's house with barely a burp in between. *And* go rummaging for a snack two hours later."

"I remember being starved all the time when I was that age." He had been in the joint, too, until he'd resigned himself to eating whatever he was given.

"I suppose if I come down to see you now, it'll have to be on a weekend."

"Afraid so. When I'm working, I only take half an hour for lunch."

"Maybe we could invite Erin this time."

"You know I don't live at her place anymore."

"But you see her, don't you?"

His sister had no idea her casual question was equivalent to smacking him with a bat.

He'd assumed he would catch sight of Erin around town occasionally, say, at the grocery store. Every now and again, he'd drive by the hardware and lumber stores, even the plant nursery, not because he was looking for her, but keeping an eye out for her Cherokee nonetheless.

He hadn't realized that in a town this size it was possible to go for long stretches *without* running into someone you knew.

"No," he said.

"What? Why not?"

"It wouldn't have been good for either of us, and that's all I'm going to say."

His sister responded, but he tuned her out.

He'd been thinking about going by Erin's house, just to see if it looked like she was still living there. Or, damn, whether she'd rented out his apartment yet. So far, he'd talked himself out of it.

"…an idiot."

Cole could fill in the part he'd missed. "So, when are you planning to drive down here?"

She huffed out an annoyed breath at being ignored, but said, "Maybe a week from Saturday?"

"Sounds good." Wasn't like he had any plans. He found the weekend hours tough to fill.

"The job still going well?"

"Yeah, I think so."

"So it looks like it'll be permanent?"

She just had to tap into one of his worries.

"I don't know," he admitted. "New construction will slow down in a couple months, once rainy weather hits. The contractor I work for is big-time enough to keep some projects going year-round, but I'll bet he throttles back. And that means letting some people go." Cole didn't want to be one of those. Being laid off might be inevitable, since he was a new employee, but his level of determination had to count for something. He didn't make expensive mistakes. He was never late; he didn't slack off when Phillips wasn't there. He didn't have a beer at lunch, he didn't bad-mouth the boss. "You know how it is. I'm the new guy," he finished.

"Jerry has relented," she said abruptly. "Worse comes to worst, you can move here."

That would be a cold day in hell. He'd bet good money that Jerry hadn't so much relented as been bullied into shouting, "Fine!" just to shut his wife up.

"Tell him thanks," Cole said.

The short silence gave him warning.

"Cole, would it kill you to call Dad?"

He bumped his forehead against the steering wheel. "Because he's finally convinced I got screwed? And, wow, I'm worthy to be his son, after all? Got to tell you, after ten years of silence, I'm not overflowing with forgiveness."

"Maybe you should think about someone besides yourself," she snapped. "My dinner's almost ready. *Goodbye.*"

She'd been a bossy little girl, too. He grinned at her snotty tone, even though her accusation rankled. His father had had over ten years to write him a letter. To visit. But no. So now Cole was supposed to call and say, "Daddy, I've missed you"?

He swore, dropped his phone on the seat beside the hard hat and put the truck back in Drive.

SINCE SHE REALLY needed groceries, Erin decided to shower in the high school locker room instead of waiting until she got home, like she usually did.

She'd taken to swimming laps at the pool here at least three days a week. Usually she came earlier, but she'd worked at the library until seven this evening.

A voice echoed in the big, concrete space. "It's fun playing, but Mr. Whittaker doesn't know any more than Mrs. Fisher does."

"I don't think I'm going to play this year," another girl said.

Walking from the shower room to her locker, Erin saw a bunch of preteen to teenage girls filtering into the locker room from the gymnasium. Oh, no. They had to be taking the more advanced of the two volleyball sessions she'd read about on the Recreation Department website. How had she let herself forget? This session met twice a week, Tuesday and Thursday evenings, six to eight o'clock, allowing for teenagers who held summer jobs.

She reached her locker, only to have two girls saunter after her, stopping just a few feet away to open lockers of their own.

"If we all suck at setting the ball," one of them grumbled, "how are we supposed to spike it?"

Good question. And sad, because what everyone enjoyed most was slamming the ball over the net.

Voices rang out from every direction, echoing in the big, concrete space. Dressing hastily, Erin couldn't help listening to the two girls talking.

The dark-haired girl started pulling clothes out of her locker. She had to untangle panties from skinny jeans. "You're really not going to play?"

The other was a tall, athletic blonde with hair

cut short. "Why waste our time? Anyway, you know Mrs. Fisher doesn't even want to coach volleyball. She only did it last year because Mr. Hoffer leaned on her."

"They get paid extra, you know."

"I heard her telling Mr. Ellis she didn't care about the money."

It took as little as this conversation, seeing two younger girls snapping towels at each other outside the shower room, the sound of a high-pitched giggle from nearby, to pierce Erin's heart. It was all so painfully familiar.

She hurriedly fastened the buckle on her sandals and shoved her suit, goggles and wet towel in the tote. She had to get out of here.

Since she was apparently invisible to the girls, they kept talking. "Last year, she said she'd watch films and, you know, study skills. So maybe…"

"Oh, sure."

A shriek of laughter came from the other side of the bank of lockers. Erin slammed hers shut. The clang was achingly familiar, as were the bits of other conversations drifting her way.

I miss this.

Forcing an apologetic smile, she slipped by and went to the row of mirrors. She was lucky to get one. The younger girls headed out with wet hair, like she was planning to, but the older ones waited in line for outlets to plug in their hair dryers. Some were carefully applying makeup, because God forbid a hot guy should see them without.

The ache she felt was bittersweet. She could help the girls who really did want to play the game well. Memories flickered like a campfire leaping to life. The laughter, the frustration, the childish moments and the graceful, mature ones. Even though it hurt, Erin was glad. She didn't want to forget the girls, ever.

She hadn't thought in a long while about the good times with her team.

If she coached at the high school level, she wouldn't drive to games; the district would provide bus transportation.

It's too soon.

In another year, she might think about applying to coach. Or even teach a class or two at the community college. Not too big a commitment.

But not yet.

Given the emotions that had pummeled her, Erin's enthusiasm for grocery shopping had waned by the time she reached the parking lot, but the pickings in her kitchen were getting skimpy, and she couldn't imagine she'd jump out of bed in the morning and think, *Wow, I can hardly wait to go to the grocery store!*

Plus, she was working tomorrow afternoon.

So get it over with, she decided.

Sad to say, she never walked into Safeway without looking for Cole. Which was totally stupid, when she didn't even know where his apartment was or if he was still working at that development between West Fork and Arlington. He could be living and working on the other side of the county by now.

Tonight, she nabbed a cart and started in the produce department, barely glancing at the checkout lanes. It wasn't as if they'd be that busy after nine in the evening.

Except…there was Cole Meacham, unloading the contents of his cart onto the belt.

Was she hallucinating? Erin closed her eyes and opened them again. No, that was definitely him. She couldn't mistake those shoulders, the muscles moving under a thin cotton tee, the power in the arms bared by short sleeves.

Transfixed, she stared hungrily. His hair had grown enough not to be spiky anymore. Instead, it was rumpled, as if he shoved his fingers through it. She would give anything to slip *her* fingers into his hair, feel the texture of it now. Have him turn, his sharp blue eyes locking on her, narrowing purposefully…

Dear God, what if he saw her gaping?

Her cheeks flamed with humiliation and she moved fast enough to make her cart wheels squeak, not slowing until she was mostly hidden behind a heap of bananas. Even then, she kept her back to him.

Erin grabbed bananas and red grapes. By the time she reached the lettuce, she knew he wouldn't be able to see her if he happened to turn. Nobody was close enough to hear her whimper. Her heart hammered so hard and fast her head swam.

As much as she'd wanted to see him, she suddenly realized she couldn't afford the stress. Maybe she should start driving farther away to do her shopping. The hours she worked at the library should be safe, except she'd have to decline shifts like this evening's. She'd be smart to buy gas in the middle of a working day, when there was no way she'd run into him.

And here she'd thought she was doing so well.

She pulled herself together enough to continue shopping, although her choices were more random than they should have been. Usually she maintained a mental list of what she needed. Today, she found herself putting a bottle of extra virgin olive oil in her cart, even though she didn't remember whether she needed it or not. And never mind pausing to make price comparisons.

She had to backtrack four aisles to get a carton of eggs she did need before she went to check out.

This was close to the longest day of the year, so the sun still hadn't set. But the purplish-gray of dusk had deepened the color of the sky by the time she pushed the cart to her Cherokee. Thanks to her remote, the hatch door had already lifted when she stopped the cart. She started to pick up the first bags of groceries... and saw the man leaning against the fender.

"I thought that was you in there," Cole said.

SEEING HER JUMP six inches, he regretted not waiting in plain sight. What, had he assumed that if she spotted him out here, she'd lurk inside the store however long it took for him to go away?

"I'm sorry," he said, retreating a step. "I didn't mean to scare you. It's not dark yet, and..." And what? "I'm sorry," he repeated.

Erin pressed a hand to her chest. "No, I should've seen you. I guess I was preoccupied." She smiled, although he wasn't convinced it was genuine. "How are you?" she asked.

"I'm good." When she didn't move, he took over the job of putting her groceries in the back of her SUV. "The job's going well. Uh, I have an apartment not far from here. I could have walked, but I felt lazy."

"That's great."

"How are you doing?"

"Oh, I'm fine." This smile looked a little more...real. "Lottie drove over the other day to bring me a coffee cake, which even I have to admit was better than Nanna's."

"Lottie drove?" Guilt poked at him, because he'd never followed up on his concern. He'd meant to talk to Ryan and Michelle at least, and ask if they'd offer to pick up groceries for Lottie, or give her a lift. He knew Erin would've been willing if he'd said something.

"Well, it's not as if she could walk that far. It was kind of scary to see, though. And when she backed out—" Erin's shudder was theatrical.

"She's afraid she'll lose her independence if she has to give up driving." Cole shook his head. "I told her the neighbors would take her to the store if she asked, and there's Dial-A-Ride, but I understand her fear."

"I do, too," Erin said. "I'll see if she wants to hitch a ride next time I shop. I'd be glad to drive her when she needs to do other errands, too."

"That would be good." He lowered the hatch door as she maneuvered the cart out of the way. Should he back off now? But he hadn't gotten her out of his head in the five—no, almost six—weeks since he'd seen her, and he didn't like that she hadn't mentioned anything she was up to. Lottie, he thought, had been a diversion.

So, ask.

"You doing any more work on the house?"

She wrinkled her nose in that familiar way. "Not really. I've pretty much finished painting—yes, ceilings, too, which was an *awful* job—but I haven't done anything about the moldings or the floors." She hesitated, looking shy. "I've actually started a part-time job. Not so much for the money, just…to get me out. I'm clerking and helping with reference questions at the library. Only about half-time so far, but I feel useful."

Even as he smiled and said something that must have been close to right, Cole felt things he didn't totally recognize. Jealousy—but not quite. All he knew was that he wanted her to take those steps, but he hated that she'd done it all on her own. He'd have liked to hear about the jobs she'd applied for and why, her hesitations and hopes. He could've told her about his days, too—the occasional frustrations, the awkward attempts to make friends, his apprehension about possibly being laid off when the weather turned.

But his basic fears remained. He didn't let himself ask whether she'd kept her promise to him. He didn't say the words *I miss you.*

And he didn't want to know if someone else was living in his apartment.

"Guess we're both…" Cole paused, not sure how to finish what he'd started. *Doing okay?*

But Erin said, "Moving on?" This smile was definitely fake. "You're right. We are. It was good to see you, Cole, but I'd better be getting home."

When she reached for the cart, he took it from her. "I'll take care of this. See you around."

He had a softball-sized lump in his throat as he pushed the cart toward the closest return lane.

THE NEXT DAY, Cole made a point of getting to work fifteen minutes early. Tom Phillips's truck was already parked outside the office trailer. Cole knocked lightly and stepped in.

Alone inside, Phillips sat scowling behind a computer. He looked up in surprise. "Meacham." He rocked back in his chair, the frown lingering. "What can I do for you?"

"I need to take a couple hours off sometime in the next week or so."

"Family?"

"No. I told you I want to take some classes at the community college." At the other man's nod, he said, "I'm way past the application deadline for fall quarter. I can't figure out from the website when I'd have to apply for winter quarter. I need to sit down with an admissions officer and start the ball rolling."

"You might be able to appeal and still get in for fall."

"That's my hope." He smiled wryly. "I was out before the May deadline, but I didn't have tuition money or transportation yet. That was a little too far ahead for me to plan."

Phillips grimaced in apparent sympathy. "You have a good excuse."

"A new and improved form of 'the dog ate my homework'?"

He laughed outright, then said, "Just give me some notice of when you'll be gone." Then, humor absent, Phillips said, "You aiming for full-time?"

Cole shook his head. "An evening class or two. I need to work."

"Fair enough."

Should he ask about winter layoffs? The possibility had been preying on his mind, but this was too early to say anything, Cole decided. He should be grateful if Phillips just gave him a good recommendation if he laid him off.

Before he could leave, the boss said, "Since you're here, anyway, let's talk for a minute. Have a seat."

Oh, shit. He managed a nod and lowered his butt onto a straight-backed chair.

"Been meaning to tell you how happy I am with your work."

That was the last thing he'd expected to hear. "Thank you, sir."

"You're probably aware I downsize my crews over the winter."

"I guessed."

"You willing to stay on?"

"I'd...hoped to."

Phillips smiled. "Excellent. You know most of the guys look up to you already? You have a quiet way of taking charge without anyone noticing that's what you're doing."

Cole did know. Even in school, he'd ended up masterminding group projects. He didn't think of himself as a leader, but he really wasn't a very good follower. "All I do is put in a word when I see a way to do something easier or better."

Keen eyes studied him. "You're a bit of a puzzle." Phillips shook himself, like a dog changing moods. "You keep on like you have been, and you'll be one of my foremen before you know it."

Cole was almost as stunned as he'd been when Erin offered him a job. He stared at the other man for longer than was polite before he got out a husky, "Thank you," and excused himself.

Walking back to his pickup to get his hard hat and tool belt, he ached to call Erin. Share his good news. Knowing he couldn't left him feeling hollow—or maybe just expanded the hollow place that was always there now. The one that had him second-guessing his decision to walk away from her, even though he was still convinced he'd needed to do it.

I miss you. If he'd actually said the words, how would she have responded?

But he knew. *Guess we're both moving on.* She'd soon find herself bored working at the library. Eventually the grief would soften, and she'd want her real life back.

Buckling on his tool belt, Cole gave a helpless shrug. Had Erin resigned from the college where she'd taught? Or had they extended her a leave of absence, and expected her back in September? If that was the case, next time he drove by the house, he might see a For Sale sign in front.

When that day came, he could quit looking for her whenever he went out. Damn. Had he really held any hope? If so, he'd be smart to let it go.

CHAPTER EIGHTEEN

WITH THE NIGHT dark and eerily quiet, Erin sat in the driver's seat of the Cherokee. She'd resisted the temptation last night after seeing Cole, as she had every night since she'd promised she wouldn't do this again. She didn't even know what had propelled her out here at two in the morning. Probably a nightmare, but if so, she didn't remember it.

The key was in the ignition. The fact that she hadn't fastened the seat belt or started the engine meant she hadn't yet committed. Instead, gripping the steering wheel so tightly her knuckles ached, she closed her eyes and ran through what she wanted to do. Put the key in the ignition. Shift from Park. Roll quietly down the driveway. Turn right at the street. She imagined taking every turn, all the way to Highway 9. There, if she saw no headlights, she could press her foot down on the accelerator. The veil separating her from the girls would thin. She might even see their faces as she felt the rush, as the world blurred. As her terror climbed.

Her eyes flew open. Terror? Where had that come from? She wouldn't be afraid. She never had been, except when the animal had run out onto the highway in front of her.

On a little pop of surprise, she knew better. *I will be now.*

Erin moaned. Wrong verb tense. She *would* be scared now. The word *will* implied that it would definitely happen, which wasn't true. She'd promised Cole. Maybe only impulse had motivated him to hang around to talk to her the other night. Maybe he felt genuine curiosity about how she was doing. He might never give her a thought again, she didn't know, but he'd meant something huge to her. And now, crap, her eyes were leaking, because she'd used the wrong verb tense again. He *still* meant something huge to her. Maybe…always would.

No, she couldn't think like that. She couldn't handle mourning one more person.

So if he didn't care anymore, why *not* go for a drive tonight?

Because she'd promised. Because, while the craving still gnawed at her, the urgency had lessened. *Because I won't deliberately set myself up to die.*

She'd get there eventually, after all. Since living forever wasn't an option, the time would come, whether it was a year from now or fifty years from now. If there really was an afterlife, she'd see the girls then, along with her parents and Nanna and Grandpa.

Maybe not the girls. They might be too busy with their families, with everyone else they'd loved. Her, they'd liked, respected, trusted, which wasn't the same thing.

Staring ahead through the windshield, she accepted that they would have graduated and gone on with their lives, perhaps not even stayed in touch. Other girls would have taken their places. If she'd kept on coaching—if she *did* keep coaching—she'd care about a lot of students, feel proud when she sat with faculty and watched them accept their diplomas, when she eagerly read the alumni magazines later for updates on their lives.

She let herself cry as she hadn't since Cole had held her, and knew it to be cleansing. Living with him had been better than living without him, but she could do it.

A MONTH HAD passed since Cole had seen Erin at the grocery store. He'd caught a couple of glimpses of her. Once when he was waiting at a stoplight and she drove past right in front of him. Another time when he'd gone down her street—out of curiosity, that was all—and seen her kneeling in the flower bed in front of the porch he'd built. She had a trowel in one gloved hand, and when he slowed, he saw her drop what were probably weeds in a bucket. Her hair had been fiery in the sunlight, her braid as fat and tempting as he remembered.

There was no For Sale sign.

It really bothered him that he hadn't built the rose trellis he'd promised. Worse, he hadn't reminded her to pick up a garage door opener for him to install.

He'd made himself keep going. She hadn't seen him.

He still didn't love hanging out in a tavern, but he'd taken to doing it a couple evenings a week, plus Sundays now that football season had started. He didn't know many people except his coworkers, and this was how they spent their time. He'd never felt the pleasure in his new apartment that he had in the one above Erin's garage. This one seemed bare, whether he added anything personal or not. Solitude had morphed into loneliness. Sometimes he felt as if he'd injured a limb that was regaining feeling, the prickles more painful than hopeful.

Tonight being Thursday, football was on both big screens at Mickey's. The Seahawks were playing the Packers in Green Bay, and led 14–3 at the moment.

Just then, the ball squirted out of a Seahawk

running back's arms as he went down, and a bunch of Packers piled on. The crowd at the tavern erupted. On the screen, more bodies got into the fray as they all fought to get their hands on the football. Cole hooted with everyone else when the ref straightened up and signaled that it was still the Seahawks' ball.

Sanchez poked an elbow in his side. "You ever play ball? You're almost big enough to make it as a pro."

He took a swallow of the beer he'd been nursing since the kickoff. "You kidding? Those guys are massive. Going up against three hundred and fifty pound behemoths doesn't sound like much fun. Yeah, I played a couple of years in high school, but that's not the same."

"You weren't good enough to be recruited by any colleges?"

Too late for regrets. He only laughed and shrugged. "No place I wanted to go."

"I played in high school, too," Rico surprised him by saying. "In Toppenish. You know, near Yakima."

Cole nodded. About all he did know was that the area had a large Hispanic population because of agriculture.

Rico's grin was reminiscent. "We had a losing record every year, but we never lost hope. Me, I'm short but I'm fast. Kind of like Rawls."

He tipped his glass toward the TV. "Easy to squeak by the big guys."

Returning the grin, Cole suggested, "We should start up a league. A little touch football on Saturdays. What do you say?"

"Great—if you're on my team. I sure as hell don't want you flattening me." Rico was starting to slur his words. He wasn't usually a big drinker, although if he was to be believed, he stopped at Mickey's most days on his way home, even though he was married. His wife was here tonight, talking to her sister, who'd come, too. The sister, Soledad, was a pretty woman, with a huge smile and a wealth of wavy black hair. Cole had met her once before, but they hadn't been at the same table. Tonight, she was right across from him, and definitely flirting.

He was out of practice when it came to responding, and grateful that the football game gave him an out except during commercial breaks. Not that he didn't like what he knew of her. He did. Soledad worked for a well-drilling company, answering phones and bookkeeping. Her smile came easily, and she wasn't pushy. Rico wouldn't have gotten them a table for four tonight if he didn't think she and Cole should hook up.

But how fast would that change when he found out Cole was an ex-con? He should go for it, anyway. Worry about what would happen down the road when it *did* happen.

The Seahawks had to punt the ball and then a truck commercial came on. Soledad leaned forward and raised her voice.

"I heard you talking about playing football. I'll bet you were really good."

He smiled and shook his head. "Not dedicated enough. Or maybe I just wasn't smart enough to think about what I wanted to do with the rest of my life." And wasn't that the truth.

She made a face. "In high school? Who is?"

"There are always some serious jocks, plus the students angling for acceptance by good colleges."

"Did you go to college?"

"A few classes here and there." *Oh, by the way, while I was in prison.* "I've signed up for the fall semester at the college here, a couple night classes. What about you?"

"I got an AA from Skagit Community College. Going on would have meant leaving West Fork, and…I don't know…I like being close to family. It wasn't as if I had any big plan for what to do with a four-year degree."

He wished he'd followed the path his father had laid out as his only acceptable option, but for Soledad's sake, he smiled in a vague way he hoped she took as agreement. The game resumed, and he pretended more interest in it than he felt.

Pretended? Why would he do that when a pretty young woman was smiling at him, her eyes holding an open invitation? He'd decided a one-night stand would feel sordid, especially in comparison to what he'd had with Erin. This would be different. He could have a girlfriend. He'd spend the night at her place sometimes, or she at his. He didn't have to be lonely.

Why did he feel so sure he still would be?

But he knew. Soledad would be a fill-in for what he really wanted. *Who* he really wanted.

Despite the burst of cheers around him, he closed his eyes in resignation. None of his fears about a relationship with Erin had left him. They carried the same weight as shackles that made every step drag.

He had a long way to go before he could approach her, and by then it might be too late—if it wasn't already. But having fun with Soledad in the meantime wasn't something he could do. He'd never make love with one woman while he was thinking about another.

He pulled his phone from his pocket as if it had vibrated and looked at it. "I've got to go," he said, jumping to his feet. "Sorry to run."

Both women and Rico protested, but he just shook his head apologetically and fled.

Had running away become a habit? Didn't matter, he told himself. Better to run than get himself into something he'd regret.

ERIN SMILED AS Laura Carlson came out the kitchen door carrying a tray, calling, "Who wants s'mores?"

Even the badminton players turned at that. The shuttlecock dropped to the grass.

"Really?" asked Jeff Abbott, a nice young guy, fresh out of grad school, who was a research librarian at the West Fork branch of the county library system.

Laura, the branch librarian, laughed. "Of course I'm serious. Why let those coals go to waste?"

Accepting the invitation to the barbecue at the Carlsons' house had been another way for Erin to push herself out there. She'd been living in limbo, but that was changing.

This gathering had been good. She liked most of the people she'd met; they reminded her of her colleagues at Markham. Some she knew from the library, but those people had brought husbands, wives, friends. Laura's husband was an assistant principal at the Lake Stevens high school, so some of his colleagues were there, too.

With a fire crackling in the barbecue pit, Erin

chose a seat beside a woman named Monique Murphy, whose profession she hadn't heard. Probably in her mid- to late-thirties, Monique had come alone.

"I can't even remember the last time I made s'mores," Erin commented.

"I think I was about ten," the other woman said, laughing.

"Are you with the library?"

"No, I teach English at the high school here in Lake Stevens. Oh, and I coach basketball."

"Really? I...used to coach girls' softball and volleyball at the college level."

While they shared their experiences, George Carlson handed out sharpened sticks. In no time, they were all roasting marshmallows— or burning them to a crisp, in a few cases—then squishing them between graham crackers and chocolate bars.

She and Cole should have done this. He'd uncovered an old concrete and rusty metal grill out in the backyard that Erin had forgotten was there. Once she saw it, she remembered how much fun cooking outdoors, over an open flame, had seemed to her when she was a little girl. He might have enjoyed it.

Looking around, she tried to imagine him here. Would he have fit in? Did it matter? The answer was no, it didn't, not for her, but she thought he would've been fine. This was an eclectic crowd, with ages ranging from midtwenties to George's late fifties. Another high school teacher had visible tattoos on his brawny arms. There was also a librarian who'd transferred from West Fork to the library headquarters in Marysville before Erin started. She was a quiet woman who watched more than she spoke, like Cole. He would've had no reason to feel uncomfortable.

And why was she even thinking about this? He knew where to find her, but he hadn't stopped by, hadn't called, in the six weeks since their encounter at Safeway. *Message received.*

She pushed thoughts of him out of her mind and joined the increasingly lazy conversation. This felt like days' end at summer camp, with the glowing coals, the circle of contented people, the darkness beyond.

Suddenly uneasy, Erin stiffened. She'd meant to be home before dark. Which was totally silly, but she'd developed a sort of phobia about Highway 9. She felt as if she was breaking some rule when she had to take it. Plus, the scenery had a way of giving her flashbacks. Really, she hadn't had that many reasons to drive there since she'd given up her speeding hobby, but in a rural county like this, there weren't always a lot of choices. The Carlsons lived closer to Lake Stevens than to West Fork. She'd asked one of the women earlier, and learned that Laura had accepted a promotion to branch librarian in West Fork only a couple of years ago.

Erin hadn't minded the drive so much this afternoon, but in the dark, with her headlights spearing the road ahead... She hid her shiver and said, "I'm afraid I need to be going."

Monique went with her into the house, where they both collected dishes that had held their contributions—in Erin's case, a coffee cake made from Lottie's recipe. Both said their good-byes and thanks.

Walking back out, Monique suggested they have lunch someday, and they exchanged phone numbers. By then, others were leaving, too. In fact, she followed two other cars along the narrow country road until they reached the highway. By then, she'd almost convinced herself she could relax. She'd be part of what was in effect a convoy.

She concentrated on the taillights of the car in front of her. The highway wasn't deserted like it was in the middle of the night, anyway. There was a surprising amount of traffic. Saturday night, no wonder.

Duane—whose last name she couldn't remember, only that he was the high school band director—turned off well before she needed to. As she accelerated again, she had to squint.

An oncoming driver needed to turn down his brights. Or maybe it was one of those pickups high enough up that the headlights always blinded anyone approaching. Irritating.

Suddenly, another set of oncoming lights was in *her* lane. Really? Somebody was *that* desperate to pass? She eased her foot from the gas to give the idiot more space, but... Were the superbright lights approaching faster? Panic started to elevate her pulse, and Erin glanced in her rearview mirror to see that a big SUV was riding her bumper, too. Steer to the shoulder, she decided, hoping she didn't get rear-ended.

She tapped her brakes, flicked on her turn signal—and felt the jolt of being bumped from behind. Her Cherokee rocked. Blinded by the oncoming headlights, all she knew was that she'd lost control.

Her door crumpled inward, the impact painful. And then her car was flying off the highway. A monster evergreen tree loomed in front of her. She was going to die. Metal screamed, and she blacked out.

SHIT! DID I not set the alarm?

Cole reared up in bed, his appalled stare on his digital clock. Damn it! He'd swung his feet to the floor before he woke up enough to think, *Sunday. I don't have to get up.*

Groaning, he flopped back down. After a minute, he yanked the pillow from beneath his head and pressed it over his face. It didn't take him long to recognize that he wouldn't be able to fall asleep again.

As a teenager, he could have—and sometimes did—sleep until noon or even later, which irked his father to no end. The last ten years, he hadn't had any choice about when to rise. Now, the five-day-a-week schedule had him up at six thirty. Apparently, he was incapable of sleeping in.

Grumbling under his breath, he pulled on shorts and made his way to the kitchen, where he remembered he hadn't set the timer for his fancy new coffee maker last night. Because he was going to sleep in.

While he waited for the coffee to brew, he turned on the TV. Local news was running, something about the Seattle city council, which he couldn't care less about. He picked up the remote and was about to change channels when the newscaster declared, "One fatality and two people in critical condition after a multicar accident that occurred last night on Highway 9 in north Snohomish County." A camera panned the cleanup phase of the accident. Lights flashed atop police cars, and a tow truck had backed up to a sedan now compressed like an accordion. Cole winced. The fatality almost had to be that driver. A big pickup had its share of dents and hung halfway off the road. One of those big SUVs like a Suburban—what was left of it, anyway—was perpendicular to the road, blocking both lanes.

The camera kept moving as the on-scene reporter talked. Cole stared in disbelief at a smaller SUV crumpled around a tree. His heart slammed into overdrive. The driver's-side door had been smashed in, right where she'd have been sitting. He couldn't read the bumper sticker, but it was in the same place and the same color as the one Erin had on her Cherokee, saying, Markham College. Was that— Could it be—

Frantic, he paid attention to what the reporter was saying in a gravely concerned tone. One person involved had been pronounced dead at the scene. Another had been transported by helicopter to Harborview Hospital in Seattle. Injured passengers from one vehicle, as well as a woman driver, had been taken to the hospital in West Fork. The police weren't yet releasing names.

Had Erin gone out last night? Had she *caused* this mess? Cole had trouble believing it. As he watched, the news moved on to another story. Wishing he had a computer, Cole found his phone and tapped in some keywords. The article that came up repeated information he'd already heard—except he saw the time of the accident. Around 10:30 p.m.

Thank God. If that was her Cherokee, she would have been coming home from someplace. Frustrated, he reread the meager information, turned off the coffee maker and went back to the bedroom to throw on some clothes.

Unless she'd moved on, into a new relationship—and he didn't believe that—she'd be alone at the hospital, and she didn't have to be.

ERIN LAY IN the hospital bed, not bothering to open her eyes. The white-curtained cubicle with a machine reading her pulse and who knew what else hadn't changed.

Dazed, probably drugged, she hurt. It was hard to focus on anything else. Top of the list— her head felt like a bass drum being rhythmically pounded. Her face, probably because of the air bag. Arm. Shoulder. Chest. Breathing hurt, too. She struggled to remember what the doctor had said. The cast on her arm was a clue, but the rest was a blank. Déjà vu.

"Erin?"

At the sharp inquiry in that deep voice, she did lift her leaden eyelids. "Cole?"

"Yes. *God.*" His shoulders sagged as he gazed down at her. He looked haggard, at least a day's stubble darkening his jaw and upper lip. "You're okay."

"Don't feel okay," she mumbled.

"I know." He sounded impossibly gentle. After glancing around, he dragged a chair to the bedside and sat down, reaching over to carefully enclose her right hand in his. On the good-news front, the broken arm was her left.

"They let you in."

"I told them we're close friends."

The bewilderment was likely caused by pain-killers, but maybe not. She did know she'd been unconscious for several hours. "How'd you find out?" As if that made any difference. But the little things were a place to start.

"About the accident? You're on the morning news." His mouth twisted. "You haven't been identified, but I recognized your Jeep."

"I wasn't trying." She felt a desperate need for him to believe her. "I said I wouldn't."

"I know you weren't." His free hand lifted to her face, gently stroking. With his fingertips he massaged her temple, the undamaged part of her forehead.

Her eyes wanted to roll back. Keeping them open took a real effort. "Not my fault," she whispered.

"I know that, too," he murmured. "I talked

to a state patrol officer on the way in. They've been reconstructing the accident and talking to the people who weren't as badly injured. Another driver saw it happen, too, and pulled over to help. Apparently, an oncoming car was trying to pass a pickup, driven by an eighteen-year-old guy who viewed that as a challenge and sped up. Nobody was passing *him*," he said sardonically.

"Oh." Suddenly her vision blurred. "I thought I was going to die." It just burst out of her. "I was so scared. Why was I scared?"

Even as he swore, he shifted from the chair to the bed. He flattened his hands on each side of her shoulders and bent to touch his forehead to hers. It felt like an embrace, probably the closest he dared come with her so obviously battered.

"Because you don't want to die." Breath warm against her lips, he spoke softly, but his voice was ragged, too. "You already found that out, remember? It's not your time, Erin."

Hot tears ran down her face, blinded her. She tasted salt. "Maybe I *can't* die," she whispered.

"Please don't. Please."

She started to sob. She could, because he was here, but, oh, it *hurt*. His arms came around her and he half lifted her so she could cry against his shoulder, let him soak up her tears and her pain.

If only *he* didn't withhold so much. If only he'd let her take on some of his pain, too.

One second she savored his strength, tried to gather her weary mind. The next she slid into darkness.

WITH NO WARNING, her cheeks still wet, Erin fell asleep. Cole hoped she was actually asleep, and hadn't plunged back into the coma that had kept her unresponsive for almost four hours last night, according to the doctor.

After laying her carefully back on the pillows, he studied her. The rise and fall of her chest was slow, even. Her lips were slightly parted. Movement flickered behind her eyelids. REM. This wasn't the first time he'd seen her sleep.

Finally relaxing, he eased off the bed and settled himself in the chair again to wait. The relief he'd felt when she talked to him was so profound he was still weak from it. She was alive. Injured, but conscious and already beginning to recover.

He'd brought a day pack with his school stuff, but he hadn't been able to do anything other than stare at her and will her to open her eyes. Now that she had, he unzipped the pack and pulled out a book.

Nurses poked their heads in every so often. One brought him a chilled bottle of water, for which he murmured "Thanks." He would read a few paragraphs and look up, his concentration not the best. She was under so deep she didn't stir for nearly two hours.

When she did, she swallowed and opened and closed her mouth a couple of times. Finally, her lashes lifted, revealing confusion. She moaned when she rolled her head to stare uncomprehendingly at him.

The sound was enough to bring a nurse, who prompted Erin to press a button to give herself a shot of pain relief, then held a water bottle with a straw to her mouth.

"Thank you," she whispered afterward. "It felt like I had a mouthful of sand."

The nurse chuckled. "Not the first time I've heard that."

Erin fixed her eyes on Cole. At least he saw clarity in them, even if he couldn't tell what she was thinking. Not until the nurse was gone did Erin say, "You're still here."

"I am."

"Why *are* you here? Is this because you think you owe me or something?" She didn't give him time to answer. "Because if it is, you can leave right now." She sounded…hostile.

Cole dropped the book into his pack, grabbed it and stood up. "If that's what you want, fine."

He was ready to walk out, but her big hazel

eyes betrayed too much hurt before she rolled to face the far curtain. "Up to you," she mumbled.

This was ridiculous.

"I want to stay here with you. If you'd rather not talk, that's okay. I'd still like to keep you company." He moved his shoulders uneasily. "You should have someone here."

He thought she swiped at her eyes, but they were dry when she shifted back.

"Thank you." It was a small, husky whisper.

"Can I hold your hand?"

She looked at him long enough to make him nervous, but finally extended her hand.

He scraped the chair as close to the narrow bed as it would go, then wrapped his fingers around her much smaller, too-cold hand. "Do you remember what happened?"

Lines formed on her forehead. "Kind of." She sounded uncertain. "I was… I went to a sort of party. Mostly people who work at the library, but some teachers from Lake Stevens High School, too. I meant to come home before dark, but time got away from me. After that… mostly I remember headlights blinding me and the jolt when I braked and the guy behind me didn't, and seeing this big tree coming at me."

Of all people to have something like this happen. "I'm sorry," he said.

She gave a tiny nod and flinched. "Head hurts."

"I know." He couldn't resist stroking her face again, staying away from the places that were purple or raw. Her skin was irresistibly soft, the bones beneath delicate.

Her eyelids sagged again, and he said, "Go back to sleep if you can."

"No." Her voice was a little slurred. "Just… Feels good."

He stroked, gradually moving his hand to the nape of her neck and gently kneading. Erin made a humming sound.

"Say something," she murmured.

Cole remembered how much he'd wanted to call her after he'd talked to Tom Phillips that day, and again after the college administration decided to let him take a couple of classes now instead of making him wait until winter quarter. And then, after he'd been to the classes and realized how young most of the students were, he'd been relieved when he saw a decent proportion of students his age and older.

So he started, haltingly at first, because filling the silence alone didn't come naturally to him. When he told her he had a good shot at being promoted to foreman, her eyes flew open and she squeezed his hand. He kept on, talking about the two classes—calculus, which he was taking as a refresher before he went on to trig, which he hadn't taken in high school, and nineteenth century American literature, because it fulfilled a requirement he needed for his AA degree. He'd already read *The Scarlet Letter* and was now deep into *Moby Dick*. He lifted the battered copy he'd found at a used bookstore in town.

"We can choose from a long list. All these famous books, and I hadn't read any of them."

"Me, neither. Every so often, I make myself pick one up."

He smiled. "Even college professors have areas of ignorance?"

"Shh."

Cole laughed.

Except she looked at him in that way she had, as if she could see right down to the darkest places inside him.

And then she said, "Will you tell me? I think it's time. Don't you?"

"Time?" But that was just a delaying tactic. He knew what she was asking and it made him feel sick. He would give almost anything to be able to skip this.

CHAPTER NINETEEN

SHE WATCHED COLE'S face go blank, the way she'd seen a hundred times before. He didn't move, just wiped away all expression. Was he going to refuse to tell her? Pretend to misunderstand, or ignore what was really a question?

Muscles flexed in his jaw. "Second-degree murder committed during an armed robbery. I was convicted of shooting the guy working the night shift at a convenience store. Barely twenty-one years old. He died." His mouth curled in an unpleasant little smile. "Now you know why the local cops came straight to see me after the ampm in town was robbed."

Her mouth fell open. She couldn't help it. Completely blown away, she said, "But—" She tried to slot in the pieces until they fit, but— "I don't believe it. *You*, shoot someone? No way." Not the quiet, gentle, caring man she knew. "Even if you were high or something… No." She shook her head.

"I was convicted." He sounded odd, his voice

unfamiliar. "The prosecutor made her case, and the jury bought it."

Erin kept shaking her head. She'd guessed... She didn't know what, but not murder. Not rape. The man who'd held her every time she needed him, who'd raced to help Mr. Zatloka, who'd done small favors for the old folks up and down the street without being asked, without expecting thanks...

"No," she said again. "Will you tell me what really happened?"

He stared at her for the longest time before a raw sound tore from his throat and he bent forward, elbows braced on his knees, his hands covering his face. His shoulders shook.

Shocked, Erin pushed herself to a sitting position despite the fireworks going off in her head. "Cole?" He was crying. She wanted desperately to wrap her arms around him, hold *him*. Well, she'd have to do it with one arm, but that had to be good enough. By slow degrees, she scooted toward the edge of the bed.

He lifted his head, face wet. "Damn it, what are you *doing*? Lie down before you fall out of bed!"

"What did I say?" she begged. "I didn't mean—"

He used the corner of the white hospital blanket to wipe his face. "I'm sorry. I...can't remember the last time I lost it like this."

"But…"

He was on his feet, moving her back to the middle of the bed, arranging her until he decided she was comfortable. Or so she thought.

Then he sat back down, wiped his face with the hem of his T-shirt and gave the strangest laugh. "I should have known."

"Known what?"

"I kept thinking you had X-ray eyes. That I didn't really have any secrets from you." He laughed again, a little more naturally. "Turns out I was right."

"You didn't do it."

"I didn't." He swallowed. "Dani claims to believe me, although I wonder. Otherwise, you're the first person who has believed me. Even my father—" Cole had to stop.

Fury leaped as if it had been fed by gasoline. "I want to punch him," she muttered.

This time, he laughed at her. "You're ten years too late. And—" he sobered "—I did commit some crimes. I'd gotten into drugs—cocaine—and joined a crowd that was into stuff I didn't let myself think about." He hesitated, his gaze sliding from hers. "When a guy supposedly cheated one of my friends on a drug deal, I went along with the others and helped smash the shit out of his car. That was the worst thing I did. Got caught, too."

"What happened? I mean with the law."

"I made a deal. They don't have room in the jail for punks. It put me on the cop radar, though. After my father hauled me home, he slammed me against a wall and I hit him. I packed my stuff and moved out."

"Tough guy, huh?"

"Angry guy. I don't totally know why. He and I butted heads even before Mom died, but it got a lot worse after. I've told you that. The older I was, the harder he came down on me. Dani could do no wrong, and then there was me. It was like…I was a threat to him. He became more and more rigid. I rebelled." He grimaced. "Stupid.

"The thing is, I never liked guns. I didn't own one. I went to the shooting range with friends a few times, which might have been the biggest mistake of my life. I used this guy's gun."

"Your fingerprints were on it," she said slowly.

"You got it. I asked my attorney to find out if the range kept a video that would show me handling the gun there. She claimed they didn't keep it that long, but I think she didn't bother looking. She was more interested in making a plea deal than in defending me." Cole's voice was hard now. "The trouble with the plea was, I'd have to admit I'd done the crime, and I refused. It got so I could have served as little as three years, but I kept saying no. What a stubborn ass." He shook his head. "I was so sure I wouldn't be convicted."

He talked about his shock and disbelief, about the moment he'd been led out of the courthouse in shackles, about the sentencing and hearing the words *ten years*.

"Did your father support you at all?"

"He came to the courthouse to watch the trial. But when I turned around to look at him after the foreman said, 'Guilty as charged,' I could tell he thought I was guilty, too. He walked out looking disgusted. A week later, he wrote a letter saying I was no son of his and that my mother would have been ashamed of me."

"How could he?" she said fiercely.

His eyes met hers, so vividly blue she couldn't look away, and he said, "The road I was on, I might've gotten to the point where I'd have shot someone for a hundred bucks to buy a snort of coke. I can't say that's impossible."

"It is." Erin held out her hand in a demand he recognized. Once she had a firm grip on him, she said, "That's not the man you are. I can't imagine you hurting anyone on purpose."

He shed a few more tears, embarrassed but not trying to hide his face this time. Apparently, he could tell she was winding down, because he made her push that button for more drugs.

She said, "You know who did kill that boy."

Funny, he thought, because he'd been a boy, too, although of course he hadn't seen himself that way.

"Yeah, only one of my friends—" irony filled his voice "—was built like me. That day at the range, I used his gun. He had a cloth in his hand when he took it from me and holstered it. The surveillance tape at the store showed the shooter wearing gloves."

"Did you tell anybody?"

"You mean, did I finger him? Sure I did. I told the cops and my attorney. I didn't owe him anything after he set me up."

"But they had your fingerprints, so they were satisfied."

He inclined his head.

Drowsiness felt like warm waves lapping at her.

He could obviously tell, because he kissed her cheek and freed her hand. "Thank you," he said. "You've done one more thing for me."

The warm, contented feeling vanished as if someone had opened a freezer door beside the bed.

He was ready to say goodbye. He was grateful for her faith in him, which was good—except for the fact that now he had to swallow one more indigestible lump of gratitude. He was right that they couldn't build anything on that as a foundation.

So she tried for a smile and said, "Thank *you* for coming. I'll probably be out of here by tomorrow, and I know you have to work, so…" She let her voice trail off. "Anyway, I'm glad things are going so well for you. And hey, if Edgar Allan Poe is on that list, give him a try. You'll like his stuff."

He rose to his feet, but not as if he was eager to escape. "How about you?"

She held on to the smile, although her lips trembled, and said, "I guess I need to find a life, the same way you have."

They both heard the approaching footsteps. A nurse pushed aside the curtain. Cole looked at Erin for another long minute, nodded and left.

THE NEXT DAY, he had a little trouble keeping his mind on the job. The others gave him a hard time about being slow on the uptake, but in a friendly way.

He kept thinking, *I shouldn't have left*. Had she *wanted* him to go? Cole honestly didn't know. He hated the idea of her being uncomfortable with him, though, which meant he couldn't ignore her when she sent a clear signal.

During the night, he'd briefly questioned whether she really believed in his innocence, or whether it was an act. Make Cole feel good about himself, which was in line with her determination to help him succeed. And yet… Some people might call him naive, but he knew she wasn't pretending. Her astonishment was so open, as was her anger at his father and everyone else who'd been idiotic enough to think Cole could do something so awful.

God, it had felt good. Even here at work, every so often he'd realize he was grinning like a fool for no apparent reason. Erin *believed* in him. No one else in the world had, except maybe Dani—and that was a big maybe—but Erin did.

He made the decision to stop at the hospital to be sure they weren't keeping her another night. The woman behind the counter checked; the computer showed that Erin Parrish had been discharged.

He was pissed off that she'd been released so fast after being unconscious as long as she had, never mind the broken arm, cracked ribs and clavicle. How was she supposed to take care of herself? Struck by a real flash of guilt, Cole wondered how she'd gotten home. Had she called *Lottie* to pick her up, for God's sake? Mr. Zatloka, who probably took half an hour to make a ten-minute drive across town? And now what? Was she without any transportation of her own, or had some rental place dropped a car off?

So he drove by her house, too. All he could tell was that lights were on, so she was there. No rental car sat in the driveway, but she might not have one yet. Unless she'd hired someone to install a garage door opener? Even the thought made him feel shitty, but he shook it off. Whether she had transportation or not, he doubted she'd be up to grocery shopping or anything like that for a few days.

He went back to his apartment, which didn't feel a lot homier than his cell had, nuked a frozen dinner and turned on the TV. After a minute, he turned it back off and reached for *Moby Dick*. The story seemed kind of slow to him, but his focus wasn't the best right now.

Finally, Cole acknowledged what he'd decided to do. If his father really wanted to hear from him, he could make that call. Whether there were apologies on either side, he couldn't see having much of a relationship with the man. Still, this *was* his father. Not a great one, but Cole, in his bullheadedness, hadn't been an easy son, either.

So he picked up his phone, bounced it in his hand a few times, huffed out a disbelieving breath and entered the number he still knew by heart.

"Hello?"

The familiar voice gave Cole an unexpected shock.

"This is Cole. Dani said you had something to say to me."

Silence stretched. Maybe *his* voice had startled his father, too.

"I'm sorry," Joe Meacham said. "That's what I wanted to say."

Crap. He wanted to retort, *Too little, too late*, and hang up. But a crushing sensation in his chest held him silent. He had to concentrate on breathing for a minute before he regained his voice.

"Sorry for what?" If he sounded harsh, he didn't care.

"I didn't listen to you." Pause. "Chad Adelson was arrested for armed robbery the year after you were convicted. That time, the clerk he shot survived. She, uh, saw the color of his eyes."

Adelson had weird-colored eyes. Or *not-colored* might be a better description. So pale a gray they looked washed out.

So Cole had been right. His father hadn't concluded on his own that his beloved son would never have shot and killed someone. Nope, he'd had to be presented with hard proof.

Still talking, Dad said, "He served barely a year. Starting two months after he got out, a series of armed robberies ended with him shooting and killing someone else. A customer, that time. Now he's in for the long haul."

This was news to him, but not a surprise. All he could think was, thank God they hadn't come face-to-face in the pen. Cole had been carrying so much rage then he was afraid of what he would have done. Maybe Chad had been sent to Monroe instead of Walla Walla.

"It didn't occur to the cops to wonder if they'd gotten it wrong with me?"

"Detective Sivik tried to get Chad to confess. He was in so much trouble it wouldn't have made that much difference, but he refused. Sivik said he laughed."

Man. Cole wondered if he might be having a heart attack.

"You never got in touch," he heard himself say.

"I…thought you wouldn't forgive me."

He was right. Cole bit back the words, though. "You changed your mind because even you couldn't deny the obvious. What if he'd never been arrested? Or you'd never heard about it?"

"I don't know."

A quaver belonged in an old man's voice, not his dad's. But then…he was getting up there. He'd been almost ten years older than Cole's mother. A moment's calculation told Cole his father was now sixty-eight.

"Did you not want a son?" he heard himself ask. "Or was it something about me?"

"What are you talking about? Of course I wanted a son!" Quaver replaced by outrage.

"I always thought you hated me. The way you'd look at me—" Cole shook his head. Why bother doing this? His father would never admit to his unequal treatment of his children, and what did it matter now?

"I don't know what you're talking about," Joe said stubbornly.

Yeah, they did have something in common.

"Well, Dad, I guess I should thank you for the update on my good friend Chad."

"Dani says you're doing really well. Working full-time, even taking some college classes."

"Too bad I lost ten years of my life." He wished he could quit with the bitterness. "It never crossed your mind to believe me, did it? To believe *in* me?"

"You were running with a rough crowd. Using drugs. It was hard to believe in you."

"I get that," he made himself say, "but the worst thing I'd done was take a tire iron to a car fender. Big jump to murder."

"I'm sorry," his father said again.

"I appreciate you saying that. But if it's forgiveness you want… I don't know. I've got to go. Goodbye, Dad."

His hand shook, but he used his thumb to end the call.

Leaning back in the recliner, Cole closed his eyes. He wanted to talk to Erin like he'd never wanted anything before. Face it, he thought—no matter what happened, little or big, he wanted to tell her. When he couldn't see her, talk to her, that hollow inside him kept expanding, a sinkhole trying to swallow him.

She cared about him. He knew she did. She might hurt him badly, down the line. But maybe she wouldn't. Was he really so gutless that he'd keep letting fear hold him back?

THE FIRST ERIN heard from Cole was a phone call Tuesday evening.

He sounded gruff. "How are you?"

"I'm okay."

"I've had broken ribs before," he said, doubting her for good reason.

"They're the worst," she admitted, giving up with the "I'm fine" thing. "I can't laugh or breathe deeply—and if I accidentally bump my body with the cast… Reaching high into a cupboard, nope. And the damn cast makes me clumsy. My brain sends these automatic signals and there I go, trying to use my left hand before I know it and whacking something."

"And it hurts." He was quiet for a minute.

"Collarbone will be really painful for at least a month, too."

"That's what the doctor told me. Have you broken that, as well?"

"Ribs were at football practice. Collarbone was in a fight."

Bad enough knowing he had scars, even if broken bones didn't leave the same visible evidence.

"I don't want to bug you," he said, his voice still gruff, "but I called to say if you need a ride, I'm available."

Her eyes stung, but she was determined not to let herself sound teary. "Thank you. I've got a rental, but I haven't driven yet. I'm hoping to start back at the library later in the week."

"Call if you need me."

He was gone, saving her from saying, *I do need you*.

Making it back to work that week turned out to be fantasy, not reality. She was too miserable. The pain pills made her groggy, but she hurt too much to function without them. Sleep happened in short increments, interrupted whenever she moved. The rental car sat in her driveway, although she had yet to go anywhere in it. Her insurance agent had told her she should receive a check next week, but she wasn't up to car-shopping. Neighbors up and down the street brought her casseroles and baked goods, so at least she didn't have to cook. In fact, she had to freeze a lot of the offerings. Michelle insisted on grocery shopping for her, bringing fresh produce, milk and eggs.

Friday morning, she went online and applied for the job as girls' volleyball coach at the high school. Her heart was racing by the time she finished. They'd probably already hired someone, but she surprised herself by hoping not.

Exhausted after so little effort, she took a late-afternoon nap. She'd barely dragged herself up from it when the phone rang. Her heart skipped a beat or two when she saw Cole's name.

"Hi. You'll be glad to know I haven't gone anywhere."

He chuckled, that low, rusty sound she loved. "Good. I wondered if I could bring you dinner."

She sat down on the edge of her bed. "Is this still about you thinking you owe me?"

"No."

She waited, but that was it. *No.*

"Then—" her voice came out husky "—I'd love to see you for dinner. But you don't have to bring anything, unless you already have it in hand. Half the neighbors have brought over meals, and several people from the library, too. Tell me what sounds good, and I probably have it."

Cole laughed again. "I'm not picky. Whatever you feel like having."

"Mystery dinner."

"See you in a few." He was gone.

She raced for the bathroom. Well, moved as fast as she could. This week, she'd hardly paid attention to what she looked like, but now she saw herself with dismay. Yellow and green remnants of a bruise lingered on the left side of her forehead. She had a pillow crease on her right cheek. She'd managed to wash her hair, thank goodness, and now she brushed it, but she couldn't braid it or even manage a ponytail one-handed. Makeup... Why bother? She rarely had when he lived here, and he did see her about ten hours after the car accident. Her eyes must have been spinning like whirligigs.

Sighing, she slipped her feet into sandals and went downstairs, wondering how quick his few minutes would be.

THE FLOWERS WERE probably overkill. Getting out of his truck, he seriously considered leaving them on the passenger seat so as not to embarrass himself. But he hadn't gotten to the point where wasting money sat well with him, and anyway... He'd swear he could hear his mother telling him he had to bring a gift. The pain pills Erin should still be taking ruled out wine, and Cole was willing to bet Lottie had dessert covered. Muttering under his breath, he scooped up the bouquet and started for the front porch.

He didn't have a chance to ring the bell before the door opened. She must have heard the truck engine. Erin's face lit up with a smile that froze him in place and stole his voice. He forgot how beautiful she was when he didn't see her daily, and she looked a thousand times better than she had on Sunday at the hospital, even though tiredness left her eyes sunken and accented with purple crescents.

Feeling like an idiot, he wordlessly held out the bouquet.

"For me?"

"Who else?"

"They're gorgeous." She accepted them with her right hand. "I can't remember the last time anyone gave me flowers. Well, the college did when my softball team won a regional title, but that's not the same, is it? And I'm babbling." She bent her head to breathe in the fragrance. He'd insisted on flowers that smelled good. "You must have gone to a florist."

First time in his life. "Can I come in?"

"Oh! Of course!" She tripped as she backed up.

Cole caught her with one hand. He liked that she felt as awkward as he did. Her cheeks were pink, too. From shyness?

He followed her to the kitchen, noting the changes in the house on the way. The ceiling was a creamy white instead of brown-splotched and dingy. He couldn't imagine how she'd reached the ceiling above the staircase. Damn it, he should've been here to do it for her. He could see her leaning out over space to roll on paint, the ladder slipping...

Cole shook himself. She'd done the job and hadn't injured herself—at least not then—so he should keep his mouth shut. But he thought about how much the house still needed, and how he'd like to be the one to do the work. Unpaid, this time.

The microwave already hummed. "Do you mind slicing the French bread?" she asked, laying the bouquet carefully on the counter. "I need to find a vase."

The vases, apparently, were kept in a cupboard above the refrigerator. Erin started to drag a stepstool over. He leveled a look at her and reached up to open it.

"Which one?"

She craned her neck. "How about that yellow one?"

Ceramic and gracefully shaped, it had to be an antique. When she filled it with water and arranged the mix of roses, sweet peas and something lacy in the vase, he smiled at the expression on her face. She liked them. Mom was right.

Talking grew easier as they got dinner on the table and sat down to eat, probably because they'd done this so often before. He carried the hot casserole dish to the table instead of letting her do it one-handed.

Encouraged by him, Erin grumbled about how completely miserable she felt. "Even my legs ache! My hip is sore. I feel like a hypochondriac. It's not like I was injured below the waist."

"You hit that tree with a lot of force." He didn't tell her, but he'd driven over to see where the accident had happened. Seeing the gouges in the tree had shaken him. The highway on that stretch was raised a good five feet above the wooded ground on each side. Her Cherokee had literally flown. "Your whole body had to be traumatized. Now you're probably walking a little differently than usual, too, which can strain muscles."

"I didn't think of that."

He wasn't surprised when she told him she'd discovered what a restless sleeper she was. "I so want to lie on my left side," she said with a sigh.

"It's only been about a week. Just a few more, and you'll feel like yourself again." He almost said, *You should remember. You've been through this before*, but stopped himself in time.

Her thoughts went there, anyway, because she said, "I broke a lot of the same bones. Same side, too. It's...weird."

Cole set down his fork and reached across the table. Her hand met his without any of the earlier awkwardness. "Did this trigger nightmares?"

"A few." She twisted her mouth. "I'd probably have more if I managed to stay asleep long enough."

Cole looked down at his plate. He'd been hungry when he called her, but nerves had unsettled his stomach and now—

"I could help you get comfortable if I was sleeping with you."

Erin stared at him. God, talking had never been his best skill. When so much was on the line, talking about feelings flat-out terrified him.

Even so, worried that he'd embarrassed her, he pushed himself to say, "I miss you."

Her eyes filled with tears.

He shoved his chair back and moved fast, scooping her up and sitting down with her on his lap. "Don't cry," he said hoarsely.

Erin leaned her face against his chest, which muffled her wail. "I never used to cry! I don't know what's wrong with me!"

He was still scared, but found he was smiling, anyway. "You've been through a lot, sweetheart. You'll get your balance back."

Not until she went completely still did he realize he'd used an endearment. Worse yet, one his father had used with his mother. Cole could only wait to see how Erin reacted. He kept rubbing her back.

"I need to blow my nose," she mumbled.

Still smiling—*don't let them see your fear*—he thrust a napkin in her hand. She mopped and blew firmly, crumpled the napkin and lifted her head. The brief storm had added puffiness to her eyes and blotches of color to her freckled skin.

"You really mean that?" She searched his face. "You're not just saying it?"

Lump in his throat, Cole shook his head. "I didn't want to go. You had to know that."

"I…suspected. But then I told myself—" She shook her head, too, as if there was no point in stating the obvious.

This was up to him. Fear and shame and a bunch of other stuff tangled up as he prepared to reveal himself to her again. At least after this… he'd know. Once and for all.

"Anything that happens, I want to tell you about it. I think about you all the time. Will you let me come back?" *Home.* That was what he'd meant to say. Instead, his speech had been about as fancy as his dented, aged pickup truck.

She didn't jump off his lap. So many emotions crossed her face and enriched the color of her eyes he couldn't read any of it. Or maybe he was just too nervous.

"Do you mean the apartment?" she asked carefully.

Muscles tightening even more, he whispered, "With you."

"What changed your mind?"

"It didn't change. I always knew—" Cole took a deep breath. "It killed me to leave. But…you're a college professor. I'm an ex-con. I thought, sooner or later, you'd go back to, I don't know, if not the same college, the same kind of place. Life," he corrected himself. "If you didn't want me to go with you…" He swallowed, unable to say, *I might not survive that.*

"I'm such a mess. More than you are, and with less reason."

"That's not true."

"It is, but…I've been in love with you almost from that first day. You were so stoic, you had such pride and dignity, you knew how to do everything." A tiny smile came out of hiding. "You're sexy, and you're stubborn."

He had to close his eyes for a minute to gather himself. "You love me."

"Yes." She rested her head on his shoulder and pressed a soft kiss to his throat. "If you think I'd ever be embarrassed by you, you're wrong. You're smarter than most of the professors I've met and way more practical. None of them look like you, either. I *really* don't want to think of the women you must have trailing you on the Everett campus."

A grin broke free. "I try to ignore my followers."

Erin snorted, but then she went quiet again. Finally, she sat up straight, meeting his eyes. "Did you... I mean, have there been other women?"

"No one." Honesty compelled him to admit, "I told myself I should find someone more at my level, but...I just couldn't do it. You were always there. I would have compared them."

"With the crazy woman who kept trying to kill herself? Who screams every night, and sobs in your arms?"

"Yeah." His heart didn't feel right. Or maybe it finally did. "With her."

"Oh, Cole," she whispered.

That did it. He had to kiss her, and she seemed just as eager to kiss him back. It took everything he had to hold on to enough sanity to know this was as far as it could go until a few of her bones knit themselves back together. But this was good—kisses that were tender, that asked questions and gave answers, hungry kisses, teasing kisses.

Erin was laughing when they parted, even though her eyes shone with new tears. "You'll really come home?"

"I really will," he said huskily, "as long as

you know I want you forever. That I'll go any-where you do."

She laid her uninjured hand on his cheek and rubbed her thumb over his lips. "Works the other way around, too. We may need to move if you want a four-year degree. Or more."

Erin loved him. She believed in him.

"Damn, I wish we could go to bed," he growled.

She laughed at him. "We can. You did promise to make me so comfy I'd sleep through the night."

He kissed her again, hard, then murmured in her ear, "I can only think of one thing I'd rather do."

* * * * *

If you enjoyed this story by
Superromance author Janice Kay Johnson,
you'll also love her most recent books:

HER AMISH PROTECTORS
PLAIN REFUGE
A MOTHER'S CLAIM
and
BECAUSE OF A GIRL

All available at Harlequin.com.

Get 2 Free Books,
Plus 2 Free Gifts—
just for trying the Reader Service!

Get 2 Free Books,
Plus <u>2</u> Free Gifts—
just for trying the Reader Service!

YES! Please send me 2 FREE Harlequin Presents® novels and my 2 FREE gifts (gifts are worth about $10 retail). After receiving them, if I don't wish to receive any more books, I can return the shipping statement marked "cancel." If I don't cancel, I will receive 6 brand-new novels every month and be billed just $4.55 each for the regular-print edition or $5.55 each for the larger-print edition in the U.S., or $5.49 each for the regular-print edition or $5.99 each for the larger-print edition in Canada. That's a saving of at least 11% off the cover price! It's quite a bargain! Shipping and handling is just 50¢ per book in the U.S. and 75¢ per book in Canada.* I understand that accepting the 2 free books and gifts places me under no obligation to buy anything. I can always return a shipment and cancel at any time. The free books and gifts are mine to keep no matter what I decide.

Please check one: ☐ Harlequin Presents® Regular-Print   ☐ Harlequin Presents® Larger-Print
(106/306 HDN GLWL)   (176/376 HDN GLWL)

Name _____ (PLEASE PRINT)

Address _____ Apt. #

City _____ State/Prov. _____ Zip/Postal Code

Signature (if under 18, a parent or guardian must sign)

Mail to the **Reader Service:**

IN U.S.A.: P.O. Box 1341, Buffalo, NY 14240-8531
IN CANADA: P.O. Box 603, Fort Erie, Ontario L2A 5X3

Want to try two free books from another series?
Call 1-800-873-8635 or visit www.ReaderService.com.

* Terms and prices subject to change without notice. Prices do not include applicable taxes. Sales tax applicable in N.Y. Canadian residents will be charged applicable taxes. Offer not valid in Quebec. This offer is limited to one order per household. Books received may not be as shown. Not valid for current subscribers to Harlequin Presents books. All orders subject to approval. Credit or debit balances in a customer's account(s) may be offset by any other outstanding balance owed by or to the customer. Please allow 4 to 6 weeks for delivery. Offer available while quantities last.

Your Privacy—The Reader Service is committed to protecting your privacy. Our Privacy Policy is available online at www.ReaderService.com or upon request from the Reader Service.

We make a portion of our mailing list available to reputable third parties that offer products we believe may interest you. If you prefer that we not exchange your name with third parties, or if you wish to clarify or modify your communication preferences, please visit us at www.ReaderService.com/consumerchoice or write to us at Reader Service Preference Service, P.O. Box 9062, Buffalo, NY 14240-9062. Include your complete name and address.

Get 2 Free Books,

Plus 2 Free Gifts—

just for trying the Reader Service!